CROSS
MY
HEART

CROSS MY HEART

THE OXFORD LEGACY

ROXY SLOANE

AVON

An Imprint of HarperCollins*Publishers*

HarperCollins books may be purchased for educational, business, or sales promotional use. For information, please email the Special Markets Department at SPsales@harpercollins.com.

Originally published as *Cross My Heart* in the United States in 2023 by AAHM, Inc/Roxy Sloane.

FIRST AVON TRADE EDITION PUBLISHED 2024.

Interior text design by Diahann Sturge-Campbell

Rose illustration © vectortatu/Stock.Adobe.com

Library of Congress Cataloging-in-Publication Data has been applied for.

ISBN 978-0-06-341838-7

24 25 26 27 28 LBC 5 4 3 2 1

*For the readers who want their dark academia with a dash of wild sex parties and thigh-clenching spice.
The professor will see you now . . .*

Note to Readers

This book contains a dirty-talking hero, spicy scenarios, and plenty of blush-worthy moments (ahem, Chapter Seven).

There are also references to a prior suicide, and the past kidnapping and possible sexual assault of a supporting character, but neither event takes place "on the page" or within the current timeline of the book.

Forewarned is forearmed.

Chapter One
TESSA

O xford. The city of dreaming spires, ancient legacies . . . and *secrets*.

It's also the last place in the world I ever expected to find myself, an ocean away from my regular life in Philadelphia, dressed up in a neat blouse and skirt, sipping tea in the gardens of the five-hundred-year-old buildings that make up Ashford College. The oldest, most prestigious of all the Oxford colleges.

And the one that hides the most secrets of all.

"Isn't it incredible?" one of the other guests coos. Lacey, I think she's called, and she's wide-eyed and gasping over every detail of this place. "It was built in the sixteenth century; they shipped all the sandstone over from Florence to build the main cloisters. Can't you just feel the history?"

"Mm-hmm." I give a vague nod, scanning the crowd. It's a welcome party for all of us new graduate students at the college, and we've been stuck here an hour already: milling around the manicured lawn, drinking weak tea, and meeting the professors and staff. Everyone around me is buzzing with excitement to have finally arrived, and if I'm honest, my nerves are on edge, too.

But for a very different reason.

I look around, waiting for my chance. The crowd is an eclectic mix of graduate students in their twenties and thirties, and brainy-looking professors. Everyone has that awkward "first day of school" look, laughing too loudly at bad jokes, and eager to impress.

"Hello," a new staff member greets us, pulling me back to the conversation. She's a tall, serious woman in tweed, her grey hair cut in a severe bob. "And who are you?"

"Tessa," I introduce myself politely. "I'm here for the year, studying the social politics of eighteenth-century literature."

"Ah yes, our Ashford scholar," she says, naming the scholarship I managed to find to fund my trip. "Welcome, welcome, we're thrilled to have you."

"And I'm thrilled to be here," I lie, forcing another perky grin.

"It's always been a dream to study in Oxford," Lacey gushes beside me. "I can't believe I'm finally here!"

Neither can I. But it wasn't my dream, but a *plan*.

Carefully made, painstakingly executed, step by step that would bring me here, to Ashford College, and all its secrets.

Secrets I'm determined to reveal, no matter what the cost.

"Are you one of the professors?" I ask the woman politely.

"No, I'm the administrator, Geraldine Wesley," she introduces herself.

I perk up, recognizing the name. "So, you've been on the other end of all those helpful emails," I say, flashing her a smile.

"That's right." She smiles back. "I supervise student life and keep track of everything here at Ashford outside of your studies. So, if you have any questions or concerns, just let me know."

"I will," I say, already knowing Geraldine here is going to be very helpful. Because I have a thousand questions, and she'll give me the answers . . .

Just not the way she thinks.

Somebody taps a glass, and everyone quiets. It's the head of the college, a bumbling, tweedy kind of guy stepping into the middle of the garden. "Welcome, welcome." He beams at us. "It's so wonderful to have you all here. I'd like to share a few words, about the legacy of our college, and what an incredible opportunity you have here . . ."

People move closer to listen, all eyes on him. It's the moment I've been waiting for.

Nobody notices me carefully backing away from the crowd and slipping out of the garden, down a passageway and out to the cobblestone courtyard in the middle of the campus.

I don't have much time, so I walk quickly across the college grounds, tracing the route I memorized. It's September, and the semester has just begun, so there are plenty of other students around, going about their day or studying on the quad. Ashford College looks like something out of a magazine, with the fall leaves turning gold, and all the preppy, studious undergrads. Exclusive. Prestigious.

Dangerous.

The administrators' offices are just on the other side of the quad, up a flight of narrow, creaky stairs. I'm betting that in a place this old, they won't have installed many new alarm systems or security gear, and I'm right. Geraldine's door just has an old-fashioned keyhole set beneath the handle. And in a small, exclusive college like this, with high gates and security on the front entrance, there's no reason to keep it locked all day while she pops out to meet us new students at the garden mixer . . .

Holding my breath, I slowly turn the handle.

It opens.

Yes.

I exhale, stepping inside and closing it almost all the way behind me as I look quickly around. It's a cluttered, L-shaped room under the eaves, with a desk and computer and a long wall of filing cabinets.

I go straight to them and try a handle. Locked.

Where would I keep the keys? It would be close, for convenience, so I rifle through the desk and—*there*. A set of keys are sitting in the top drawer. I grab them and go straight to the first cabinet. Geraldine looks like the kind of woman to keep things organized, and she does: The student records are all filed by year, then alphabetical. I find the files from two years ago and flip through them until I reach the drawer I'm looking for.

"O'Hara, Patrick . . . Peterson."

I pause, snatching it out of the cabinet. *Wren Peterson.* Her name is labelled in neat letters on the top, and my pulse kicks with recognition.

My sister.

I open it, heart pounding, but the file is frustratingly slim. Just a copy of her lecture schedule and application packet. A printed page with her internet log-in details and rooming assignment . . .

Nothing with any real information.

Nothing I can use.

I let out a sigh of disappointment, but I quickly snap photos of the contents on my phone before putting the file back and locking the cabinet. I'm just slipping the keys where I found them in the desk drawer when a creak from the doorway makes me whirl around with a yelp.

"What the hell—?" I blurt, panicking. Then I blink. There's a dark-haired man leaning in the doorway, assessing me with a piercing stare. He's not just handsome, but devilishly hot: in his early thirties, maybe, dressed in dark pants and a white button-down, with his jacket sleeves rolled up casually over his forearms; a perfect scruff of two-day stubble on his strong jaw.

"Looking for something?" he asks, one eyebrow raised.

I gulp. His dusk-blue eyes are focused directly on me. Stripping me naked.

Exposed.

I back away from the desk. "My welcome packet," I blurt. "It wasn't in my mailbox, and Geraldine said I could just pick it up here."

"Did she now?" His gaze sweeps over me, blatantly sensual. Appreciative, too. I can feel my skin prickle and my nipples tighten in response, but I force myself to stay calm.

He doesn't know anything. You're just a ditzy new student.

"My log-in won't work, you see," I say, giving a helpless smile. "And, like, I can't go a single day without being online. I mean, I know this is a historic place and all, but there's no way I can function without email or social media this long. It's like the thing with the tree falling in the forest, right?" I add, mimicking Lacey's breathless tone. "How will anyone know what an amazing time I'm having here if I can't post to show them?"

It's causing me physical pain to pretend I'm a shallow idiot to this sculpted god of a man, but I don't have any choice. "So do you know where it would be?" I ask, with a dopey look. "My, you know, info sheet?"

"I'm afraid not." He glances around the office, a small smirk on his lips, like he's not buying my story for a moment. *Fuck.* But just as I'm wondering if I've blown my own cover before I've even begun, he stands aside and gestures to the stairs. "You'll want to be getting back to the party, I'm sure. So you can, *like*, meet everyone."

He mimics me, and I would roll my eyes at his condescending tone if I wasn't so relieved to have an escape.

"Right. Yes. Thanks!"

I bolt past him and down the stairs, not pausing for a second until I arrive back at the garden party, my heart racing in my chest.

How could I have been so careless? One wrong move, and all my plans would have been blown for good.

I grab an iced lemonade and gulp it down, wishing for something stronger to settle my nerves. It's not just panic making my heart pound, but the memory of the way that guy looked at me.

And how my body responded. *Wanting him.*

Hell, they say fear is an aphrodisiac. Clearly, I've got a secret kink for danger and discovery fantasies . . .

"Where have you been?" Lacey grabs me. "You missed all the speeches."

"Bathroom," I say vaguely, my body still wired with adrenaline.

"There are such amazing professors here," she continues, munching on a scone. "I'm just hoping I get assigned to the seminar with Professor St. Clair."

"Uh-huh . . ." I'm barely paying attention, recalling that teasing smirk on the man's face, and the way he seemed almost amused to find me snooping somewhere I shouldn't be.

"Are you talking about Saint?" Another new student asks, joining our group. "Anthony St. Clair, he's next in line to be the Duke of Ashford, you know. His ancestors founded this college."

"A duke?" Lacey's jaw drops.

"Yes. He's not a real tutor, he just drops in to give lectures sometimes. Perks of the family name. Probably why he gets away with it."

"Away with what?"

"Everything," the other student says, looking scandalized. "He dates students all the time, hosts wild parties, he's nothing like the other professors. Look," she says, nodding across the lawn.

I glance over to see who this infamous tutor is, and find myself staring directly at *him*. The man who just interrupted me. He's standing apart from the crowd, his jacket slung over his shoulder now, looking so cool and composed that it reminds me of that song lyric, about a guy walking into a party like he was walking onto a yacht.

Because this is clearly a guy who's strolled onto plenty of yachts in his time. He has that rich guy confidence just radiating off him, and he's watching us all with what looks like amusement on his face.

Handsome. Dark. Sensual.

The kind of man who knows exactly how to make you moan . . .

His eyes meet mine across the lawn, and there's something so direct in his gaze, blatantly assessing. I feel a shiver of awareness, like he can see right through this innocent role I'm playing.

But that's impossible. I look like every other eager new student in this place. Nobody knows why I'm really here—and I'm going to keep it that way.

I turn away.

"Not your type?" Lacey asks.

I shrug, acting unimpressed. Because even though this Saint guy would be anyone's type . . . he's definitely not mine. I've come to Oxford looking for a man, but not for some illicit fling.

There's only one man I'm interested in, and I'm going to hunt him down, no matter what.

The man who attacked my sister, and made her take her own life.

Chapter Two
TESSA

What happened to you, Wren?

My sneakers pound the cobblestones as I run through the center of town, passing quaint cafes and bookstores, the city just coming to life for the day ahead. It's barely six a.m., and dawn is still streaking the sky, but I couldn't sleep. I don't sleep much these days, my head filled with the same questions that have haunted me for the past year now.

Questions I've crossed the world to answer, no matter what.

I keep running, trying to exhaust the anxious buzz in my veins. I turn off the High Street, past the old colleges, with their high walls and ancient turrets. Oxford is like a federated system of schools, made up of over two dozen individual colleges, each with their own staff, rules, and students, dotted around the city like little walled kingdoms.

And Ashford College is the richest, most exclusive kingdom of all.

I remember Wren clutching the letter in triumph when she got the offer of a placement to continue her research there. A cutting-edge biomedical program, some neuroscience center that would revolutionize the field. I never could follow exactly what she was researching. My older sister was always the brains in the family, not me.

She got straight As, while I stumbled along as a B-average student. She got a full ride to college, then medical school, while

I bounced around liberal arts programs, changing my major a dozen times over—and partying more than I studied. After graduating, she was head-hunted to do research for a major biochem company, while I strung together odd jobs, working in a coffee shop, volunteering at charities and non-profits in Philadelphia, falling in and out of love with toxic tortured-artist types.

But Wren never judged me, or acted superior because she had her life together. She loved hearing about my misadventures whenever I'd go stay with her. "You're really *living*," she would say enviously, and I would feel like maybe I wasn't a loser for not having my shit figured out, like her.

My whole life, she was the person I looked up to, my first emergency call after every bad breakup or minor win. My brilliant, kindhearted, optimistic sister. Just twenty-seven, and ready to change the world. At least, that's what we all thought, when she packed up and moved to Oxford with her bright future ahead of her.

A year later, she was dead. Walked into Lake Michigan, leaving me nothing but a scribbled letter of tear-smudged apologies.

> *I'm sorry. I can't go on like this.*
> *It hurts too much, not knowing.*
> *Forgive me.*

I swallow back the lump in my throat and keep on running. I turn off the main street and back through the Ashford gates, nodding my hello to the uniformed security guys that mind the front entry. The Ashford College sweatshirt I'm wearing seems over-the-top, but I figured it would bring me the fewest questions as I come and go.

Sure enough, they wave me through as I head past the quad, all the way to the back of the buildings, where a path winds off, down to the river. I roamed every inch of the place the first days I arrived, and found that the college grounds sprawl out a couple more miles beyond the main dorms and libraries—into woodland

and fields, so still and pretty in the dawn light, it could almost calm the storm raging in my chest.

Almost.

Who did this to you, Wren?

That's the question that's been haunting me, to the point of obsession. No, way past that point. To *vengeance*. Ever since Wren showed up on the front steps of my apartment building, barely a few months after she'd left for Oxford. She'd quit. Come home early. And for the longest time, she wouldn't say why.

I knew something terrible had happened, I could pinpoint it to the day. Her calls and FaceTime chats from Oxford had started out so happy, brimming with stories of her amazing lab partners and all the history and architecture here in town. She was making friends, having fun, devoted to her work.

And then . . . something changed. Her calls grew less frequent, and when we did talk, she seemed strained. Hollow. She still tried to keep up the act, pretending like everything was going great, but she couldn't fake it with me.

I knew her better than anyone.

The Oxford job was supposed to be for two, maybe three years, but suddenly, it was Christmas and she was there in Philadelphia, on my doorstep with a lame story about losing her direction and burning out after too much work.

There was something burned about her, alright. Ashen and brittle. Dark shadows under her eyes. So tense, every slamming door made her flinch. And the cheerful, hug-loving, ambitious, "glass half full" sister I'd known all my life?

She was gone.

This Wren, I didn't recognize. She stayed out all night, partying with strangers. Drinking to the point of oblivion—and more than just alcohol, too. Pills that glazed her expression. Powder that made her shriek with too-loud laughter. She was quick to anger, and she burned with resentment.

A stranger I couldn't look directly in the eye.

The trees blur past me as I reach the end of the footpath, and I finally slow to a stop. Bent double, gasping for air. My heart pounding in my ears as I look out over the riverbanks, remembering that night too clearly.

The night she finally broke down and told me the truth.

I was supposed to be working, a late shift bartending at a dive down the street. But the owner never showed, and I didn't have the keys, so I left the place closed and headed home.

Wren was on the bathroom floor, wasted out of her mind. A razor blade sliced through her left wrist.

I don't think I've ever been so terrified, seeing her body crumpled there, pooling blood. But she was breathing. Somehow, the cut wasn't that deep. I managed to get her bandaged and in a cold shower to sober up, and when she finally surfaced, red-eyed and shivering, I made her tell me everything.

It had been a night out with her friends, at the end of her first semester. Just a fun drink at the college bar, the way she'd enjoyed a dozen times before. But someone knew someone else who'd heard about a big blow-out party in the countryside; Wren just *had* to come. It would be an adventure.

And that was all she remembered—everything else after that was just . . . gone. Who she'd left with, if they'd even made it to the party at all . . . Wren's brilliant mind, that could hold dates and facts and figures like it was nothing, was now a black hole, empty of every detail that might have helped. She swore she hadn't been drinking. One glass of wine, maybe. I believed her. Back then, Wren was always the designated driver, the cool head that made sure everyone else got home safely; held back your hair while you were sick and supplied the morning-after coffee and snacks.

Just one glass of wine, but that was all she remembered. She woke up back in her room at the college, sprawled out on her bed in her best party dress. Her body aching. Bruises on her wrists and thighs. Her roommates didn't know where she'd gone to after the bar, they couldn't even recall who she'd been with, if they'd been strangers or friends.

A whole twenty-four hours had passed.

A full day. *Gone.* For my sister, so used to knowing everything, planning everything, that was the part she couldn't get her head around. What had happened? Where had she been?

With whom?

She took herself to the ER, but whatever drugs had been in her system, they didn't show on any tests. A rape kit was inconclusive. The nurses gave her a lecture about drinking too much and sent her on her way. She tried to retrace her steps from that night, but nobody had been paying much attention, too caught up in their own deadlines and romantic dramas, and a fun night on the town. Everywhere she turned came up blank.

And then the flashbacks started.

Nothing solid, no names or faces or anything she could hold onto. Just brief images. People in formal wear, dancing in a garden. A dirty cell somewhere, no windows. A bare mattress. Restraints on her wrists and ankles. A man, looming over her, with a distinctive tattoo on his thigh: a crown encircled with a serpent.

Half of her wished she could remember, Wren sobbed to me that night. It was the not-knowing that was driving her mad. But the other half . . . it knew that the mind is wired for self-preservation.

Maybe there was a reason her brain was blocking it out. Repressing the truth.

Maybe it was trying to save her from whatever horrors had really happened in that cell.

After that night, I tried to help her, any way I could. Finding therapists, support groups. Rehab programs. But Wren rejected them all. It was like finally talking about what happened to her out loud had pushed her over the edge, and she needed to forget, more than ever. She went off the deep end, disappeared for weeks at a time. Our parents went out of their minds with worry, and

I spent every night wondering where she was. If she would be coming home.

Until the day she didn't. And we got the terrible call from the cops, instead.

She was gone.

* * *

I FINALLY TURN away from the river and start walking back toward the college, my limbs aching from the run. But I barely feel it. I'm already thinking ahead to my next step. The next part of my plan to find whoever did that to my sister—and to make him pay.

Because whoever drugged her, held her captive, did God knows what to her for those lost twenty-four hours? He's the one who killed her. Snuffed out the life and hope in my sister's eyes, turned her into a shell of her former self, until she couldn't even bear to draw another breath.

He as good as murdered my sister, and I won't rest until I track him down—and make him suffer, the same way that he hurt her.

That's why I've moved heaven and earth to get here, to Oxford and Ashford College. The scene of the crime. Lying and snooping and pretending to be someone I'm not. I'm going to find out everything about Wren's life here: her friends, her lovers, who hosted that party, and every person who attended. Every last fucking detail, until I can avenge her death.

I don't have much to go on yet, but the information I got from the administrator's office is a start. Her schedule and room assignment. I'll begin with them. A place like this, people stick around. There's bound to be people who knew her, who can point me in the right direction—

I'm so deep in thought, I barely look where I'm going. Until I collide, face-first, into a solid mass of man.

"Woah, easy there!"

I hear a crisp, English accent, and look up to find myself inches from an all too familiar face.

Him. Anthony St. Clair. That future duke everyone was swooning over. The man whose family name is etched in stone above the gates of this very college.

The man who came dangerously close to blowing my cover here, before my mission has even begun.

"Sorry," I blurt, stumbling back. "I didn't see you."

"Good," he says, flashing a charming smile. He's still dressed in last night's clothes, but of course, the disheveled morning-after look still looks great on him. "And if the Master asks after me, I'd appreciate you sticking to that story."

"Why?" I can't help asking. "What have you done this time?" Despite everything, I'm curious—why this guy is so out of place here, the least likely Oxford tutor in the history of the school. *Saint*, the girl called him.

But this guy is a sinner, through and through.

Saint's mouth curls in a sensual grin. "I see my reputation has preceded me."

He looks so handsome, irritation burns me. He's probably used to women falling at his feet. Or straight to their knees to suck him off.

Well, I won't be one of them.

"Oh yeah, I've heard all about you," I say directly. "The partying, the booze, the women. Kind of a cliché, isn't it?" I add, as revenge for how dismissively he looked at me the other day. "Bad boy professor dating every hot coed in town. It doesn't make you look half as cool as you think. Let me guess, you drive a classic sports car, too? Red or silver. Anyone would think you're insecure about your manhood."

Saint's jaw drops in surprise. That I called him on his bullshit or was brave enough to say it to his face, I don't know. Either way, I don't stick around to find out.

"I won't keep you," I add with a smile. "You'll want to shower before class. You stink of sex."

And then I turn on my heel, and keep on running.

Chapter Three
TESSA

I head back to my student housing, a cozy apartment in an old red brick building just across the street from the Ashford College grounds. I'll be taking my classes with the undergraduate students here, but thankfully, I'm rooming with the other grad students my own age instead of being stuck in the freshman dorms. I open the door to the sound of playful bickering coming from the kitchen, and when I go to investigate, I find my new roommates arguing over a jar of pickles at the ancient, wonky dining table.

"Are you out of your mind? I'm not drinking that!" Jia protests, wincing as she combs her fingers through her wet, choppy dark hair.

"It's a miracle hangover cure!" Kris swears, his lanky, slim frame folded into a chair. "Just one shot of pickle juice and a cold shower and boom, you feel like you never drank at all."

I kick off my sneakers and stretch as they argue. Jia and Kris are British students, here for graduate programs too, and so far they seem to split their time between the library and the many pubs and drinking spots of the city.

"Do you believe this nonsense?" Jia asks me.

"It's true," I agree with Kris. "Something about the acids? I don't know the science."

"Ha! See? Works like a charm." He beams.

"Then you drink it," Jia argues.

"I'm not the one who did whiskey shots all night," Kris reminds her as I cross to the refrigerator and grab a bottle of water, gulping half the thing down while Jia lets out a pained groan.

"The guy from my poetry seminar was buying. He was so hot, Tessa," she adds. "Very 'consumptive Edwardian ghost boy,' just the way I like them. You should have been there."

"So hot, he gave *me* his number," Kris says smugly.

"What? So this hangover is all for nothing . . . ?" Jia sighs, shakes her head, then downs a gulp of the pickle juice. "Ewww! Fuck. I'm never drinking again."

"Except we have that college mixer tonight," Kris reminds her.

"Right. I'm never drinking except that," Jia corrects herself, laughing. "You should come, Tessa. It'll be fun!"

"Maybe," I say vaguely, as they drag themselves up and collect an assortment of jackets, books, and study materials. "I have a ton of reading to do to get ready for my first class. I mean, tutorial," I correct myself, using the Oxford term for the small discussion groups I'll be learning in.

"You know what they say," Kris says, mock scolding. "All work and no play . . . There's more to Oxford than dusty old books, you know. You're here for the full experience!"

They clatter out, leaving me in the early morning peace of the old apartment; sun falling through the iron-paned windows and warming the scuffed wooden floors.

He's right, I'm here for more than study. Which means I don't have time for regular student amusements. I quickly shower and dress in comfortable jeans and a T-shirt, then grab my bag, and head back to Ashford.

The college is waking now, and the front quad bustles with students, and tourists snapping photographs of the famous buildings and neat, manicured lawns.

". . . founded in 1583, by the first Duke of Ashford in tribute to his patroness, Queen Elizabeth the First," the tour guide announces, "Ashford has produced dozens of leaders in media, industry, and even the government. Three British Prime Ministers attended here, soon to be four, if Lionel Ambrose wins his current bid for leadership . . ."

I weave past them, through the wrought iron gates and into the squat gatehouse lodge, where the college custodians direct all visitors and mail in their smart maroon uniforms and peaked caps. *Porters*, they're called, and I add it to the list of lingo everyone throws around here so casually. I go to check my mail cubby. It's stuffed with flyers for student events, junk mail, and— yup, my official class schedule.

I look at the list of seminars and lectures, and feel a tremor of nerves.

Once I decided to hunt down the truth about what happened to Wren, I knew that just hopping on a flight to England wouldn't be enough. Places like Ashford College are closed to outsiders. If I just showed up asking questions, I'd be like one of the tourists at the gate: peering through the bars from the outside, not ever glimpsing what secrets the college is hiding past those crumbling, ivy-covered walls.

No, I had to get inside. Walk the same stone hallways, the way Wren did. See what she saw. Follow whatever trail she might have left behind.

Which meant I needed to become a student here, too.

I've never excelled academically. I always cared more about clubs and sports and volunteering around town. But it turns out, I just needed the right motivation, because once I had my target in view, I stopped at nothing to find a way here. I searched for weeks until I found an obscure scholarship for "non-traditional" (read, B-average, older) students. It's a special year-long individual study program where I'll take lectures and tutorials alongside the regular undergrads. I badgered every vaguely impressive person I knew into writing me glowing recommendations and, yes, bullshitted my way through every interview and application with my fingers crossed behind my back as I talked about my love for eighteenth-century literature, Gothic fiction, and subversive philosophy—trying my best to make it sound like I hadn't been studying on Wikipedia all night long.

Somehow, I pulled it off. The lies and exaggerations were worth it when that letter arrived telling me I'd won the spot at Ashford—with a full scholarship for the year. But now that I'm actually here, staring at my printed schedule, it's sinking in that I'm actually going to have to fake it full-time—and somehow make it through all the classes that I'm signed up for.

"Uh-oh." A jovial voice breaks me from my anxiety, and I look up to find one of the porters distributing mail around the room. "I know that look," he continues with a wink. "It's the first year, 'what on earth have I gotten myself into?' look."

I exhale with a rueful smile. "Grad student, but yes. It's . . . a lot."

"Everyone panics, don't you worry," the man says, friendly. He's got a weathered face and a local accent, with *Bates* printed on his polished nametag. "I've been here twenty years, and you all look like scared little mice the first week, but you'll find your feet."

"I hope so," I say, as he arrives at my cubby.

"Peterson?" he asks, holding out another piece of mail to me. I nod, and then he pauses, studying me for a moment before snapping his fingers. "Peterson, the American. Name like a bird . . ."

I blink, surprised. "Wren?" I ask.

"That's it." He smiles. "I never forget a face. Relation of yours?"

"My sister," I reply slowly, my mind racing. Peterson is a common enough name that I didn't think about changing it on my applications. "You knew her?"

Bates nods. "Nice girl, always up early to go get that coffee of hers," he adds, and I trail him back out to the main reception area, which is busy with students coming and going. "How's she getting along these days?"

"Great," I lie brightly, feeling an ache in my chest. "She's back home in the States, deep in some big research project."

"Good for her," Bates says. "Tell her this old man says hello, and to watch her blood pressure with all that espresso," he adds.

"I will." I pause as people bustle around us. "You know, you're the first person I've run into that knew Wren when she was here," I say, trying my hardest to keep my voice casual. "You don't remember any of her old friends, do you? I'd love to get some embarrassing stories about her, to make her suffer at the holidays."

He chuckles. "Sorry, I can't recall. Maybe check the yearbooks," he suggests.

Yearbooks! Of course. I brighten. "Where could I find them?"

"Try the library," he says. I'm still blank, so he adds, "Across the main quad, take a right, then a left. You'll be spending plenty of time there, mark my words."

"Thanks."

My gratitude is drowned out by another student asking about a food delivery, so I slip away, following his directions across the campus to the library, which is just as imposing and beautiful as every other building in the college, with ivy-covered walls, stained glass in the windows, and a huge vaulted roof with a bell tower nestled on top.

I only arrived on campus a couple of days ago, but I feel like I know it already—thanks to Wren. She loved this place. From the day she stepped foot in Oxford, she couldn't stop texting about the ancient architecture, sending me constant updates about the cute period details and artwork scattered around campus. Now, I feel a pang, thinking of how happy she could have still been here, if things had turned out differently.

If she hadn't gone to that party. If she'd stayed up studying, or chosen to hang with her friends and watch a movie in the common room instead.

If some monster hadn't done unspeakable things and broken her good, pure spirit forever.

I swallow back my familiar rage and step inside the dim, hushed building. The librarian directs me to the stacks along the back wall, where I find a dusty row of yearbooks, stretching back forty years and more. I grab the volume from her year and settle in at a desk in the corner to search. Leafing through the pages of student pics, I feel a jolt when I first come across a photo of Wren, gathered in the back of a group of beaming students, out on the front quad. She looks so happy that I spend a long moment just staring at her smiling face, remembering the sister I used to know.

The sister I lost.

When I read the caption at the bottom of the picture, I realize it's from a welcome mixer at the beginning of that fateful school year. I absorb the photo, trying to memorize every face in the frame, desperate for even the smallest breadcrumbs. I want to know who she was talking to, who she hung out with—who might know anything about what happened to her.

I go back to flipping through the pictures, searching carefully in every shot for more glimpses of her. There are a few: a group picnic on the quad, a formal dinner in the grand hall. There she is, in the back of a shot of some other students, sitting in the shadow of one of the old elm trees, head bent studiously over a book.

The ache in my chest grows. God, I miss her so much.

But I force myself to keep searching, jotting down the other names listed in every photo she's in. There are a couple of other students that keep popping up in the same shots with her. A short redhead with dimples standing arm-in-arm with Wren in one pic and raising a toast at a group dinner in another. *Lara Southerly.* I make a note of her name. There's a tall, tow-haired boy, too, caught smiling at Wren with a look of adoration clear in his eyes. *Phillip McAllister.*

Maybe I'm clutching at straws here, imagining they might remember more than Wren even did herself, but I'm going to follow every clue I can find. Somehow, I'll piece it together, what happened to her. Then, maybe I'll find the answers—and some peace.

I'm at the end of the yearbook when I find it: Wren, dressed up in a floaty pink cocktail dress, caught in a blur of motion, spinning around. Her face is hidden from the camera behind a waterfall of dark hair, and there's no name in the caption, but I'd know her anywhere.

I remember that dress. We picked it out together at an expensive boutique when she was preparing for her trip. Wren balked at the price, but I convinced her. After all, I teased, who knew what fancy parties she'd be invited to, rubbing elbows with the cream of the English aristocracy in Oxford?

Sure enough, in the photo, she's in the lavish gardens of some sweeping country house. It looks like she's having the time of her life.

She didn't know that it would soon be over.

I stare at the photo and feel a deep shiver. A grand house in the countryside . . . a formal event . . .

Was this the night she was taken?

My heart is in my throat as I scan the page for information. Wren couldn't remember anything useful about this mysterious party, no matter how hard she tried. Where it was, who was there, how she even wound up attending at all . . . she wondered if she'd been dreaming about the glimpses of ballgowns and champagne glasses, but this picture in the yearbook matches up with those shattered fragments of memory.

Here it is, I realize, right in front of me: The first evidence that she was even at the party at all.

So what was the event?

My hopes rise. If I knew where the photo was taken, then I could try to find a guest list, photos, build a timeline, and figure out when she was taken—

I eagerly check the yearbook for any more information, but there's no photography credit, and Wren's name isn't even listed by the snap. Her face is hidden, so only I would recognize her in the shot.

My heart sinks. A dead-end. But it's something, I remind myself: one more piece of the puzzle. And with so little to be working from, every small detail might prove important. So I snap a photo of the page with my phone. But I'm just about to start Googling those other names from the yearbook when the muffled chime of the church bells sound nearby. It's noon.

Shit.

I bolt to my feet and hunt for the crumpled schedule I stuffed in my bag. *12 noon, Libertines and the Law: Cloisters 5.*

Double shit.

I grab my things, shove the yearbook back on the shelf, and race from the library. The Cloisters are clear across campus, and I break into a run, weaving through groups of students milling on the quad.

"Watch it!" someone yells when I knock them aside, but I don't slow down. I'm panting by the time I find the right room, up a narrow staircase above the chilly stone cloisters, with a heavy old door that sticks when I push it.

Come on! I heave it again, putting my full weight behind the push—

—which means that when it gives way suddenly, I stumble clumsily into the office and nearly tumble straight onto my ass. I grab at the nearest solid surface for balance, a coatrack beside the door. And it's not so solid. The coats and jackets clatter to the ground.

"Shit, I'm so sorry," I blurt, gathering them up quickly. I finally straighten, flushed and panting, to find I'm standing in an elegant book-lined study, with five other students staring at me with smirks on their faces.

And one handsome, enigmatic professor, smirking the most of all.

My nerves catch, taking in the now-familiar broad shoulders and searching, wry gaze.

Of course it would be him.

"Ms. Peterson, I presume?" Professor St. Clair looks at me with amusement. He's clearly had a shave and change of clothes since I caught him strolling home at dawn. Now, he's devastatingly clean-cut, his dark hair curling damp over his piercing blue eyes, lounging on a vintage Eames chair in a rumpled button-down and dark-wash jeans. He could pass as just another student here—if it wasn't for the simple power and confidence radiating from his body.

There's no doubt that he's the one in charge of this room.

"Professor." I swallow hard, getting my breath back—and trying to ignore the way my pulse kicks dangerously at the sight of him. "Yes. Hi."

There's a free chair on the other side of the room, and I try to edge over to it, stepping over bookbags and people's outstretched legs.

"What are you doing?" Saint's voice is lazy and even.

I blink. Is this a test? "I was just going to take a seat for the class . . ."

"You're late," he cuts me off.

"By all of four minutes," I can't help shooting back. He arches an eyebrow, and I remember I can't afford to draw attention to myself.

Especially not from this guy.

"I'm sorry," I apologize again quickly. "I was at the library, and I lost track of time. It won't happen again," I promise, finally reaching the corner and sinking down on the spindly chair.

"No, it won't," Saint agrees pleasantly. "I don't stand for lateness. Which is why I'm going to have to ask you to leave."

"What?" I stare. "Now?"

"If you wouldn't mind, Ms. Peterson." He gives me another lazy smile. "You've already disrupted this seminar enough, don't you think?"

"But, I'm here now. Ready and eager to learn." I sense the nudges and looks the other students are exchanging, and I wait for one of them to speak up for me and say they don't mind.

But nope, they just sit there, looking smug. Like this is some kind of contest, and I've been disqualified at the very first round.

"Please, Professor?" I add, forcing myself to look contrite. Remembering his reputation, I flash him my most innocent smile, and even bat my eyelashes a little. Sure, I'm not exactly a blushing freshman, but if he has a thing for students, maybe I can sweet-talk my way out of this. "Couldn't you make an exception? Just this once? I'd be *so* grateful," I add, all breathy.

But Saint just takes a slow sip of his coffee and gives a careless shrug. "What kind of example would we be setting, letting you stay?" His gaze sweeps over me, like he can see right through me—like he can see that I don't really belong.

"You can't expect to waltz in here late, bat those pretty eyelashes, and expect to have everyone bend to your whim," he continues. "It's such a cliché, don't you think? It doesn't make you look half as cool as you think."

The words are familiar, and then I realize: He's quoting my own quip right back at me!

I narrow my eyes, meeting his smug stare. So, that's what this is about. I wounded his delicate male ego this morning, and now he's turning the tables and reminding me who's really got the power here.

"Go on," he says, nodding to the door. "Shoo."

Shoo! Like I'm some kind of pet, for him to order around!

I bite back my furious retort just in time. *Remember, you're undercover.* Keeping a low profile. Which means not pissing off the star professor on my very first day.

So, I get to my feet, forcing myself to move slowly and casually. Like I'm not really burning with embarrassment under everyone's scornful glares. I saunter back the way I came—not trying nearly so hard to avoid trampling on the other students as I go this time.

But despite the voice in my head reminding me to shut up and take whatever public humiliation this annoyingly handsome asshole wants to dish out, I can't help pausing by the door. "Does this ban on attending your seminar last all semester, or just for the day?" I ask, fixing him with an icy look. "I really would like the chance to learn *something*," I add, unable to keep the sarcasm from my voice. "Since that is your actual job, isn't it? As opposed to, well, all the rest of your *extracurricular* activities."

I don't wait for an answer—or another put-down. I turn on my heel and walk out.

And yes, I let the door slam shut behind me. Immature? Maybe, but there's something about that Saint guy that's already getting under my skin.

Like the fact he clearly gets off on ordering people around, like he's in total control.

And the inconvenient fact that I felt a rush of heat while he was doing it. Because if he'd instructed me like that outside of official class time . . .

In a bedroom, perhaps . . .

Tempting, sexy scenes flood my mind before I can stop them: Saint laying me out on that crushed velvet couch, sending the coffee cups crashing to the floor. Damp skin sliding, fingers pressing just *there*. His cut-glass English accent murmuring filthy whispers in my ear, ordering me to my knees, to be a good girl for him—

"Wait up!" There's laughter and voices down the hall, and I snap out of my reverie as a group of students bustle past.

Down girl, I scold myself, blushing. Just because I like my romance novels on the spicy side, it doesn't mean this man isn't a smug asshole for talking to me like that in real life.

Besides, when has a real man ever measured up to the breath-less, sexy scenes that fill my Kindle and keep my highlights tool working overtime?

Precisely never.

* * *

I PLANT MYSELF down on a bench opposite the stairwell, pull out my reading for the week, and wait. The hour passes quickly, and soon, the other students are clattering down the stairs, gush-ing over their first amazing experience with the great Professor St. Clair.

"He's one of the youngest members on staff," a blonde girl is saying as they sweep past. "You know he's published already?"

"And have you seen the Ashford estate out in the country?" another girl pipes up, red-cheeked and flushed from a whole hour in the great man's company. "It was featured in *Town & Country* magazine last year, it's gorgeous!"

They disappear without a word to me, but I stay planted right there, until the man himself finally descends. He's pulled on a navy peacoat, and with an armful of papers, he's every inch the dashing academic—although the gleam in his eye when he sees me is anything but studious. "You waited for me," Saint says, smirking.

"For your assignment," I correct him crisply. "Something tells me my classmates aren't going to fill me in on what I missed."

"Snooty little suck-ups, aren't they?" he agrees, and I bark a laugh in surprise. "Sometimes I wonder why I even bother teaching here," he continues, producing a printed reading list and dropping it on the bench beside me.

And I realize: he likes this. Me talking back to him. Giving as good as I get. Not swooning and sighing like all those other stu-dents, who actually care about impressing him for their grades.

"Because you like to lord it over everyone, and savor what small, pathetic scraps of power you can wield?" I suggest sweetly.

Saint grins wider, and damn if it doesn't make him even hotter: the sudden flash of mischief in his eyes, the promise of some reckless pleasure in his plush, sensual lips . . .

"I can see that you're going to be trouble, Ms. Peterson," he says softly, and I feel a shiver of lust that's impossible to ignore.

Red alert. Danger ahead.

"No trouble here," I lie, getting to my feet and packing the reading list away. "Well, only when provoked."

"Should I consider that a warning?" Saint asks, arching an eyebrow.

"That's up to you. Plan on being an asshole to me in class again?" I ask.

"I think you've learned your lesson," Saint replies, eyes still sparkling with amusement.

"Don't be late, and that the professor is a power-hungry jackass." I tick them off on my fingers. "Yup, just about got that covered. And they said Oxford would challenge me."

He chuckles, a warm, rich sound that rolls all the way down my spine.

And lower still.

"Is that why you're here?" he asks, his gaze drifting over me again, like he's trying to place me. "The challenge?"

I swallow hard. "Something like that," I lie vaguely. "What about you? Why literature and philosophy? You're not exactly 'teacher of the year' material."

"My student feedback would say otherwise," Saint replies.

I snort with laughter. "Sure, it's your *teaching* they love. No, really, why?" I ask again, curious now. "You don't exactly need the paycheck. Aren't you already set for life as some swanky duke?"

"If you mean, am I heir to the Ashford duchy, the answer is unfortunately yes," Saint says, with a flash of what looks like annoyance in his gaze. *Interesting.* "As for my position here at the college . . . consider it a favor to a friend. Keeping me out of trouble. Idle hands and all."

"So, you were here last year?" I ask.

"No, I was traveling in Europe. Working on my book," he replies, and I mentally cross him off my list for investigation. He wouldn't have crossed paths with Wren at all.

"And you left all that behind?" I reply. "Clearly, you missed the fame and glamor here in Oxford."

Saint smirks. "Academia has its perks. Molding young minds."

"Sure, it's the young *minds* you enjoy," I can't help muttering, and he laughs again.

"We'll see, Ms. Peterson . . . you should keep an open mind, about your classes *and* your professor. You did say you were eager to learn."

With a wink, he saunters away, leaving me buzzing from our brief, charged banter.

Not that it matters, I remind myself, hoisting my bag and marching in the opposite direction. He might be sexy and annoyingly intriguing, but he's also a distraction.

I'm here for Wren, to find a way to avenge her. That's what matters.

It's the *only* thing that matters.

And I won't let anything stand in my way.

Chapter Four
SAINT

Tessa Peterson . . .

I wait by the front gates, idly scrolling through her file on my phone. But there's not much to see. American, here on fellowship . . . She doesn't exactly fit the profile for the usual Oxford student, who are straight from the most exclusive schools in the world—or with a family name to make up for it—

"Excuse me, Professor St. Clair?"

I look up from my phone to find one of those pampered, rare-fied students hovering nearby.

"That's me." I glance her over. She's blonde and coltish, and not a day over nineteen, glancing back at the coterie of other whispering girls nearby who clearly urged her to come over.

"I wanted to say, I'm a huge fan of your work," she says con-fidently. "I just loved your book on the libertine movement."

"Really?" I arch an eyebrow. "Even my editor didn't love that book. Despised it, actually. Thought they would be lowering the tone of the whole publishing company to print the damn thing."

Of course, he was more than happy to accept the fat promotion after it became a surprise bestseller, but even he had to accept that sex sells—now, as much as it ever did in the eighteenth century.

"Oh no," the girl gushes quickly. "I thought it was insightful. Moving, even."

"Is that so?" I regard her, amused. "Which part *moved* you, in particular?"

"Well," she gives me a coy little smile. "Your perspective on sexual debauchery as political rebellion for one." She gives me a flirty smile. "It changed my whole outlook on the period. I tried to get in to one of your seminars," she adds, "but there's already a waitlist. I was wondering . . . perhaps you could send me a copy of the reading list, all the same. That way I could still benefit from your teaching. In private . . ."

She trails off and fixes me with another suggestive, flirty smile. There's no question what kind of "private teaching" she's angling for. And there's also no question that I should be happy to instruct her. Give her a personal tour through the teachings of Rochester, and Cleland, *Les Liaisons Dangereuses*—with, perhaps, a cautionary detour into the work of the Marquis de Sade to round out her education.

After all, I have a reputation to live up to.

Libertine. Rake. The professor who practices what he teaches.

But instead, I give her a cool smile. "You can find a subject list on the college website," I say.

Her face falls. "Oh. Of course, you must be busy."

I nod curtly. "Was there anything else?"

"No. Sorry. Thanks." She scurries away, back to her friends, cheeks flaming, and I can't help thinking of Tessa's breathy little act back in class. Fluttering her eyelashes, pouting those pretty lips . . . If I didn't know better, I'd write her off as some wide-eyed student angling for a forbidden fling, just like this one.

Too obvious. Too innocent to tempt me.

But then I remember the look on Tessa's face when I busted her snooping in the administrator's office: that flash of sharp calculation in her eyes before she put on the airhead act.

Yes, there's something different about her. Some secret she's determined to hide.

Good.

I could use a fresh diversion, and she's not the only one who needs a challenge. The term has barely begun, but already I'm feeling a restless itch, craving something—or someone—to jolt me out of the ordinary. Inspire me, provoke me, do anything to break up the endless monotony of idle pleasure that somehow has become my life.

And now I might just have found her.

I look back at my phone, to Tessa's student snapshot, taking in those unreadable grey eyes and a smart-talking mouth just made for sin.

What's your game, Ms. Peterson?

"So, *that's* why you're slumming back at Oxford. All the adoring coeds."

I look up to find my cousin, Imogen Alcott, approaching, brisk and polished as ever. She's a few years younger than me, but we grew up like siblings. She air-kisses me on both cheeks. "Who's the poor girl this time?" she teases good-naturedly as we leave the college and head along the cobbled street toward our favorite lunch spot in town.

"You mean, who's lucky enough to be graced with my attention and expertise?" I shoot back, smiling. "There's nobody yet. Except . . ."

I think of Tessa again, the grace she's hiding under those baggy college sweatshirts. How her silky ponytail would feel wrapped around my fist, her body arching under me, gasping in pleasure . . .

Imogen snorts with laughter. "Aren't you getting tired of it yet?"

"My freedom? Adventure? Indulging every whim at a moment's notice?" I reply. "Yes, you're right, it's a dreadful bore."

"I meant the way you're avoiding the real world," Imogen corrects me. "I mean, come on. You graduated from this place years ago, but you still find a way to loiter here like some eternal Peter Pan."

"Have you been talking to my parents?" I say lightly. "And I'm not loitering. I'm a sought-after guest lecturer. Published. Awarded. The Master of the college himself asked—no, *begged*—me to come teach a class."

She gives me a look. Imogen doesn't buy my "enigmatic professor" act for a second. She knows the real reason I'm just wasting time with idle amusement, fine wines, and the occasional seminar. Delaying the inevitable as long as I can.

"What about you?" I change the subject as we arrive at the courtyard café, and head for our regular table. "What brings you up to Oxford? Tea parties and tipple?"

"Now who's giving the family lecture?" Imogen scowls. She runs a successful party-planning business down in London, but in our world, the fact she's still single at twenty-seven is the only thing that matters. "Mum sent me a list the other day: ten of the most eligible bachelors in Europe. Apparently, I'm supposed to pick one and get to work, before it's too late."

"She's right," I tease. "Are those new frown lines I see? Better get those taken care of soon before those minor European princes get snatched off the market."

"Says the perpetual bachelor rotting his liver with Chateau Lafite wine." Imogen grins.

"Not at all. I'm more of a Domaine Leroy man myself," I joke, naming another vintage red wine. "Speaking of . . ." I beckon the waiter, then order wine and food.

Imogen's smile fades, and she sighs. "They're serious, you know. Never mind that the business is doing great, the only thing they care about is me marrying a man with the right name and breeding."

"I'm sorry." I give her a sympathetic smile. For all our joking around, we both know the pressure that comes from our family legacies. "And I know you do more than host tea parties. What's the event today?"

Imogen gives a wry laugh. "A tea party. Floral wonderland. Ten thousand pounds worth of designer roses and fine tableware."

I whistle.

"And the guests are all five years old!" Imogen exclaims, shaking her blonde hair. "Sometimes I wonder . . ."

She doesn't finish. She doesn't have to. We both have harbored those what-if fantasies—what our lives would be like if we didn't occupy this particular place in society, with all the expectations and legacy that comes along with it.

Now, Imogen regards me thoughtfully. "You can't avoid them forever, you know. London is only two hours away. Less, the way you drive like a bat out of hell."

I give a casual shrug, as if the St. Clair name isn't hanging around my neck like a deadweight. The gravity of my birthright I won't ever be able to escape.

Not now, anyway.

"I've been summoned," I admit. "The right honorable Duke of Ashford requests my presence at the company HQ as soon as fucking possible."

"Which is why you're out chasing freshers and drinking yourself into an early grave." Imogen rolls her eyes. "You may as well get it over with, you know. Short of divorcing your family, there's no way around it."

"Or dying," I say bleakly. "But Edward got in there before me. Typical big brother," I add darkly. "Always stealing the glory, one step ahead—and into an early grave."

Imogen knows to ignore my black humor, especially where family is concerned. "Look at it this way," she says brightly. "The sooner you go get lectured about your wayward libertine lifestyle, the sooner you can ignore every word of it, drink yourself senseless in one of those clubs of yours, and be in bed with one of your adoring freshers by dawn."

"Well, when you put it like that . . ." I take a gulp of wine and brace myself for battle. "Wish me luck."

"I think your new student might need it more." Imogen smirks.

* * *

AFTER LUNCH, IMOGEN goes to set up her lavish tea party, and I collect my Aston Martin for the drive.

Let me guess, you drive a classic sports car, too? Red or silver. Anyone would think you're insecure about your manhood.

I have to smile, remembering Tessa's pointed insult—and the smirk on her face as she delivered it. So, I'm predictable when it comes to my motor. But I'm guessing she doesn't know how *unpredictable* I can be in other departments . . .

I hit the road. There's a longer route that winds through the pretty countryside, but I reckon there's no point delaying the inevitable, so I take the motorway instead, speeding fast to chase away the tension already settling in my limbs as the open fields and woodlands turn into the city sprawl—taking me closer to the destiny I've been fighting for years now.

My family. My father. My future.

It was never supposed to be me.

Heir to the dukedom, future CEO of the family business . . . Nobody expected me to be next in line to inherit it all. After all, I was the second son.

The spare, as they so eloquently put it.

My older brother, Edward, was the one who would make them all proud. And God, he did. He was the golden boy: intelligent, kind, a natural-born leader, even back when we were kids. My parents doted on him, and I didn't even hold it against him for being their obvious favorite, not when it got me off the hook of familial responsibility.

Not when Edward himself would wink and say I got the easy job—chasing pleasure instead of glory. He was even happy to follow in our father's footsteps: studying medicine at university, ready to take his place at the head of Ashford Pharmaceuticals, the world-leading corporation my father (and his father, and his father) built. But, of course, he insisted on taking a year out to volunteer for Doctors Without Borders before he took his seat in the boardroom. He wanted to do some good in the world. Give back.

He was a good man. A better man than me in every way.

Even 'til his last breath.

Maybe that's why I don't even try to be good anymore. Nothing I do will ever live up to his shining legacy.

Nothing I do will make up for the fact it should have been him carrying on the famous St. Clair name.

Not me.

* * *

THE ASHFORD PHARMA headquarters are in Central London, a towering chrome-and-glass monstrosity bragging our status to the world. I don't come here often. In fact, I try to avoid it as much as possible, but the doormen and security still know me on sight, and leap to open doors and show me up to the executive level, high above the city.

"Tricia," I greet my father's ancient secretary with a charming smile. "You're looking lovely today. Is that a new hairdo?"

She gives me a tremulous smile. "Saint. You can go straight through."

I pause. "Everything alright?"

She swallows. "Oh, you know. Things are a little hectic right now, that's all."

I look around. She's right. The company is never fun and games, but everyone's looking more stressed than ever, and there's a buzz of frantic activity in the air.

But damned if I want to know what's going on. I'm not a part of running Ashford Pharma, by choice, and I'd like to keep it that way.

I saunter into my father's office without knocking.

"You took your time." My father barely glances up from his computer screen.

"Lovely to see you too, Dad," I reply, relaxing into one of the oversized armchairs that look out over the stunning city view as I settle in to wait.

And wait.

I stifle a sigh. Clearly, he needs to show how important he is, so I pull out my phone and idly scroll through my messages and schedule—checking when Ms. Tessa Peterson is due in my office again. Not until next week, I'm sorry to see. But I'm sure I can find a way to engineer another meeting sooner . . .

Finally, my father looks up and removes his reading glasses, regarding me with the same expression of disappointment that he's given me for the past ten years. "I hear you've been having fun," he says, disapproving. "That business in Paris last month, with the Vanderbilt girl . . . It was all over the papers. Hardly discreet."

"What's the matter, Dad?" I ask, acting casual. "You used to love hearing about my wild conquests."

He scowls back at me. "You're a grown man, Anthony. It's time you acted your age and started giving a damn about this family. This company."

But it's not my age that's the problem. We both know what really changed. My reckless adventures were all fun and games to him before Edward died, just something to brag about with his aristocratic friends, the grand adventures of his wayward second-born son.

Until I was suddenly heir to it all, and nobody was joking anymore.

"This nonsense at Oxford has gone on long enough," my father continues. "That's why I'm making arrangements for you to join us. Something in acquisitions or marketing, let you get your feet wet. Learn the ropes before you need to step into a larger role."

I fold my arms. "Thanks, but no thanks."

"It wasn't a suggestion, son."

"I didn't think it was, *father*," I echo, holding his gaze. "But why bother pretending like either one of us wants me here? You have Robert, trailing your every move," I add, naming my younger brother. The baby of the family, he just turned twenty-five, and is still fresh-faced and eager to prove himself. "Let him handle things."

"You think I don't want to?" My father scowls. "But unfortunately for the both of us, that's not how entailment works. You're the oldest. That means that you're the future of the Ashford dynasty—and I would prefer you didn't bring it into any further disrepute with your . . . *activities*."

I smirk, knowing it'll only piss him off more. "I'm discreet," I say. "Well, most of the time. It's not my fault the Vanderbilt girl has a thing for personal movies . . ."

He glares, and I have to hide a chuckle. My father already thinks I'm a reckless troublemaker, and he doesn't know the half of my more *provocative* pastimes. Now, if those adventures wound up on the front page . . .

Nobody would forget the Ashford name in a hurry, that's for sure.

"Are we done?" I ask, getting to my feet. "I have places to go, scandals to start . . ."

My father snorts in disdain. "Not so fast. As much as I'd prefer to keep you well out of the public eye, we have some big events coming up and need to present a united front. Tricia will be sending you a schedule."

"Events?" I frown.

He sighs. "Haven't you been reading the company reports?"

I shrug. "They're not exactly gripping literary material."

My father grits his teeth. "We're near the end of clinical trials on the new drug. Everything's on track, and as soon as we announce the results . . . Well, Ashford Pharma will be changing the face of medicine. There'll be press attention, scrutiny, celebration . . ."

"In other words, you need me to show up and shake hands at all the stuffy conferences and cocktail parties." I wince.

"I need you to do your duty."

"Don't I always?" I ask lightly. At the end of the day, it's a tight-rope walk: toeing the line enough to keep my parents off my back, so I can maintain my freedom to live life how I choose.

The phone on my father's desk interrupts us, and he scoops it up, already frowning as he answers. "No, I told you, I need the raw data going back to '02 . . ."

Clearly, I've been dismissed.

I turn and saunter out, but the word echoes in my mind.

Duty.

I know what it means to my family: continuing the legacy of wealth and privilege our ancestors have built. Running Ashford Pharma. Marrying an appropriate, titled woman who can stand by my side at all the charity events and awards galas, burnishing the hallowed Ashford name.

But I have a different definition of the word. My duty is to pleasure. Adventure. And I'm not about to give that up so quickly.

I think of Tessa, and that rebellious spark in her eyes. A spark that could ignite, given the right . . . *instruction.*

I smile and keep on walking. Let my father bluster all he wants. Nothing about my life needs to change.

Chapter Five
TESSA

By the end of my first official week at Oxford, it feels like I've bitten off more than I can chew. I'm not trying to be a star student here, I'm just trying to keep my head above water long enough to find out more about what happened to Wren, but even so, I'm drowning in reading and lectures, working through the night just to keep up with my all-star classmates and not earn dirty looks from the professors. Every tutorial just leaves me scrambling to catch up, and I've barely had a chance to dig into my sister's experience here at all.

I feel like I'm letting her down somehow; letting the truth stay hidden with every passing day.

Patience, I try to remind myself. I'm here in Oxford, that's the most important thing, and I'm already making progress. Thanks to the yearbooks, I have a list of names to try and track down. They may have graduated or moved on, but England's a small place.

I'll find them, one way or another.

"Already studying late?" The elderly clerk at the Ashford College library gives me a sympathetic smile on Friday night, as I slouch in, tired, past the main desk. "Remember to pace yourself. It's early days, yet."

"I work better at night," I tell her truthfully. "It's quieter, I can focus."

I haven't been sleeping great since Wren died, so I may as well make use of the time.

"If you want a hot tip, there's a café just up Cornmarket Street that stays open until midnight," she adds. "But don't go wandering around alone. It's still a big city, and you should stay safe."

"Thanks, I'll be careful!" I reply. I'm just about to head upstairs to study when another student arrives, looking panicked.

"I forgot my pass, but I have to check this out," she says, brandishing a textbook. "My essay is due first thing in the morning!"

"It's alright," the clerk chuckles. "I just need some ID, and I can replace it for you."

"Oh, thank God!" The girl rummages in her bag and produces a driver's license. The clerk taps a few things on her computer, then hands her a fresh card.

"The passcode is 0000, so you'll need to reset it," she advises. "But it's all set up to your original account."

"You're a lifesaver!" The panicked girl checks out her book, and then races away.

I pause, suddenly getting an idea. "Shit, I forgot my pass too," I lie. "Can I get a replacement too. Please?"

"Seems like a running theme around here," she says with a tired smile. "ID?"

"Right here." I find it in my purse—but it's not mine. It's Wren's old driver's license, the one I "borrowed" back in college to use as a fake ID and sneak into bars. It's expired, but it doesn't matter. The librarian barely looks at it before making me a new library card, just like I hoped.

"Thanks!"

I bolt upstairs and find a quiet corner to unpack my laptop and settle in. I bring up the library system and enter Wren's ID number and the default passcode.

Her library borrower history flashes up on screen. A record of everything she checked out during her time here. It's a thin connection, but I'm leaving no stone unturned, so I eagerly scan the list of obscure science journals. *Neuroscience Today. Microbiology Quarterly. Secret Societies of Oxford . . .*

Hold up.

I scroll back, frowning at the list. In addition to all her coursework, Wren checked out a bunch of books on local history, about Oxford. But not just tourist stuff, no, these were books about secret societies and conspiracies here at Ashford.

Why did my sister care about that?

Curious, I head to the stacks to track them down, skimming the shelves, not sure what I'm looking for or why Wren would've been interested. I pick up one of the books that she checked out: it's a dry, academic overview of the history of Ashford College, from the founding of the school by some bigwig in Queen Elizabeth the First's court, all the way up to the present day. *Saint's ancestors . . .* Apparently, there were rumors that the college was a front for radical political thought, and all kinds of politicians, nobility, and intellectuals would secretly meet to plot about the future of the country.

I can't imagine why Wren would have been reading this stuff, not even for fun—she was more into thrillers and mystery books. Maybe she was just interested in finding more out about the school?

I flip through the rest of the books, sighing. I said I'd leave no stone unturned, but it feels like I'm clutching at straws here. And mixing my metaphors. Maybe I should give it up for the night and try again with a fresh mind tomorrow.

I pack up, and head out. Kris and Jia made me promise to meet them for a drink, so I walk the short distance through town. Despite the librarian's warning, Oxford is warm and buzzing on a Friday night, with people spilling out of the bars, and the cobblestone streets busy with new students out to party. I find the right address, which is a historic pub with crooked, Tudor-style beams and a packed beer garden out front. I duck inside and try to weave through the crowds of students inside, packed ten-deep around the fireplace and scuffed, ancient bar.

"Tessa! You came!" Jia greets me with an excited hug, almost spilling her beer.

"I said I would."

"Yes, but you've been so busy, we didn't believe it." She grins. "Isn't this place cool? It's supposed to be one of the oldest pubs in the city. At least two of your presidents got high on the patio."

"Together?" I joke, but she's already gripped my arm and is dragging me through the packed room to where Kris has claimed a tiny table under the eaves.

"Look who I found!" Jia announces as we squeeze in to fit.

He slides a full pint glass over to me. "Take this. I can't even look at beer right now."

"Tequila, on the other hand," Jia cracks.

"It's cleaner. Agave, right?" Kris says, before launching into a story about his lecture and a new crush who asked him for his notes.

I'm content to sit back and let their gossiping chatter wash over me. It's nice to feel included, and to switch off from all the stress of my classes and investigation, just soaking up the atmosphere. Kris and Jia are fun, too, already comparing notes about drunken exploits with the men in their study groups.

". . . I heard he's off the list."

"What? We had such high hopes, all that brawn."

"Turns out there's a reason the man's called the Tiny Texan when he's a whopping six-foot-two," Jia sighs mournfully.

I look between them and have to laugh.

"What?" Jia asks.

"Nothing." I smile. "You guys just aren't what I expected, that's all. I thought Oxford students would all be, you know—"

"Nerdy academics who do nothing but sit around, having stimulating intellectual debate?" Jia replies with a smirk.

"Well . . . yeah!" I laugh.

"We contain multitudes," Kris jokes. "But no, that's just the reputation. The truth is, there's nothing hornier than a bunch of grad students."

"It's like an arrested adolescence," Jia agrees. "I was too busy being a perfect student to ever really date or have fun in school, and then undergrad was just all study, all the time. So now . . . ?"

"Now we're making up for lost time," Kris declares.

"Well, I'll toast to that," I say, raising my glass. "Vicariously."

"Just you wait," Jia says. "Some hot British man will sweep you off your feet."

I snort. "I'm not looking for anything right now," I reassure them. "I can barely keep up with my studies. I don't need any distractions."

"You say that now . . . !"

They return to their scorecards, and I idly watch the crowds, but then the conversation turns to outrageous Oxford traditions.

"You know the Bullingdon Club members fuck a pig?"

"What?" I nearly choke on my beer.

"It was a pig's head," Jia corrects him, laughing. "At some formal banquet. Allegedly, the old Prime Minister had to, you know, penetrate it. For a dare."

"Is this why he just resigned?" I ask, blinking.

"No, this one groped some Parliamentary intern," Kris says, rolling his eyes. "But it's typical, all these old-school boys, doing whatever the fuck they like."

I pause. "So, it's like a secret society?" I ask, remembering Wren's extracurricular research.

"Bullingdon isn't exactly secret, it's like the most famous drinking club around," Jia replies. "But there are a bunch of others, sure. Piers Galveston, the Nocturnes . . ."

"What do they do?" I ask.

"What does any group of rich assholes do?" she says, taking a gulp of beer. "Play dress up, get their cocks out, and lord it over the rest of us."

"It's all about money and power," Kris agrees, sighing. "Just another way to feel special and scratch each other's backs."

"That's all?" I ask, disappointed. "I mean, they must be hiding *something*, right, or else it wouldn't be secret?"

"You mean like sacrificial rituals and blood oaths?" Jia giggles. "You're giving these people way too much credit."

"The inbreeding gets out all their imagination," Kris adds cheerfully. "Trust me, there's nothing so boring as a man named Frederick Scottsworthy the Fourth after too much tipple. Barely capable of missionary, at best."

They howl with laughter. Clearly, they're way ahead of me in the drinks department. "Want another?" I ask, getting to my feet. "My round."

"Yes, please!"

I head for the bar and have to elbow my way in to get near the bartender. "Ouch," a guy curses beside me.

"Shit, I'm sorry!" I exclaim. He's got sandy hair and wire-rimmed glasses and gives me a friendly smile.

"It's OK. Every man—or woman—for themselves."

I try to make eye contact with the bartender with zero results. "Clearly, I haven't cracked the code of getting attention," I tell the stranger with a sigh.

"You certainly got mine," he says with a grin. "And I'll have the bruise to prove it tomorrow."

"Are you angling for me to buy you a drink to make up for it?" I ask, amused. It's been a long while since I flirted with anyone, but this guy seems nice enough.

"Well . . . now that you mention it."

I laugh.

"No, I wouldn't dream of it," he continues. "Besides, with your shoddy drink-ordering skills, we'd be here all night."

"Hey," I protest lightly, and he grins at me. Definitely flirting.

"I'm Frederick," he says, and I have to cough to hide my snort of laughter. "What?" He frowns, and I shake my head.

"No, sorry, just something my friend said . . . I'm Tessa," I add quickly, and his smile widens.

"Lovely to meet you, Tessa with the incredibly sharp elbows."

I'm just shaking his hand when someone slides in by the bar behind me. "Causing more trouble, Ms. Peterson?"

A shiver of awareness rolls down my spine.

Saint.

I turn and find him leaning there, all rumpled dark hair and a cut-glass jawline. Again, I feel that electric pulse of uncertainty, like a live wire just hitched a spark, but I keep my cool and fix him with an even gaze. "You know me," I say archly. "Always disrupting things."

Saint smirks. His eyes drift past me to my new friend. "Freddie, good to see you."

"Professor St. Clair." Frederick's eyes widen, and he clears his throat. "I, umm, hi."

"I'm surprised to see you out tonight," Saint says, giving him a lazy smile. "If I recall, you have a paper due first thing Monday, and based on your recent performance in my seminar . . . well, I would suggest you have better things to do than flirt with pretty girls in bars. However disruptive they might be," he adds, giving me a smirk.

Frederick's face turns red, and the man practically deflates in front of us. He looks from me, to Saint, and back again. "He's right. I, um, I have to study," he mumbles, and then hightails away so fast, he's practically a blur.

"Really?" I ask Saint, giving him a pointed look. "You had to pull a little power move?"

Saint gives a careless shrug. "What can I say? I care about my students' academic futures."

"Sure you do."

"I'm surprised at you, though," he adds, gesturing to the bartender with his sharp gaze still fixed on me. Of course, the guy
materializes to take his order right away: a glass of some ancient
scotch, neat.

He doesn't offer to get me anything.

"The boy's still a first year," Saint continues. "But I guess you
like them young."

I narrow my eyes. "Actually, I do," I say brightly. "Less attitude,
for a start. They don't walk around, acting like they expect
everyone to drop to their knees and obey every word."

Saint arches an eyebrow, and too late, I realize the double
entendre. *What it would feel like on my knees in front of Saint,
awaiting his instruction . . .*

My cheeks flush, but I pretend like I don't notice. "Besides,
younger men have far more stamina," I continue sweetly. "They're
insatiable. While with age comes . . . infirmity. Wouldn't you say?"

Saint laughs at the insult. "There's certainly nothing lacking
in my . . . firmness."

"Oh?" I let my gaze drift lower, over his pressed shirt and black
jeans. "Lucky you."

"I find luck has very little to do with it," Saint replies, amusement
tugging at the edges of his plush mouth. "Some things in life are
just better with skill. Experience. For example, the maturity to
know when stamina is necessary, and when a more *immediate*
gratification is required."

His voice drops, confidential, and it feels like he's standing
closer to me, even though he hasn't moved an inch. "When pleasure shouldn't be delayed," he continues, eyes still fixed on mine.
"When the shock of being overwhelmed is the most exquisite
release of all. I dare say, young Freddie has no idea what it takes
to satisfy a woman. Not the way she truly needs."

My body tightens, and I feel a rush of heat. I can't help it. Still,
I fight my reaction.

This is his regular routine, I remind myself. He's probably used that line a dozen times already—this week.

So, I give a shrug and act unimpressed. "You Oxford men really love hearing yourself speak, don't you? What do the Brits say? 'All talk, and no trouser.' I'll take my chances on a man of action, any day."

I angle my body away from him and finally manage to flag down the bartender to order in another round. Saint lets out a low chuckle, but just as I'm expecting another sizzling comeback, he walks away instead, leaving me off-balance.

Again.

I shake my head, trying to push the unsettled sensation away, but I can't help tracking his path through the crowd as he moves to join someone. A beautiful woman, who's waiting for him in the corner. She's blonde and polished, and dressed so elegantly that she couldn't be a student.

I feel a treacherous stab of disappointment. Of course, he has a date. A man like him doesn't go home alone. Which is why I'm keeping my distance. I have zero interest in being just another conquest to the campus Romeo.

However tempting his talk of pleasure might be . . .

"Tessa!" Jia's voice pulls me back. She's pulling on her jacket and handing me mine. "Change of plans. We're starving, let's go get something to eat!"

* * *

WE HEAD BACK toward Ashford, stopping at one of the food trucks pitched up along the main street. Jia and Kris swear by a concoction of fries smothered with curry sauce, which turns out to be delicious. "An Oxford institution," Kris declares, a little unsteady on his feet. He gestures wildly with a fry, sending sauce splattering to the ground. "No finer food on earth!"

Jia and I exchange a look. "Lucky there's no lectures in the morning," she says, patiently steering him toward our building. "He can sleep it off."

Lectures. Shit. I stop. "I just remembered, I need to grab my mail," I say, relieved to spot a light still on over in the Ashford gatehouse. "I might have an extra class tomorrow."

"On the weekend?"

"I need it," I say grimly. "Can you get him back OK?"

"I'll manage. Oi!" Jia yells, as Kris stumbles over to a clueless couple and asks them for a cigarette. "Behave!"

She goes to keep him out of trouble, and I cross the street, ducking into the gatehouse lodge. I head back to my mail cubby and flip through the flyers to see if there's anything from my literature tutor.

Instead, there's a stiff envelope tucked inside, with my name written in inked calligraphy on the front. The paper is heavy stock, thick cream with gold edging, and when I open it, I find a luxurious invitation inside.

You are cordially invited . . .

The Mulberry Park Hotel. Masks required.

Discretion presumed.

It has tomorrow's date.

I turn it over in my hands, confused—and intrigued. *Masks?* Is this some kind of Oxford welcome event? But there's no return address, or any hint of who the invitation is from.

Then I see a handwritten note, scrawled on the back of the card, and my heart stops in my chest.

Meet me by the fountain at 11:30 p.m.
I know what happened to Wren.

Chapter Six
TESSA

I spend a sleepless night tossing and turning as my mind races over every detail of the cryptic invitation, but by the time dawn breaks over the city and my feet pound the pavements on another restless morning run, I'm no closer to any answers.

What does it mean? Who could have sent it to me?

And why?

Nobody's supposed to know I'm digging into Wren's history here. I've been so careful to be discreet and keep my true motivations hidden—lying to everybody about why I'm in Oxford, and the fact that we're even connected. I thought only Bates the porter knew we were related, and even then, I told him she was happy back in the States.

I think over our conversation in the gatehouse, trying to remember if anyone could have overheard. I recall a tall boy, asking about a delivery . . . a blonde woman dropping something off . . . but their faces are a blur, and I can't even remember if they were around when I mentioned Wren. A dozen people were coming and going while we talked, any one of them might have listened in. Or maybe it wasn't my chat with Bates that gave me away. Either way, somebody knows more. And even though the anonymous invite makes me nervous, a part of me is excited, too.

It's a clue. Some path that may lead me closer to the truth.

I have to follow where it leads.

* * *

I SPEND THE rest of the day preparing for this mysterious event. A quick search online reveals that the address is for a fancy hotel in the countryside, about forty miles away, so I have to figure out the best way to get there and blend in at the party. But despite my hunger for answers, I can't help the nerves growing, sharp in my stomach, and by the time evening rolls around, I'm wound tight, on edge, wondering if I'm walking into some kind of trap—or reading way too much into this.

A knock on my bedroom door startles me, and I let out a yelp. "Woah, sorry." It's Jia, sticking her head into the room. "Are you OK?" she asks, frowning. I'm pretty sure I've been pacing a hole in the old rug in here, going over everything in my mind.

"Fine!" I lie loudly, flashing a smile. "Just thinking over this essay I have due."

"Want to take a break?" she asks. "We're heading over to college for movie night."

"I need to finish up here," I say, "but maybe I'll swing by later."

"OK, see you there!"

She retreats, and soon, I hear her and Kris clatter out, leaving me alone.

My pulse kicks.

As soon as I have the apartment to myself, I jump in the shower and start getting ready for the event. I didn't pack any gowns for my trip, but I do have a long black silk slip dress that looks formal enough when I pair it with some strappy black sandals, and I twist my hair up into a sleek chignon style. I found a costume store in town this afternoon and bought a simple black silk masquerade mask. A slick of red lipstick and some smoky eyeshadow, and I'm ready for action.

Even though I still don't know exactly what kind of action it'll be.

I pack some cash and my keys in a tiny clutch purse, cover my dress with a silky wrap, and head out. It takes two local buses and the better part of an hour, plus a long hike up a gravel drive-way, before I arrive at the hotel, and by the time I'm standing on the grand stone steps, my anxiety is working overtime.

It's a huge old country house, lit up in the moonlight, but the place looks deserted. Weird. There are no guests or staff in sight.

I pause for a moment, wondering if I've got the right place—or date—but then a taxi pulls up, and a group of people spill out, dressed in gorgeous gowns and elaborate masquerade masks. They saunter up to the front entrance, and a burly security guy appears to check their invitations, before they're ushered inside. I hear a burst of music emerge before the doors swing shut again.

It's game time.

I remember to pull on my mask, then follow in their footsteps to the main doors.

"Private party, ma'am." The man blocks my path.

As if I could be here in the middle of nowhere in a mask for any other reason.

"I have an invitation." My hand trembles with nerves as I pull it from my bag and show him.

A curt nod. "Phone?"

"Excuse me?" I blink, confused.

"Your cellphone," he explains, holding out a velvet bag. "No electronic devices are allowed in the premises."

"Oh." I feel a flicker of unease giving it up, but I slip my phone into the bag and receive a small, numbered token in return. Finally, he stands aside. "Enjoy your evening."

"Thanks."

I take a deep breath, and step inside.

I'm not sure what I was expecting, but the minute the door swings shut behind me, I find myself in a dimly lit, classical wonderland. The cavernous hotel lobby has been transformed, with what must be hundreds of candles alight on every surface, dripping wax in rivers to the floor. Antique urns spill vast armfuls of antique roses beside the elaborate chandeliers and candelabra, but as I draw closer, I realize, they're all dead and preserved—their crumbling, dried petals adorning the marble floors.

The effect is lush and atmospheric, almost like a mausoleum. I can hear classical music playing, the sound of an orchestra deeper in the hotel, so I follow the music down a long hallway strewn with more decaying flowers and candles, the light dim and flickering, until a man in elaborate historical dress suddenly materializes in front of me. He's masked and wigged in a pastel-colored brocade coat and knee-high boots, dressed up like something from the court of Marie Antoinette.

"Oh, hi," I blurt, startled. "I'm sorry, I was looking for—"

Wordlessly, he swings open a pair of double doors, revealing a grand ballroom, filled with masked guests, music and laughter. "Thank you—" I turn, but he's already melted into the crowd.

OK then.

I edge into the ballroom, looking around. It's an elaborate spectacle, alright: hundreds of people, all dressed to the nines, with staff and performers circulating in more of the same historical outfits. Plumes of feathers, rich satins and silks, wild colors . . . It's a feast for the senses at every turn, and I drink it all in, wide-eyed.

I've never seen any party like this before. Even the costume bashes I've attended are amateur hour compared to this extravagance. Crystal chandeliers reflect off the silverware, champagne flowing, and groaning tables of the most delicate cakes and pastries imaginable. At the head of the room, a full orchestra performs—dozens of masked musicians dressed in brocade coats and gowns, led by the conductor up on a podium, dressed head-to-toe in dazzling white satin with a bouffant powdered wig.

It feels like a movie set, some hundred-million-dollar production that a crew has staged, just for us. And the guests . . . !

My simple dress is nothing compared to the costumes on display here tonight. Lavish gowns, white tie tuxedos, and elaborate masks disguising every face. They drink and dance together, a whirl of color and activity. The energy is electric in the room, full of anticipation.

But I'm not here to party.

I grab a glass of champagne and take a sip to steady my nerves. *Focus*, I remind myself, taking another calming breath.

Someone at this party knows what happened to Wren.

I could mingle, just watching everyone for hours, but it's coming up on eleven thirty, so I make a beeline for the wall of open French doors, leading out onto a candlelit terrace. People are talking in groups, and the air is crisp and cool, sobering me fast as I look around to find—

There. The back steps lead down to a rolling lawn, and an ornate fountain burbling in the middle.

I pick up my skirts and make my way across the dew-wet grass. It's quieter here, away from the main building, lit only by soft spotlights in the hedgerows and more candles set around the lip of the fountain. I take a seat on the concrete ledge to wait, letting my fingers skim the surface of the water, tracing over rose petals as my mind races with excitement, alert to every footstep nearby.

Who am I meeting? And why did they need to bring me here?

Will I finally learn the truth about what happened to Wren tonight?

The minutes tick past as my nervous anticipation only grows. I have a view of the ballroom terrace from here, and people occasionally drift out to talk or flirt in the shadows, but nobody crosses the lawn to meet me.

I check my watch impatiently.

11:30. 11:40. 11:55 . . .

The minutes tick past, infinitely slow, but still, nobody comes. My excitement slowly fades until I'm left shivering in the cool night air, my shoulders slumped and the metallic taste of disappointment bitter in my mouth.

A member of the waitstaff drifts over with a silver tray of drinks. "No, thank you," I tell them, but he keeps the tray offered.

"For you, ma'am."

I notice there's a card on the tray, and a sprig of white flowers. Another message. I take them, excited, and wait for the man to leave before I open the note up to read.

Legacy is our gift, and a sworn bond.

The single line of text is written in the same handwriting as the last note. I turn the page over, confused, but there's nothing else on it.

That's it?

A thorn from the sprig of flowers pricks my finger, and I wince. I suck on it, my hopes deflating as I look around.

Whoever sent me the invitation isn't going to show. Maybe they got cold feet for some reason. Or maybe this was all some kind of sick joke from the start. Either way, I feel like a fool. I got all dressed up, and came all this way, for another weird, cryptic note? I just want to go home and forget that I even came here.

Midnight is approaching as I make my way back past the terrace and into the ballroom. The party is still in full swing; if anything, the mood is even more hyped up, with a buzz of whispers and conversation in the room. I push through the crowds, heading for the door, when someone catches my arm.

I whirl around, startled. It's a short man, impeccably suited, with a red silk mask covering his face. "Where are you going?" he demands, sloshing champagne from his glass. "The fun's just getting started!"

"Thanks, but this isn't really my scene." I politely pull away.

He lets out a cackle of laughter. "This? This is just the prelude, my dear. Haven't you experienced midnight before?"

Midnight? I pause, confused. "Umm, sure. It comes every night."

"Then you're a lucky girl," he says, smirking. "The rest of us have to wait for that very special invitation . . ."

I'm just about to ask what on earth he means when the music suddenly stops. A low drumroll sounds, and the whole crowd stills, hushing in clear anticipation.

"Here it is," the man says with delight. "The stroke of midnight..."

The ballroom doors swing open, and a procession of masked performers in their elaborate historical costumes and wigs slowly walks in as a clock chimes midnight. I wonder if they're about to perform some kind of dramatic reading or musical number, but when they reach the center of the room, they pause there, as if basking in the attention.

All eyes are on them. You could hear a pin drop. And then, they each slowly move toward the performer closest to them and start to undress each other.

Unlacing the gowns. Peeling off the ruffled shirts and cummerbunds. Clothing falls to the floor—and it doesn't stop.

Wait a minute. My eyes widen, watching as the performers closest to me begin unlacing each other's petticoats, slipping the sheer fabric over their shoulders and off their chests, fingers tracing softly; touch caressing bare skin and stiff, peaked nipples as the last scraps of silk drift to the polished floors. *They're not going to ...*

But they are.

Before the chimes of midnight come to an end, the group is standing in front of us, completely naked, save for their masks. They stand there, posing, proud, drinking in the attention of the rapt, expectant crowd.

And then the music starts, and I realize that this is only the beginning.

Chapter Seven
TESSA

What kind of party is this?

I stand there, frozen in thrilled shock, as the elaborate ball turns into . . . well, I'm not really sure, but I'm guessing it's the reason for the anonymous masks and the confiscated phones. The orchestral music turns seductive, the naked performers acting like guides in this new, decadent scene of debauchery. They move through the crowd, pulling guests onto the dance floor and into dark corners, undressing them and pairing them off with other newcomers. One of them tries to take me by the hand and bring me to a couple who are already stripping off their formal clothes, sensually touching each other as they peel the fabric away. The woman glances up, beckoning me to join them, but I shake my head, blushing furiously, and scamper back into the shadows where nobody can see me.

What the hell is going on?

My heart is racing as I watch the party turn sensual and explicit before my very wide eyes. A woman in sheer black lingerie lays back on a velvet chaise as two men pour champagne over her, licking the liquid from her damp skin—and then parting her legs to feast even more. Behind them, a couple is slow-dancing a tango, completely naked in the center of the room, the air between them shimmering with tension and heat. More of the guides are passing out platters of party favors, and when one comes close enough, I can see the silver tray is set with condoms, lube, and silk restraints; sex toys and accessories being circulated like hors d'oeuvres amongst the guests.

I watch it all, mesmerized. Never in my wildest dreams did I imagine that things like this actually happened! Between the pages of my spicy romance reads? Sure.

But in the real world?

Apparently so. If you have the right connections to make it past the door.

I grab another drink and take a long gulp, working up the courage to venture out of my hidden corner and stroll slowly through the crowd. My initial shock is giving way to the bright spark of curiosity now, and even though a part of me still wants to bolt for the exit, a larger part wants to drink up every shocking sight and sound that I can.

I've always wondered . . . imagined . . . *fantasized* . . . what it would be like to experience all the things I've only read about. How it would feel, to taste those things for myself. And now, with these incredible scenes unfolding all around me, I can't resist.

I want to see it all.

I circle the ballroom and find that there are many doors leading off the main space into smaller rooms, more intimate environments. Hidden behind my mask, I don't feel shy about peeking in and discovering just what these rarified guests will do with no limits or consequences holding them back. In one room, I find a group of women, tending to just one man. Holding him down, devouring him with their hands and mouths, riding his cock and mouth, as he writhes and cries out with hoarse pleasure. In the next, a woman is bent over a low table, her mouth wrapped around one man's cock, sucking him down greedily as another fucks her slowly from behind: skirt flipped up and bodice tugged down to reveal pert breasts, damp with the sweat that a third masked naked woman is licking from them.

It's shocking. Sensual.

Sexy as hell.

And I'm not the only one observing, I realize. For every breathless couple—or threesome, or group—writhing in sensual delight, there are people just like me, sitting on the edge of the room, watching every thrilling moment. Touching themselves, and each other.

Taking their pleasure, in every possible way.

My body tightens, humming with desire as the wild, erotic scenes unfold all around me. I can feel my own breath become labored; my core aching with that telltale curl of need. I'm just wondering if there's a private spot I can steal to, to help relieve the ache, when I see him.

Saint. Professor St. Clair.

He's masked, just like the rest of us, but I swear that I would know him anywhere. He's dressed in a black suit and shirt, the expensive fabric draped perfectly on his tall, powerful body as he moves with slow purpose down the hallway.

Instinctively, I sink back, out of sight, as he passes me by. What's *he* doing here?

Of course, it makes sense. A man like him, devoted to libertine pleasure. What could be more rakish than this?

As if drawn by some invisible force, I find myself following him to a small, dimly lit room at the end of the hall. One wall is made up entirely of windows, and the moonlight outside glitters, reflecting with the candlelight on the glass and casting shadows on the few people gathered, sprawled on the couches and antique rugs inside.

Saint heads straight for the plush, circular divan in the middle of the room. A couple is grinding there, kissing softly as the woman rides her partner, but as Saint approaches, the man rises to his feet—literally handing the woman to him and moving to a seat to watch instead.

I slip into the room and find a seat in the shadows. I settle there, burning up with unfamiliar desire and curiosity, as the woman turns her attentions to Saint.

She unbuttons his shirt, kissing her way down his chest and

unbuckling his pants. He sits back, resting on his elbows, that plush mouth curled in a powerful smile as she sinks to her knees.

"That's right, darling." I hear his voice, low in the breathless silence of the room. "Swallow my cock. Just like that. Ahh . . ." His groan echoes as she frees his cock, and the sound sends a shiver rolling through my entire body.

To hear him groan like that, it feels like I'm witnessing something out of bounds.

So intimate. So *raw*.

I shudder with heat, watching as the woman eagerly settles between his knees and lowers her head, taking him deep into her mouth. God, he must be big, I can see her struggle to accommodate him.

Saint just laces a hand in her hair. "Every inch, don't stop," he orders softly. "Shh," he adds, gripping tighter. Pinning her in place. "You can take it."

The woman moans in answer, and soon her head is bobbing, sucking him deep.

Oh God.

I'm so turned on, watching them, I can hardly stand it. I press my thighs together and wriggle in my seat, wishing I could touch myself. Craving some release.

What would it feel like to be the one on my knees, making him groan like that? His hands gripping tightly in *my* hair, his enormous cock buried down *my* throat in front of a dozen watchful eyes . . .

And then Saint glances up and catches my eye across the room.

I freeze, my blood pounding hotly in my veins. He can't know that it's me, can he?

No, I tell myself, as Saint's gaze drifts over my body and back up to my face again. *That's impossible.* I'm wearing a mask, hidden here in the shadows, and besides, I have no connection to this world. No way of knowing this kind of event even exists. To him, I'm just another stranger in the party.

A woman watching as he gets his cock sucked in a crowded room.

Saint holds my gaze and gives me a piercing smile. "Watch," he instructs me, as if I could even think about looking away. The woman on her knees does something to make him sound another low, pleasured groan, and I almost moan right along with him. "Spread your legs," he tells me, low and even. "Let me see you."

Oh my God.

I can't believe I'm doing this, but in my dim haze of lust, it feels like the most natural thing in the world to sit back and part my knees wider, hitching up the silk of my skirt until I'm baring myself to him, only a whisper of silk underwear covering me between my thighs.

Saint exhales in a hiss of satisfaction, and I swear his eyes darken, even behind their mask. "Good girl," he murmurs, and fuck if those words don't send a fresh wave of desire flooding my core. "Now touch yourself. Show me how you like it. Play with that sweet, wet cunt."

Fuck.

This time, I can't hold back the moan that slips from my lips. My hand slides between my spread thighs and I touch myself through the silk of my panties, lightly petting my swollen clit.

God, it feels good.

I sigh in pleasure, tilting my head back against the chair as my fingers rub slowly, teasing myself. Saint's dark gaze stays locked on me, watching every hitched breath and shift of my body, the woman on her knees still working on his cock.

My heart pounds in my chest as slowly, I slide my fingers under my panties and stroke against my bare, wet heat. I moan again, louder, shocked by my own brazen actions, but still loving every minute of this.

I sense attention shift in the room, people turning to watch me now, but I don't break the stare. Saint is the only one who matters now, and this wild, sensual connection between us, driving me higher with every touch of my fingers and hoarse groan from his lips.

"Deeper," he growls—to me or the woman, I'm not sure. It doesn't matter. I dip my fingers inside myself, grinding my palm against my clit as I pulse. I'm spiraling closer to the edge now, my whole body shaking with a sweet electricity, desperate for release. My other hand moves automatically to my breasts, palming them through the silk of my dress, plucking and squeezing at my nipples as I pump my fingers deeper.

"Goddamn." I hear Saint sound a ragged curse. He's breathing faster now, labored, eyes blazing wild and fixed on mine. It's like we're the only two people in the world, urging each other closer to the brink, delivering pleasure even though we haven't laid so much as a finger on the other's body. "Don't stop," he demands, gripping the woman's head, moving her mouth faster on his cock, his eyes burning in the dim light. "Don't you dare fucking stop now."

I moan in answer, arching up against my own hands. I'm out of my mind, lost in this exquisite rush of forbidden pleasure as I touch myself, sliding my fingers through my wetness and rubbing my aching clit in a breathless rhythm. "Oh God," I cry aloud, feeling the flames start to lick at the base of my spine. "Oh my God!"

"That's right, baby." Saint growls, thrusting his hips, panting hard. "Come for me. Let it all go and come for me. *Now.*"

At his command, my body breaks. Pleasure slams through me, so hard and sweet, I scream.

Holy shit!

And as I writhe there, mindless, I see Saint's jaw clench, and his body rise. Sounding a cry of release, he pulls his cock from the woman's mouth and pumps, spurting his climax over her bare chest in a ribbon of cum as my own orgasm crashes over me, leaving me breathless and dizzy from hands-down the most intense sexual experience of my life.

And not for one moment does he look away.

Chapter Eight
TESSA

Touch yourself. Show me how you like it. Play with that sweet, wet cunt...

Saint's voice echoes in my mind, sending fresh waves of pleasure rolling through me. I toss and turn alone in bed back at my student apartment. I have a ton of work to do in the morning, but there's no way in hell I can sleep, not after the night I've just had. My body is still wired, humming with the illicit memory of his crisp, tempting orders, and the wild blazing passion he drew from me. Passion I'd never even known I could feel.

Did that really just happen?

I lay there, my heart still pounding in wild exhilaration. The moment my orgasm faded and the haze of lust lifted, I came to what was left of my senses and bolted from the party, spending a jaw-dropping amount on a taxi back to Oxford and the safety of the real world, far from extravagant sex parties and the man who can apparently draw earthshaking climaxes from my body without a single touch.

I didn't say a word to Saint before leaving, and he didn't try to follow.

Besides, what could I say? *Thanks for my first public sexual experience, Professor. You were right, you really do have incredible expertise?*

I can't help but giggle, lying here in the dark in a state of total disbelief. Already, it feels like a dream. An out-of-body experience...

Except my body remembers everything. The way he gripped that woman's hair, calmly controlling her movements. The casual way he leaned back, his eyes devouring my every sinful movement. How thrilling it felt to bask in that reckless gaze, making me wanton. Making me wild.

And oh, that ragged groan when he came . . .

Christ. I have to smother my giddy laughter in the pillows so I don't wake my roommates—and invite their questions about what's making me act so crazy.

Because it was—crazy. This whole night. Dressing up and donning that mask. Making my way to the hotel, and then sticking around when the lavish clothing fell to the floor and I first realized that my investigation had taken an unexpectedly illicit turn—

Wait a minute . . .

I sit up, remembering clearly for the first time since the stroke of midnight exactly what sent me to that party in the first place. Or rather, *who.*

Somebody planned for me to be there. They sent me that mysterious invitation and led me on a wild chase by dangling the promise of information about Wren.

I pull the two cards out and set them side by side.

I know what happened to Wren.

Legacy is our gift, and a sworn bond.

The handwriting definitely matches, but I can't figure out what the second note means. I try searching online on my phone, but there's no match for that phrase.

So, what happened? What are they trying to tell me? And why the mysterious cloak-and-dagger routine?

Did they get cold feet about meeting me, or was it all some elaborate ruse to lure me to the party so that they could . . . ?

What exactly? Introduce me to the debaucherous British sex scene? Or was the party itself a clue? I can't imagine my strait-laced sister ever taking part in something like that, but I would have said the same thing about myself, up until a few hours ago.

Saint flashes in my mind again, the way his gaze glittered in the dim light as he watched me touch myself.

Deeper . . . Don't you dare fucking stop.

I shudder, and it's like he's here in the room with me all over again. Urging me to spread my legs beneath the covers. Tempting me to reach under my nightshirt and slide my fingers to find my wet heat . . .

I muffle my moans in the pillows and relive the pleasure, over and over again until sleep finally claims me.

* * *

". . . AND THEN HE asked about you, Tessa. Tessa?"

"Hmm? What?"

I snap out of my reverie, blushing, to find that Jia and Kris are looking at me across the table, crammed in the corner of a steamy breakfast café in town on Monday morning. "I said, a guy from my poetry seminar asked about you," Jia repeats. "He wanted to know if you were seeing anyone."

"Oh, umm . . ." I take a gulp of coffee, trying to collect myself. I've been a million miles away from reality all weekend, lost in memories of the party. "I . . . I don't know," I reply without thinking.

Does what happened with Saint count as "seeing someone"? I mean, I saw plenty of him, after all.

His thick, straining cock . . .

I find myself giggling and cover it with a cough.

"You *are* seeing someone!" Kris exclaims, eyes widening.

"What? No!" I blurt, but it's too late. They're both looking at me excitedly, our greasy bacon sandwiches forgotten on the table between us.

"Who is he?"

"How long have you been sneaking around?"

"Does he have any hot friends?"

"Guys, no!" I cut them off firmly. "It's nothing. Less than nothing. I . . . saw a guy, from a distance," I say carefully, "but we've never talked. He doesn't even know who I am."

At least, I hope he doesn't.

The thought that Saint might have recognized me behind my mask makes my stomach lurch dangerously—half in fear, and half in reckless anticipation.

"It's nothing," I repeat again. "I'm too busy for that kind of thing, anyway. I haven't dated in . . . God, it's years now."

Since before Wren died.

Jia sighs, clearly disappointed that I don't have any hot gossip to share. "Me either."

I arch an eyebrow.

"Dated," she emphasizes. "Hookups and situationships don't count."

"If they did, my numbers would be sky-high," Kris agrees. "You really haven't been involved with anyone in years?" he asks me curiously.

I shake my head. "I mean, I'm not a total nun," I tell them, rolling my eyes. "I had a few relationships after college that kind of fizzled out. Then I had some family stuff I was dealing with," I say vaguely. "So I wasn't in the right headspace to get close with anyone."

That's an understatement. Emotional intimacy hasn't exactly been my strong point, and after Wren died, it was just about impossible to think about opening up—not when it was taking everything I had not to fall apart. It was only deciding to come to Oxford and hunt down the truth that lifted me out of my fog of grief. A welcome ray of clarity cutting through the pain.

Now, men should be the last thing on my mind.

"Well, if you change your mind, poetry guy isn't that unfortunate looking," Jia offers. "And OK, he has this weird sneeze, but he's really very sweet!"

"Thanks." I smile. "I'll keep it in mind."

* * *

WE FINISH UP with breakfast and they head off to the library, while I make my way back to Ashford College in plenty of time for my next seminar.

It's Saint's class.

I climb the narrow stone staircase to his office, my nerves and anticipation skittering in my chest. I have no idea what to expect this time around—especially considering everything that happened over the weekend. But no matter what, I won't let him lord it over me and exclude me from class again.

I've done all the reading, submitted my essay last night with plenty of time to spare, and now I'm so early that when I step into the room, I find it totally empty: I'm the first one here.

OK then.

I take a seat on the most comfortable-looking battered armchair, pull out my notes, and wait. It's a charming old room, packed with bookcases and mismatched furniture. Sunlight falls through the iron-paned windows and the sounds of birdsong and passing student voices filter in from outside. It would be relaxing if I wasn't already on edge, wondering what's about to go down.

Does he know it was me?

There's a clatter of footsteps on the stairs, and then the other students arrive, followed by Saint himself. His hair is damp from the shower, and the sleeves of his cashmere sweater are rolled up to reveal lightly tanned forearms with a dusting of hair.

He sets down a coffee cup and a battered leather satchel. "Ms. Peterson, I see you're on time today," he says, giving me an inscrutable smile.

"And you're all of three minutes late," I reply lightly, flashing a smile. "How about that? I guess you won't ask yourself to leave."

He smiles wider, amused. "Not unless you'd like to lead the group in discussion today?"

"Thanks, but I'm here to learn." I sit back, playing it cool even though my heart is racing.

Is there a glint of recognition in his eyes? Or is this just his usual enigmatic charm?

I'm not sure, but as the session gets underway, I'm on high alert, watching him for any sign—and trying my best to keep pace.

"A common misconception of the libertine writers is that they were focused solely on pleasure," Saint is saying, discussing the essay topic he posed. "But in that era, to even publish works depicting explicit or sexual content was a truly radical act. We can read these works not just as explorations of desire, but as political statements, too. Standing against all established social conventions and challenging the moral authority of the church."

He pauses, looking around the room. The other students are rapt, scribbling notes from his every word, but I'm sitting back, listening carefully. Saint's gaze lands on me. "Thoughts, Ms. Peterson?"

"On . . . ?" I prompt him.

"The topic at hand. Your essay was certainly interesting," he adds, flipping through the papers beside him to find it. "Why don't you share your ideas with the group?"

Shit.

I feel a bolt of insecurity as everyone turns to me. The other students in the group are all serious scholars who deserve to be here. I'm the imposter, trying to cover my ass for as long as I can.

"Well . . . I . . ." I stammer, checking my notes. "I guess I just find it interesting that these are all accounts of male pleasure. What we think of as libertine philosophy—what your reading list and all the critics cover—is just men writing about their own desires and fantasies. I understand that women were rarely published in the era, or even able to access education enough to write, but it's still a limited framework. Theses authors are seen as revolutionary and provocative, but what would be really revolutionary is a woman's account of the same thing."

"There's plenty of discussion of female pleasure, too," Saint corrects me. "*Fanny Hill*, for example. *La Nouvelle Justine* . . ."

I can't help but roll my eyes. "All written by men. Their perspective, their fantasies. They're not the same thing."

"Are they not?" Saint arches an eyebrow at me. "I would guess there are common themes. Shared ideas that both sexes enjoy. *Shared experiences* . . ."

He lingers on the words, just long enough. Our eyes meet, and there's no mistaking the smug recognition in his eyes.

He knows.

Oh my God. My heart stops, and my cheeks burn. I want to disappear right down the back of this chair, but instead, I have to sit here, clutching my crumpled essay pages while Saint smoothly moves the conversation on to one of the other student's essays.

He knows it was me!

My pulse races and my blood runs hot in my veins. Suddenly, I'm aware of my body in a whole new way: every shift, every brush of fabric against my skin. I can't help flashing back to that dim, candlelit room and the way it felt to have all eyes on me.

Saint's eyes, watching me.

Watching me come undone.

". . . it was the challenge to religious authority . . ."

Saint glances over as one of the other students speaks. He meets my eyes and gives me a slow, cryptic smile, allowing his gaze to pour over me, like he's replaying his own filthy memories of that night, right here in the sunlit office.

I inhale in a rush, suddenly feeling naked, like my skirt is hiked up around my waist again.

Like I'm spread to him, on display.

Saint's lips curl. He's enjoying this.

And so am I.

An illicit, rebellious thrill rolls through me. Slowly, deliberately, I cross my legs. I'm wearing jeans and a sweater, but still, I see his jaw clench in reaction. I smile, and casually nibble the cap of my ballpoint pen.

Saint stares at my mouth, his gaze turning dark, as if he's imagining my lips wrapped around something very different.

I shiver with lust, picturing it too. Taking his cock deep, hearing him murmur filthy instructions, urging me on.

Good girl . . .

". . . to judge the era. Right, Professor?"

Saint doesn't skip a beat. "That's right, Flora." He gives a curt nod, finally dragging his eyes away from me. I'm almost disappointed to lose his focus, but I feel the tension shimmer between us for the rest of the class, stirring something inside me.

Something reckless. Something wild.

Down girl, I remind myself as he wraps up the discussion, and sets the reading for next week. Flirting with Saint like this is just asking for trouble—especially when I've sworn to avoid all distractions from my mission.

No matter how filthy and tempting they might be . . .

"That's all," Saint finishes, getting to his feet. "Essays will be due Sunday night, and try to review at least three of the journal articles, as well as the main texts."

The other students take their time packing up, chatting about certain points from the session, but I just grab my things and bolt from the room. I hurry back down the staircase and into the drafty cloisters, my cheeks still flushed and heated.

"Ms. Peterson? Tessa?"

The sound of my name on his lips for the first time stops me in my tracks. I turn as Saint catches up with me. "You forgot your essay," he says, holding out the pages, which I can see are marked with comments in blue ink.

I take a breath. If he's expecting me to blush and act ashamed by what happened, I won't give him the satisfaction. I draw myself up to my full height and casually take the pages. "Thanks."

"I have to say, I enjoyed your performance," he continues, lips curling in a knowing smile.

"In the class," I clarify, teasing.

He smiles wider. "That too. You're right, I think. A man's perspective on female pleasure will always be at a distance . . ."

"As if he's watching from across the room?" I can't resist shooting back.

"Exactly." He laughs in surprise. "Have dinner with me."

Now I'm the surprised one. "What?" I ask, thrown.

"Dinner. Tomorrow night," Saint continues, raking back his dark, tousled hair. "I know a great Italian place, here in town. It's delicious, discreet . . . you'll enjoy it, I promise."

"You don't know what I like," I say, buying time. Dinner with him, like a real date? I try to picture us sitting across from one another in a restaurant, making small talk about our hobbies and families, when I already know how the muscles in his abdomen leap just before he comes.

Saint gives me a slow, molten smile. "Oh, I think I do, Tessa." He says my name softly. Intimate.

The way he would murmur in my ear as he thrust deep inside.

"At least, I've had a glimpse of a few things," he continues. "But I daresay you're hiding a whole lot more. I'd like to find out. So, dinner?"

I'm tempted. Hell, everything about this man is tempting me to throw caution to the wind and dive headlong into the world of illicit pleasure that he promises.

But he's right. I am hiding something—from him, and everyone else here. And I can't forget the real reason I'm in Oxford, not for one second.

"No thanks," I tell him, giving a breezy smile. "The party was fun and all, but I don't think it's an experience that needs repeating. Been there, done that, you know? Anyway, I'll see you in class next week."

And then I turn and walk away. Straight back to my apartment to spend some quality time with my vibrator.

Chapter Nine
SAINT

Be careful what you wish for . . .

The saying taunts me as I go through the rest of my day on autopilot. Luckily, I just have a few essays to mark and a lecture that I could deliver in my sleep, because my mind couldn't be further away from the stuffy hall and all the students hanging off my every word.

No, my thoughts are back at that hotel, in that dim lounge, watching Tessa Peterson spread her thighs wider and bring herself to a gasping orgasm as I watched every move.

She was incredible. I've never seen a more captivating sight. Her flushed cheeks and wet, open lips; the spark of reckless pleasure in her eyes as she surrendered to the pleasure. Fuck, when she started touching her breasts, pinching her nipples through her dress and moaning out loud . . .

I couldn't hold back a second longer. My climax ripped through me like a fucking tidal wave, spilling out of control as I watched her come undone.

That was my second surprise of the evening, after the delicious shock of recognizing my new student amongst the crowd. How she scored an invite, I can't imagine. The parties are top-secret, and the most exclusive ticket in town—or even the world. Nobody knows how they make it onto the guest list, not even me. But there she was, slipping through the crowd, those curious eyes searching out every detail of the sweaty, explicit scenery.

Lingering. Exploring. *Savoring* . . .

She didn't hesitate, taking a seat to watch me with that woman. Her eyes burned into me, giving me a raw sexual thrill that I haven't felt in years. A public scene like that is usually fun, but hardly novel to me now. But under her gaze, it felt brand new.

I felt brand new, as if I was experiencing every sensation for the first time.

Yes, Ms. Peterson is full of hidden talents—and one of them is clearly driving me out of my mind. I rarely lose control. I'm the instructor, the voice of experience. But that night at the party . . .

She was opening *my* eyes, pushing me further, driving my pleasure higher with every illicit caress of her hands. I'm used to being one step ahead, but a single glimpse of the wicked passion that woman has lurking beneath her surface, and I already know I would follow Tessa wherever she chose.

Except she seems not to want the company.

I frown, reminded of her cold turn after burning so hot. First, she disappeared from the party before I could approach her, and now she's acting like it was no big deal: just another Saturday night's amusement, too insignificant to be repeated.

It's an act—it has to be. The chemistry between us is impossible to deny, and our flirty, provocative banter in the seminar this morning makes me even more certain that we're on the same page. My plan was simple: a romantic dinner date, an invitation back to mine for a nightcap . . . soon enough, we would be picking up where we left off at the party. And this time, it wouldn't just be her own hands caressing that gorgeous body, making her moan.

But as I'm coming to realize, this woman is anything but simple.

Luckily, I'm more than game for the challenge.

* * *

I FINISH UP my teaching duties for the day, and then go to meet some buddies of mine at a private members' bar in the old part of Oxford. We all attended college together here, years ago, and now they're back for some alumni event, rubbing shoulders and reminiscing with old pals.

"Here he is, the most eligible professor in all of Oxford!" My friend Max Lancaster greets me with a whoop, drawing looks from all the other staid, older men drinking in the room.

I snort with amusement, joining his table. "That's hardly an achievement. The average age of the tutors here is pushing eighty."

"But still, you have those silver foxes beat." Max grins from under a shock of blonde hair and pushes a glass of scotch over to me. "You have to try this. Thirty year, barrel-smoked. My father loved the distillery so much, he bought the whole place."

"What's a newspaper man doing making scotch?" our other friend Hugh Ambrose asks. He's wearing his trademark spectacles, dressed down in battered corduroy trousers and a casual sweater, just the way he always looked when we were students, haunting the library and drinking late at every pub in town.

"Hell if I know." Max shrugs. "You know my father. It's not enough to admire something from afar, the man has to own it, every last drop."

"Newspaper man" is an understatement. Max's father, Cyrus Lancaster, is a powerful media mogul whose empire spans the globe. Magazines, TV news, movie studios, and more. He can move markets and bring down governments, all before breakfast—which is why Max can whoop it up like an overexcited playboy and nobody here will voice a word of complaint. Still, I remind him to keep it down as I take a sip. The scotch is smoky and rich, burning my throat with a pleasant glow. "Nice." I nod approvingly and fill the glass higher.

"Aww, is life as a brooding academic getting stressful?" Max teases. I give him a look.

"And what is it you do all day, exactly?" I banter back. "Didn't your father dump you in some godforsaken local news division to keep you out of trouble?"

"I don't need to follow the news," Max brags. "I make it."

Hugh and I snort with laughter. "I thought your PR team was trying to keep you *out* of the headlines," Hugh jokes. "Funny how that story about you and the Vice President's daughter was magically wiped offline . . ."

"What did Annabelle say about that?" I tease, naming Max's perky society fiancée.

"What Belle doesn't know won't hurt her." Max raises his glass. "Isn't that right, boys?"

Hugh and I exchange an exasperated look. But Max has always been like this. He makes no secret of his playboy ways, and Annabelle has to know what she's marrying by now. Their families have known each other forever.

We all have, from boarding school to winters skiing in the Swiss Alps and summers at each other's family estates in Barbados and St. Tropez. Our aristocratic circles are small and rarefied, and everyone has history. We've fallen in and out of love, shared first illicit drinks and joints, and supported each other through every success and quiet tragedy. Max and Hugh were at my side the day I buried my brother—and that night as I drank myself to oblivion in the VIP section of a Mayfair club. They've always had my back, and even though we've gone our separate ways in the world now as grown men, we're all still connected, as if by blood.

"So tell us, Professor, who's this term's tasty treat?" Max asks with a smirk.

"My cousin is a fresher, and she says all the girls are positively swooning after you," Hugh adds, teasing. "As per usual, of course."

I give a careless shrug. Nobody can compare to Tessa now, but I'm not about to draw her into our banter, so I just give a vague smile. "Not sure yet. To be honest, the whole scene here is getting pretty stale."

"So, what, you're finally going to join Ashford Pharma?" Hugh asks, looking interested. "It's a great time for the company, exciting stuff ahead. My father can't shut up about it. 'Ashford is a shining example of British innovation,'" he quotes.

"I heard that . . . a dozen times, in every speech he gives," I laugh—avoiding the question. "How long now until the election?"

"Another couple of months," Hugh says, sighing. His father, Lionel, is a respected politician in Parliament, and in the running to become the next leader of the party—and Prime Minister. "I can't wait for it to be over, to be honest. All these reporters sniffing around, trying to find a scandal. You want to have your Lancaster Media people give us a break?" he asks Max lightly. "They ran our old holiday pics on the front page, for Christ's sake. I don't need to see my mother in a bikini before breakfast. Or after it."

Max chuckles. "Easy there. We have to pretend to be fair and balanced. But Lionel's got it sewn up. All the polling says so."

"Still, he's wound tighter than ever these days. Lecturing us all about keeping our noses clean, as if any whisper of a scandal will keep him out of the top spot." Hugh rolls his eyes.

"To fathers, and their eternal disappointment," I say, raising my glass, and we toast. All three of us know what it's like to live with the weight of family expectations. I drain my drink and look around. "Another?"

"Sure. The night's just getting started."

I head for the bar, but I'm intercepted by a woman in a chic knit dress. She's tall, brunette, and leggy, with familiar-looking features. "If it isn't the sinner himself," she greets me with a lingering kiss on both cheeks. "I haven't seen you in forever."

"I've been busy, causing trouble," I reply lightly, searching for her name.

"Vivian," she supplies, looking amused. "You dated my sister back in school. Well, 'dated' might be stretching it, but you certainly broke her heart."

"Vivian Prescott." I snap my fingers, finally placing her. "Wow. You've certainly grown up. The last time I saw you, you were in pigtails on that pony of yours."

"I ride in the English Olympic team now," she says, tossing her glossy hair back. She gives me a sultry smile. "I'm just in town for a while before heading off on training again. I don't suppose you'd get a drink, catch up . . . keep me entertained?"

There's no question what kind of entertainment she's suggesting, not with the flirty sparkle in her eye.

"I'm not sure how entertaining I'd be," I reply with an easy smile. "I have quite a course load this term. Can't leave my students neglected."

Especially not the intriguing American with perfect lips.

Vivian gives a shrug. "If you change your mind, you know how to find me," she says, "Good seeing you, Saint."

"You too. And say hi to your sister," I add. I continue on to get our drinks, but when I return to the table, Max and Hugh are looking at me in shock.

"You turned her down?" Max asks, disbelieving.

"Viv Prescott, champion rider?" Hugh echoes.

"And he's not just talking about her equestrian skills," Max cracks. "Since when do you pass up a fine filly like that?"

Since Tessa Peterson made me realize just what kind of excitement I was missing.

I shrug. "Maybe I'm ready for something new," I say, thinking of her rebellious wit and breathy moans. "Something unpredictable. Different."

Max whistles. "In that case . . . you won't mind if I go say hello."

I laugh. Typical Max. "Knock yourself out."

* * *

I CALL IT an early night with the guys and head home to the town house I keep in the city on a quiet cobbled street. I pour a nightcap and sit, enjoying the peace of the simple, well-furnished rooms.

Tessa is certainly unpredictable. Clearly, I can't just sit back and wait for her to come to me. She already knows my reputation, and—

I pause. Maybe that's the reason for her reluctance. She assumes I'm just looking for another idle fling. But she's wrong; I want to get to know her. Find out what makes her tick, what secrets are hiding behind those watchful eyes. I haven't felt drawn to a woman like this in . . . well, I can't remember how long. Even now, I find myself replaying the sight of her head tipped back in pleasure, the rebellious sass in her tone.

Who are you, Tessa? And why do I already feel so connected to you?

I mull the question all night, and by morning, it's clear I need to step it up if I'm going to get any closer. So, after a brief stop at the Ashford administrators' office to charm her address out of the clerk, and a detour to the best florist in the city, I show up at her flat, ready to sweep her off her feet.

But when I ring the bell, Tessa isn't the one who answers.

"Hi?" the petite woman asks, juggling a thermos flask in one hand and a stack of books in the other. Then she gets a proper look at me and pauses. "Oh. Hello."

I flash a friendly smile. "Hi there. I'm looking for Tessa?"

"She's out," a male voice adds, and the door swings wider. A rangy guy is also pulling on his jacket, and he stops too, clearly checking me out. "But maybe there's something we can help you with?"

"Do you know when she'll be back?" I ask.

"Not until later. She went down to London," the woman explains. "I think she said she would be back tonight. But we can tell her you stopped by."

"Thanks," I say, passing her the flowers. "I'm Saint, by the way."

The guy smirks. "Oh, we know who you are, Professor. But we didn't know you knew Tessa. She's clearly been holding out on us!"

"Nice meeting you," I add, before leaving.

I may have struck out this time, but that just makes me more determined to win her over.

That party was just the beginning of what's happening between us, and I can't wait to discover what comes next.

Chapter Ten
TESSA

After the distractions of the party and Saint, it's almost a relief to get some distance from Oxford for the day, heading down to London by train. The green, lush countryside blurs outside the windows as I check my text messages and confirm everything's still set for the meeting.

See you at 2pm.

The message is from Lara Southerly, one of the girls I found in the yearbook photos with Wren. With a little internet sleuthing, I managed to track down her information and reach out, saying I would love to chat. She works in publishing in the city, and agreed to meet for a coffee, so here I am, speeding toward the capital, wondering if my investigation is finally going to lead somewhere. The two of them seemed close, and as I look again at the pics I snapped of them laughing together, I wonder if Lara will be able to fill in any of the blanks about my sister's time in Oxford. She could know who Wren was hanging out with, where she went. Maybe she was even at the party that night, when Wren was taken . . .

I take a deep breath, trying to get my nervous expectations under control. It was a while ago, I remind myself. Lara may not know anything that can help me in my quest. But still, it feels good to be moving forward in my investigation. Whoever sent me that note hasn't contacted me again, and I can't just sit around and wait for them to reach out.

I need to track down the answers another way.

The train pulls in at Paddington Station, and I navigate my way to the Underground, buying a ticket and following the color-coded maps to catch a subway train over to the Bloomsbury neighborhood. The trains are packed, and the city bustles with hectic activity, a big change from the sedate, peaceful vibes in Oxford, but I like the crowds. I'm anonymous here, no need to lie or pretend to keep a cover story going.

At least, not quite so many lies.

"Tessa?" Lara waves me over when I arrive at the café, greeting me with a friendly hug. She's a petite, curvy redhead wearing smart pants and a chunky gemstone necklace, already settled at a table with a pot of tea and a tray of little scones. "I figured you'd enjoy the full English afternoon tea," she says, smiling. "It was Wren's favorite, too."

I nod. "She always did have a sweet tooth."

Lara looks at me sympathetically. "I couldn't believe it, when you said she passed away. What happened? If you don't mind me asking."

"It was an . . . accident," I say vaguely. I decided to take a risk and share the news of her death with Wren's old friends. It seems like the right thing to do, especially when they might decide to log online and reconnect with her. But still, I'm keeping the full truth under wraps. "Just a tragic accident. Nobody saw it coming."

"God, how awful." Lara shakes her head. "And she was so young. I'm so sorry for your loss."

She reaches across the table and squeezes my hand. I blink, struck with a sudden, fresh pang of grief.

"Thank you," I manage, swallowing back the tears that threaten to flow.

Even after all this time, the ache of Wren's loss still has the power to blindside me.

"Anyway." I take a breath and force a casual smile. "I'm over here studying, at Oxford, actually. She always talked about how much she loved it here. I wanted to follow in her footsteps. You guys were friends, back then?"

"Oh, the best of friends." Lara smiles again. "Not that I had a choice in that. It was literally the first day I arrived in Oxford, I was still unpacking my things, when there's a knock on the door, and Wren is standing there with a bottle of cheap wine in one hand and the biggest smile. She said that since she was going to be living just down the hall, we were going to be friends, and that was it. We had the best time . . ."

"Any wild stories?" I prompt her gently.

"Oh, a ton!" Lara laughs. "There was a guy living on the floor below us, this math genius from Berlin. Anyway, he swore he could only focus late at night, playing the most godawful techno music. It was impossible to sleep! Wren and I tried everything— begging, pleading, bribery—but he wouldn't quit. So, we broke into his flat one night . . ."

"And broke his stereo?" I ask, smiling.

Lara grins. "No, that was my idea, but Wren thought bigger. She brought in some mold cultures from the lab and spread them in all his pantry cabinets! Soon enough, the college declared it a hazard zone and moved him to another building. And we got to spend the rest of the semester in blissful peace!"

I laugh, just picturing it. "That sounds like Wren," I say, smiling fondly. "She could think up the wildest pranks. And nobody ever suspected her," I add. "Because she seemed like such a good girl."

"Yes!" Lara laughs. "Oh, and then there was the time she wanted to see some of the countryside, but our rental car broke down, and we wound up hitchhiking . . ."

* * *

WE SIT AND chat over tea for another hour. I get swept up in all her stories about late-night study sessions and drinking at the bars in town. I miss Wren so much and hearing about her from someone else's perspective is a gift I wasn't expecting to receive.

"It sounds like you two had a great time at Oxford," I say, a little wistful. It's lovely to hear about the good times my sister got to experience, but there's a sadness, too, when I think about all the joy that was stripped away from her. Burned to ashes by some unknown assailant in a dark cell room.

Lara nods, but her smile fades. "We did. At first." She pauses, giving me a careful look. She's clearly trying to gauge just how much I know about the change in Wren, so I nod.

"I know things changed for her," I say carefully. "It was before Christmas, right? She seemed pretty stressed. The workload, her experiments in the lab . . ."

Lara looks relieved. "Something changed with her. She withdrew, started blowing me off."

"And she didn't say why?" I check.

Lara shakes her head. "I was pretty mad at her for ghosting me like that, but we were all so busy. Oxford can be intense," she adds. "Then the next thing I hear, she dropped out and went back to America. I tried reaching out, but . . . she never got back to me."

"I'm sorry," I tell her honestly. "There was a . . . family emergency. Everything was pretty rushed. I'm sure she would have talked if she'd been in the right headspace."

Lara nods slowly. "I wish she had. And now, with her gone . . ." She sighs. "It really is a tragedy."

It's not the word I would use. A tragedy is when there's nobody to blame.

What happened to Wren was a crime.

"Did Wren have any other close friends at Oxford?" I ask, steering the conversation back to my research.

"A few. We hung out with some people who lived in our building," Lara says, frowning as she tries to recall. "Wren was serious about her work though, so she spent most of her time at the lab. You should talk to Phillip."

"Phillip McAlister?" I ask, remembering another face from the photos.

Lara nods. "He was a post-doc, doing some big research project at the lab with her. Nice guy, one of those brainy scientist types."

"I think she mentioned him," I say, thinking back. "At least, she said she had a work husband with a really dorky sense of humor."

Lara grins. "That's Phil. I think he might still be there. I can look up his number, if you want?"

"That would be amazing," I say gratefully. Then I pull a page from my notebook and place it on the table. "I don't suppose you recognize this?"

I show her a sketch, with the crown and snake tattoo Wren remembered from her assailant. I had her draw it, back when we were searching for answers together. Now, I'm the only one left to search for justice.

Lara takes a closer look at the sketch, puzzled. "No, I don't think so. What is it?"

"That's what I'm trying to figure out." I place the cryptic note from the party down beside it. "What about this, does it ring any bells?"

"'*Legacy is our gift, and a sworn bond.*'" Lara reads it aloud. "I've never heard it before. It sounds like some kind of motto," she adds. "You know, all the Oxford colleges have them. *Constantia omnia vincit*," she adds. "'Constancy conquers all.' That's Ashford's motto."

"A motto . . ." I repeat thoughtfully. Then I tuck the pages away. "Thank you so much for meeting me. And if you remember anything—or anyone—who was important to Wren, then let me know. I'd love to talk to whoever I can."

"Of course."

Lara has to get back to work, so we finish up and exit the café, but just as she's about to leave, she pauses. "I don't know if he was *important*, but she did start hanging out with Max Lancaster right before the holidays."

"Max . . ." I think back, but I don't recall seeing that name in the yearbooks. "Was he another student at Ashford?"

Lara sounds a peal of laughter. "No. Lancaster, as in, Lancaster Media? He's the son and heir. Real big shot. At least, he likes to think so. His father endowed some big multimedia center to the college, so he was in town for the opening. I think they went out a few times. He can be pretty charming. An asshole, but charming."

"Lancaster . . ." I repeat, making a mental note to look into the guy. "Wren never mentioned she was dating anyone."

Lara grins. "She never told me either, but . . . I could have sworn something was going on. She seemed all flustered and glowy, like she had some big secret. Anyway, you take care of yourself, OK?" She gives me a quick hug. "Wren thought the world of you."

I give a sad smile. "The feeling was mutual."

* * *

MY TRAIN BACK to Oxford isn't for another couple of hours, so I take a wander through the streets of London, lost in memories of Wren. The stories that Lara told brought her back to life for a brief while. Not the angry, bitter, broken Wren from the end, but the girl she used to be, full of life and sweetness.

That's the Wren I miss. The sister who helped me sneak out past curfew and stayed up late to quiz me with flashcards before the SATs. The sister with a bright, shining future ahead of her, who worked so hard and always had time for a kind word or a generous gift.

The sister who was taken from me.

My grief wells in my chest, but this time, it's hot and sharp, edged with pure rage.

Somebody did this to her. Someone took my brilliant, kindhearted sister and broke her into a thousand pieces; left a shattered mess so splintered, none of us could mend the damage. Not her, or my poor grief-stricken parents.

Not even me.

I look out over the Thames, chilled by more than just the wind. The guilty questions bubble in the back of my mind, the same traitorous whispers that haunt me now.

Is there something I could have done to save her?

If I'd seen the signs sooner . . . if Wren had opened up . . . maybe I could have found a way to pull her back from the edge . . .

No. I stop myself before I can spiral into the familiar abyss. What-ifs won't lead me anywhere now. I'm not to blame for this, and neither is Wren. Whoever took her, hurt her, they're the one who needs to pay.

And I'm going to find them, no matter what.

I'm on the right path here. If Lara is correct and those words are a motto, perhaps I'm not just looking for some random evil monster, maybe it's bigger than that. Because it's clear that whoever attacked Wren wasn't just some drunk frat boy. It was organized. The isolated cell, the drugs slipped into her drink, the way she was kept there—and then carefully returned to her student rooms without a shred of evidence to track the perpetrators down.

Whoever did it had resources. Planning. Connections.

Could it have been some kind of secret society? I feel a chill, remembering Wren's odd reading list. Did she have the same suspicions, too? Her attack could have been a hazing or initiation ritual. Or just some sick game those bastards enjoy to pass the time—no matter what the cost. And then there's the mysterious note with that motto. Somebody sent it to me for a reason. They wanted me to know those words. To look in a new direction.

I can't be sure of anything just yet. All I have are wild theories and assumptions. But there are clues hidden here somewhere, I can feel it in my bones.

* * *

I FINALLY MAKE my way back to Paddington and take the train to Oxford. The sky darkens with every passing mile, and by the time I step out of the station, it's raining hard, a torrential

downpour splattering the High Street and sending shoppers fleeing for cover.

Ashford College is a couple of miles away, but there's a soggy
announcement pinned to the bus stop announcing that services
have been suspended. It looks like I have no choice but to walk.
Damn. I wish I'd worn a waterproof jacket; my woolen coat and
sweatshirt offer zero protection from the rain, and I haven't even
made it to the end of the block before I'm soaked through. My
budget doesn't stretch to a cab, not after that trip back from the
country hotel, so there's no option but to trudge determinedly
through the rain, trying my best to ignore the cold water trickling
under my collar and running down the back of my spine.

The sound of a car horn breaks through my miserable hike.
A car has slowed at the curb beside me. It's a sleek, silver sporty
number.

I pull my soaked coat tighter around me and walk faster.

The car follows, flashing its headlights at me.

Shit. I'm just about to try and cross the street to get away
from them when the window closest to me rolls down, revealing
Saint behind the wheel, looking annoyingly warm and dry—and
handsome. His blue eyes twinkle at me, amusement clear on his
chiseled face.

"You know, tryouts for the swim team were last week," he jokes
as I squelch along.

"Thanks for the tip," I say, cursing the fact he looks so damn
handsome. Already, I feel that kick of adrenaline that sparks
whenever he's around, my mind going back to the illicit moment
we shared at the party—

SPLASH.

I distractedly step straight into a puddle. Cold water flies up,
soaking my jeans all the way to my knees. I wince. "Any other
advice, or are you just out enjoying a pleasant drive?"

He chuckles. "Come on, I'll give you a ride back to college."

"No thanks," I answer automatically, still walking.

Saint sighs, keeping the car in pace with me—despite the ve-hicle honking angrily behind him. "You're soaked through. Come on, it's a two-minute drive, not a date."

"I'm fine," I insist stubbornly. My teeth may be chattering from the cold, but something tells me that getting in the car with this man might be a choice I can't take back.

And won't want to.

Suddenly, Saint angles the car, mounting the curb and driving straight onto the sidewalk in front of me to block my path.

"Are you crazy?" I exclaim, shocked, but Saint just reaches over and opens the passenger door, fixing me with an exasperated look.

"Get in the damn car, Tessa."

A shiver rolls down my spine—and it has nothing to do with the rain. *Damn.* He says my name like we're already something, fondness mixed with irritation, as if we've had this fight a hundred times.

I hate to admit, I like the way it sounds.

It is raining, after all. And it's just a friendly ride . . .

Saint waits there behind the wheel, exasperated, so finally, I give in to temptation and get in the car.

Chapter Eleven
TESSA

F inally, the woman sees sense."

Saint steers back onto the road, reaching over to turn up the heat as I settle in the passenger seat, dripping water all over his fine leather interior. "Nice car," I remark, amused as I take it in. "Silver, sporty . . . looks like I was right about you."

Saint looks over, grinning. "Don't gloat, it's not polite."

"Then I guess I'll just have to be the rude, uncouth American," I say, sitting back. "It's kind of early for a midlife crisis car, don't you think?"

"I inherited it," he replies, and his smile slips, just for a moment. Then he focuses on the radio dial. "Now, how about a little music to set the mood . . ."

"'It's Raining Men'?" I quip. "'Umbrella'?"

"Ah, here we go." He settles on a station, and I'm surprised to hear smoky jazz emerge from the speakers.

"Aren't you more of a classical guy?" I ask. "You know, snooty and elitist?"

He chuckles, a warm, rich sound that slides over my skin like molasses. "I can be snooty and elitist about jazz, don't you worry. Now, where am I taking you? Back to college?"

"Yes, please."

"And I don't suppose you'd be interested in a detour . . . ?" he asks, his voice full of promise. "For a quick drink, perhaps?"

"No." I fix him with a stern look. "Ashford. Thank you."

"As you wish." Saint nods and makes a turn, heading down the familiar High Street. I relax, but I can't deny the electricity that crackles between us, just being close to him.

I sneak a glance over at Saint. His hair is curling from the damp weather, and he's wearing a navy jacket that brings out the blue of his eyes. But it's not just the way he looks that's affecting me. The man has a presence, an enigmatic energy that radiates from him in the small car, drawing me in.

Making me feel bold and reckless all over again.

He shoots me a playful look. "I have a dry sweater in the back, if you want to change out of those wet things."

I smirk. "I expected a little more finesse, if you're trying to get me naked."

"That's right, I forget," Saint replies. "You prefer candlelight and a crowded room."

A bolt of lust goes through me at the memory.

"I wasn't the naked one," I remind him, keeping my voice casual, even as my body goes up in flames. "That was your friend. I didn't catch her name . . ."

"Neither did I." Saint grins wider. Our eyes catch, and I realize it's the first time we've acknowledged out loud what happened at the party. It's thrilling, not to be dancing around it with suggestions and double entendre anymore.

"So," I begin, giving in to curiosity, "is that kind of thing a regular event for you?"

"The Midnight parties? Occasionally." He nods, still casual, as if we're talking about a book club or poker night, not an extravagant sex party full of your wildest fantasies. "They started this year. Nobody knows who's behind them, just that the invitation arrives out of the blue . . . if you're lucky."

"Are they all themed like that?" I ask.

He nods. "Every event is different; you never know just what you're going to find. Or *whom*," he adds, glancing over at me.

I flush, despite myself. I can play it cool all I want on the outside, but this is all new to me. New, and wildly exciting.

But I don't want Saint to know that my previous sexual experiences can't hold a candle to what we did last weekend, so I just give a casual shrug. "It was a fun time, I guess. Nothing I haven't seen before."

Saint chuckles again, and I can tell, he's not buying my jaded act. "And you saw plenty, didn't you?"

My blush deepens, but luckily, he's pulled up outside of my building. "Thanks for the ride," I blurt, already reaching for the door. "See you in class!"

"Wait, Tessa—"

I pile out before he can stop me and sprint through the rain to the door. Upstairs in my apartment, I quickly strip off my wet coat and sweater, then kick my soaked sneakers aside. I'm still shivering, so I fill the tea kettle and grab a hand towel to blot my wet hair—

There's a knock at the door. It's Saint.

"You forgot something," he says, leaning in the doorway.

Like kissing you?

I stare at him blankly, fighting the urge to run my hands through his dark, tousled hair.

To touch him, full stop. For the very first time.

"I . . . What?" I stammer.

He holds up my wallet. It must have fallen out of my purse.

"Oh, thanks!" I exclaim in relief, taking it from him. "I would have freaked out if I thought it was missing. You know what a hassle it is, having to call your bank and cancel all your cards and order replacements—"

I know I'm babbling here, but somehow, I can't stop. The teakettle sounds with a whistle, and I go to take it off the heat. When I turn back, Saint is in the doorway, watching me with an expression of pure hunger in his eyes.

The lust on his face stops me in my tracks and transports me back to that dim, candlelit room, and the way his eyes devoured me.

Ignited me.

I inhale in a rush, as slowly, his gaze slides over my body. His jaw clenches with a new tension, and I realize my white T-shirt is soaked through, revealing the clear outline of my purple bra. And the taut peaks of my nipples, stiff from the cold—and his slow, seductive gaze.

My heart races. "Thank you," I say again, my voice sounding like it's far away under the thunder of my heartbeat. "For the wallet. And the ride."

"Anytime." Saint drags a hand through his hair as his eyes meet mine again. Full of tension.

Full of desire.

I find myself taking a step toward him, and another. The tea is forgotten now. I feel drawn like gravity. Wondering how it would feel to have his body pressed up against mine, pinning me into the mattress.

Wondering how he would *taste*.

"I'm having a dinner party tonight," Saint says suddenly, breaking the stare. He takes a ragged breath, like it's an effort to stay on the other side of the room. "Come."

My pulse skips at the low order.

An order he's given me before.

Fuck.

"I don't know if I should," I say honestly, feeling intoxicated. Because God, if this is the effect the man has on me with ten feet of space between us, what will it feel like to be closer?

In his arms . . .

"It's a just small get-together," he continues. "A few of my friends. You'll hit it off with my cousin Imogen," he adds with a wry grin. "And my buddies, Hugh Ambrose, Max Lancaster and his fiancée . . . I'd like you to meet them."

Lancaster.

I feel a jolt of recognition at the name. The man Lara said had been seeing Wren!

"OK," I agree slowly, hiding my new eagerness. "I'll come."

Saint looks surprised—then he smiles. "Great. Here, give me your number and I'll text you the address. I can send a car for you," he offers, but I shake my head.

"I'll be fine. Thanks."

He's just tapping his details into my phone when there's a clatter of noise and voices in the hallway, and then Kris and Jia appear through the open door. They stop by the threshold, looking delighted.

"Professor. You found her, then?"

Saint looks . . . bashful? "Uh, yes. Thanks." He nods at me, then heads for the door. "I'll see you tonight," he adds, shooting me a quick smile. Then he strides out.

The minute the door shuts behind him, Jia gives me an arch look. "I knew it!" she crows. "You've been holding out on us!"

"What? No!" I protest, flushing, then turn to busy myself with the teakettle again. "Who wants a cup? Kris, one of your herbal blends?" I offer, hoping to change the subject, but my gossip-hungry roommates won't be distracted so easily.

"Yes, and also, nice going," he applauds me as he strips off his coat. "I hear great things about that man's teaching style, if you know what I mean. Excellent reviews."

"I'm not interested in his reviews," I lie. "He just gave me a ride home from the station, that's all."

"The flowers he brought over say otherwise," Jia pipes up.

"Flowers?" I pause.

"They're in your room," she says, smirking. "He came by looking for you, earlier."

"He didn't say." I feel an unfamiliar glow, and when I go check my room and see the gorgeous bouquet, it only grows.

But fancy flowers and expensive gestures don't mean anything, I remind myself. I'm not going to this dinner party for fun tonight.

I'm on a mission.

* * *

I SHOWER AND blow-dry my hair, and pick out a chic, simple sweater dress, doing what I can to make myself seem less bedraggled before I head over to the address Saint sent for his get-together. The wayward hormones and lustful looks from earlier will *not* be repeated, I decide sternly, as I walk briskly past the Ashford College gates. Tonight, I'm purely there to gather information about Max Lancaster and Saint's other guests. The host can keep his brooding good looks to himself.

I inhale the crisp scent of rain-damp trees and hedges. The rain has stopped, and the city is washed clean, streetlights reflecting off the wet pavements and painting the night with inky color. It's pretty out, peaceful, and I take the chance to brace myself, pulling on my mental armor and getting ready to lie through my teeth again.

This is for Wren. It's all for Wren.

I check the directions again, but this is it: a chic town house on an exclusive cobbled street, just a stone's throw from the college. Not exactly your typical faculty housing, but of course, Saint isn't your average professor.

I ring the doorbell, and he answers with a smile. "Tessa. You made it."

"You thought I wouldn't come?" I ask, trying to ignore how good he looks in a pair of washed classic jeans and a casual button-down, the sleeves rolled up.

"Well, you do like to keep me on my toes," he replies, standing aside and inviting me in.

Inside, the house is warm and elegant, with pale walls and vintage art. "Let me get you some wine and introduce you," Saint says, taking my coat. He leads me past a staircase and down the hall to the back of the house. "Everyone's here."

I take a deep breath and follow him, pasting a pleasant smile to my face. The house opens up to a big open-plan living space, with tall ceilings, packed bookshelves, and an old fireplace blazing—where a group of people in their late twenties and early thirties are hanging out.

"I opened another bottle," a tow-haired man announces, brandishing the wine.

"He picked the most expensive one, too," a perky blonde in a pink Chanel jacket pipes up, rolling her eyes. "Sorry if you were saving it. Honestly, Hugh," she scolds him, as a man sporting a designer watch wanders over and plants himself right in front of me.

"Well, who do we have here?" he asks, giving Saint a look.

"Everyone, this is Tessa," Saint announces. "Tessa, meet Hugh"—the tow-haired, friendly man—"Max, and his fiancée, Annabelle"—Rolex guy, and the perky blonde—"and this is my cousin Imogen."

He finishes with a polished blonde woman who I recognize from the pub that night. *His cousin.* I shouldn't feel relieved, but I do. "Great to meet you." I give a wave, and then steal a look back at the famous Max Lancaster, heir to an empire.

Except, I guess they all are, in a way.

Max smiles at me, every inch the charming playboy. "Delighted to meet you," he says formally, taking my hand—and raising it to his lips to kiss.

"Oh, knock it off." His fiancée, Annabelle, gives him a little shove before greeting me. "Hi," she exclaims, dropping air-kisses on both of my cheeks. "Don't mind him. He's genetically predisposed to flirt with every woman around. And some of the men, too, if he gets drunk enough."

"Hey!" Max protests. "Are you calling my masculinity into question?"

"No, she wasn't," Hugh calls across the room. "Just your hetero-sexuality."

"Don't believe a word they say," Max says, giving me a wink. "He's all talk, no trouser."

My eyes find Saint's, and he chuckles at the memory. Max looks between us. "What?"

"That's what I told Saint," I admit, and Max chortles with laughter.

"I like her already," he says, slapping Saint on the back and going to pour a glass of wine.

"Are you a student at Ashford?" Annabelle asks, friendly, drawing me over to the fire. She's the kind of pretty that I'm used to seeing on the pages of magazines: sparkling blue eyes, pouty lips, and an aristocratic nose.

"Graduate student," I correct her immediately, not wanting them to think I'm just another one of Saint's adoring conquests.

Except, you want to be . . .

"I'm here on fellowship for the year," I add.

"Oh, fun! I was at Magdalen, back in the day," she continues, naming one of the other old, exclusive colleges. "And these guys will never let me hear the end of it. Old college rivals," she explains.

"Booo!" Hugh calls. Annabelle gives me a look.

"See?"

"So, what do you do now?" I ask, beginning to relax. This group seems fun enough, and I just need to keep a low profile and ask a few questions, to get a sense of who these people are—and how their paths might have crossed with Wren.

"Do?" Annabelle echoes. "Oh, you know, this and that." She makes a fluttering gesture with her hand. "I'm on a couple of charity boards, and of course, planning the wedding is a full-time job all on its own!"

"Of course," I echo, hiding a smile. I forget that these people live in a very different social class than me—the kind where jobs and careers are voluntary, and not necessary to pay for rent and groceries. "I can't imagine. Is the date soon?"

"A couple of months," Annabelle replies. "I have a wedding planner, but she's more stressed than Mummy, and I'm spending all my time trying to calm the both of them down! And then there's the florist—"

"Dinner is served," Saint announces, interrupting Annabelle's monologue of wedding prep.

"And don't worry, he didn't cook," Imogen says with a smirk. "I saw the caterers leaving just as I arrived."

"Only because my famous lamb takes a good three hours to roast," Saint protests, smiling broadly.

"You mean, the famous lamb that gave half of us food poisoning last year?" Hugh teases him.

"I still say that was the dodgy kebabs you had on the way home!" Saint meets my eye and gives me a wink. I smile back, surprised. Seeing him relaxed among friends is a new side to him, warmer and more at ease.

And even more tempting.

The others make their way through to the dining room, and I follow. "Don't believe a word of it," Saint tells me, sounding amused. "I'm an excellent cook, I can promise you that. I make a world-class omelet."

"Offering to make me breakfast already?" I give him a knowing smirk. "Isn't that kind of cheap pickup line beneath you?"

He smiles. "That wasn't my intention at all, but it's interesting that's where your mind went . . . Straight to bed."

His hand settles on my back for the briefest moment as he guides me into the room, and I feel a rush of heat.

It's the first time he's touched me—on purpose, at least.

How is that possible? I wonder. After everything we've already shared . . .

"Here." Saint shows me to a chair at the formal dining table and pulls it out for me. "You're right next to me." His voice is low, and when I glance up, sliding into the seat, I see my own heat reflected in his eyes.

He feels it too.

I look away, flushing, and gladly snatch up the crystal water glass waiting at my plate. I take a long gulp, reminding myself to keep cool. If I melt down in a pool of desire every time the man's hand brushes against me, I'll barely make it through the night. So, I collect myself and offer a vague smile to the others as the food is brought in and dinner gets underway.

". . . I'm telling you, she tanked that company on purpose . . ."

". . . no, it reminded me of that time in Chamonix, remember? On the ski lift?"

". . . and then he said, it's a good thing *I'm* president . . ."

The conversation washes over me as I pick my way through a delicious, family-style spread of roast duck and vegetables. Saint clearly goes way back with this crew, and they chatter on about old vacations and new business scandals, easily namedropping glamorous European cities and VIP events.

I've felt like an outsider ever since I stepped foot in Oxford, but hearing their casual, wealthy escapades, I feel even more out of place.

I couldn't be more different from these people. Max's father is one of the most powerful people on earth. Hugh runs an entire nonprofit division of his family's foundation. Plus, of course, there's Saint: heir to an empire. A future *duke*, for Christ's sake!

". . . and what about you, Tessa?" Imogen looks over at me, clearly curious. "What brought you to Oxford?"

I pause. "Actually, it's my sister, Wren," I announce, keeping one eye on Max. "She studied here, so I wanted to follow in her footsteps."

"Wren . . . Peterson?" Max's eyes spark with recognition. "Why didn't you say? You remember Wren," he adds, gesturing to Hugh. "American girl, brainy as hell." Hugh gives a baffled shrug, sipping his wine, and Max continues, smiling. "I ran into her at Ashford, back when Dad was opening that media wing. Or rather, she ran into me, full force, trying to get away from one of the swans."

"Ohhh." Everyone at the table makes a noise of understanding.

"The Ashford swans," Saint explains, leaning closer. "Vicious, nasty beasts. Every year they almost maul some poor tourist, but the college won't ever let them go."

"Apparently, it's in the original founding documents that they always have to have a home there," Max agrees. "Anyway, I bravely beat them back for her, we went for lunch, and then she proceeded to confuse the hell out of me with talk of her research project." He flashes me a smile. "I've never felt so dumb."

Saint smirks. "I find that hard to believe."

"So, you two were friends?" I ask, trying to sound innocent. Just a curious younger sister, learning more about Wren.

Max gives a casual shrug. "Oh, I wouldn't go that far. I've got my reputation to think of, after all," he adds with a teasing wink. "What would people say if I was out palling it up with a girl who thought the *Fast and Furious* movies were the height of cinematic achievement?"

Everybody laughs, and I manage to smile and giggle along with them, but inside, my mind is racing. Because Wren's love for big, loud action movies? That was her hidden guilty pleasure, the indulgence she only confided in her closest friends. She was surrounded by intellectuals all day, people with snooty, highbrow taste, she would explain. She would never hear the end of it if she told them she was at the movie theater opening weekend for anything starring Vin Diesel and a fast car. That's why she would only admit the truth when she really knew someone, well enough to be honest about her tastes.

I always thought it was hilarious, that she held her Netflix habits like a well-guarded secret. Now, I'm glad for it. Because it tells me beyond a shadow of a doubt that Max is lying.

However casual he's being about their friendship, it's clear that he knew my sister far better than he claims.

"Wait, when was this?" Annabelle gives Max a suspicious look.

"Last year," I reply, still trying to gauge his reaction. He doesn't seem suspicious, but what am I expecting, him to leap up and declare that he secretly kidnapped and assaulted Wren?

"While we were dating?" Annabelle presses.

"It was all perfectly innocent!" Max protests immediately, but I don't believe him anymore. "How is Wren doing these days?" he asks me.

I swallow my wine, ready to trot out the same old line about her being happy back in the States, but something makes me pause. "She passed away, actually. A tragic accident."

There's silence.

"I'm so sorry," Saint murmurs beside me, and Max nods.

"That's awful, my condolences."

"Thank you." I look around the table, not sure what to say next. The vibe is suddenly seriously awkward.

Way to be a buzzkill.

Imogen catches my eye and seems to understand my discomfort. "Annabelle, please tell me you've talked Max out of this wild elopement idea," she says, swiftly changing the subject, and soon, they're all chatting wedding plans again, and how Max wants to say his vows while leaping off a cliff somewhere.

I exhale in relief, glad not to be derailing the fun, but when I turn to glance at Saint, he's watching me with a new intensity in his eyes. "I'm so sorry about your sister," he says in a low voice. "I had no idea."

I give a vague shrug. "How could you? It's fine," I reassure him, taking a gulp of my wine.

"But still . . . if you ever want to talk . . ."

Saint's sincerity is making me feel off-balance. I'm used to charged banter and sizzling quips, not this new tenderness on his face. Something in my chest twists.

Something dangerous and raw.

I bolt to my feet. "Bathroom?" I ask brightly.

"Upstairs. First door on the right."

"Great!"

I slip out of the dining room and down the hall. Upstairs, I find the small powder room right where Saint said, but I keep moving. I figure that I have a little time, with everyone distracted over dinner.

I want to take a look around.

There's a neat guest room down the hall, and then I find Saint's primary suite, taking up the back section of the floor. It's clean and uncluttered, with polished wood floors, a thick antique rug, and a king-sized bed made with crisp navy and white linens.

I pause, unable to block the image of the two of us, tangled up in those luxurious sheets. My hands pinned to the plush pillows; Saint's body arched and straining above me, driving me deep into the mattress with every commanding thrust . . .

My cheeks burn hotter, and I quickly slip out of the room. The last door on this level leads to a cozy library lined with photographs, the bookcases full of leather volumes and curios. There's a club chair by the fireplace, and papers stacked on the desk. Clearly, this room isn't just for show. I check a couple of titles, and realize they're first editions: Swift, Balzac, Mantel . . . even a yellowed Jane Austen novel, just sitting on the shelf like it's nothing to pull down and read.

He really does live in a different world.

I keep browsing, idly looking in the desk drawers in case there's anything interesting hidden, but it's just paperwork and reading materials, so I move to study the artwork that's framed on the wall, curious to learn more about my enigmatic host.

It's an eclectic mix of contradictions, just like Saint himself: shockingly erotic sketches and vintage prints, side by side with photos of Saint with family and friends. I pause over a picture of him taken maybe ten years ago, fresh-faced with Max and Hugh in their formal Oxford robes, along with some other boys I don't recognize. Beside it, in a place of pride over the desk, is a photo of younger Saint arm-in-arm with a blonde man, grinning widely for the camera, his silver Aston Martin in the background.

There's something about the other man's face that looks familiar, and I look closer, wondering if he's a relative—

The sound of footsteps comes from the staircase, and I freeze.

Shit! Somebody's coming.

Chapter Twelve
TESSA

I have no time to come up with an excuse for my snooping as the footsteps approach. *You're just a dinner guest*, I remind myself. Nobody knows I'm here chasing answers, but my heart is still pounding as I grab the nearest book from the shelf and pretend to be reading. The door swings open, and Saint steps into the room.

"There you are," he says, looking around the room, as if he's wondering what I've found.

I give a breezy smile. "Sorry, I got distracted by your collection. Is this really a first edition?"

He strolls over and takes the book from me. "It is. You like Austen?"

"Sometimes." I give a little shrug. Saint is still looking at me a little warily, so I turn flirty. "Her books are kind of sedate though, all that restrained passion and control."

"And you prefer your passion unrestrained?" Sure enough, Saint sets the book down and gives me a smoldering look, my trespassing forgotten.

"Maybe . . ." My voice turns breathy—and it's not part of an act. Saint is close enough to touch me now, just inches away, his gaze dark and glittering on mine. Again, I feel his presence like a force field, and I can't help swaying closer, wanting him.

Wanting everything.

"God, I've been dreaming about doing this," Saint says, his

voice low. "Touching you . . ." He reaches out and slowly pushes a lock of hair back from my eyes, not breaking the stare. His fingertip traces my cheek, and I shiver, feeling it everywhere.

"Holding you . . ." His hands go to my waist, moving me back against the desk, the hard length of his body pressed against me. I inhale fast, feeling the solid mass of him.

"Kissing you . . ." Saint's head dips closer, and his mouth finally finds mine.

Fuck.

The rush of heat is like wildfire, suffusing my body the moment his lips make contact, making me gasp at the giddy spark. Saint makes a noise of satisfaction, low in his throat, and yanks me closer, his mouth hot and sure on mine as he eases my lips wider and slides his tongue deep into my mouth.

God, it feels incredible, and I find myself eagerly surrendering to the flames: my hands in his hair, my body arching against him, an impatient ache between my thighs. Saint presses me back against the desk, his body pinning me in place, and I feel a fresh shudder of lust when I feel him, hard against my hip.

Saint lifts his head, drawing a ragged breath.

"Now I want to taste you."

Blood rushes to my cheeks. "Here?" I blurt, shocked—and wanting it too. Fuck, I'm already wet and clenching for him, my blood thick and restless in my veins.

"You looked so perfect when you came for me before . . ." Saint dips his head to whisper kisses along my neck and collarbone. "It's fucking burned on my memory. Show me again, Tessa. Be a good girl and let me hear that moan."

Oh God. My legs practically give way at his urging, but rational thought still struggles at the edge of my mind. "But . . . they're all downstairs," I reply breathlessly, even as his hands slide over my hips, exploring. *Teasing.* "Anyone could find us . . ."

"It won't take long," Saint promises with a knowing smirk, and I can't help giggling.

"Someone's confident," I tease, my head still spinning.

"I'll let you be the judge of that."

Saint kisses me again, hot and sensuous, and I melt into his arms. To hell with it. The rest of the world disappears, until all that's left is this wild rush pounding through me, and the curl of pure desire tugging me into his undertow. Tongue in my mouth, he grips my hips and lifts me, setting me on the edge of the desk before taking hold of each knee and slowly, deliberately, opening them wider.

I shudder.

Saint breaks the kiss, nipping my lower lip as his hand slides under my dress, caressing my bare thigh as he moves to the very apex.

"Quiet," he orders me softly, lips brushing my ear as his fingers find me, hot and damp through my panties. "Unless you want an audience again . . ."

I clench at the memory, spread in that chair with strangers watching. Saint chuckles against me. "So, you like that, hmmm?"

His knuckles brush my clit softly, and I bite back a moan. "I . . . I guess. I did. I don't know . . ."

"But I thought parties like that were no big deal to you?" Saint teases as he slides his hand beneath my panties and strokes me again, skin-to-skin.

God . . .

"I . . . I lied," I admit, as he finds his pace, rubbing my clit in slow, long strokes that make it impossible to keep up any pretense.

"Then you're a natural, baby." He cups my cheek with his spare hand, holding my face in place to watch as his fingers rub and circle, delving deeper, driving me wild. "God, you're so fucking wet . . ."

I whimper, lost in his dark gaze as Saint slowly slides a finger inside me. "How many?" he demands softly, as I clench around him.

"I . . . What?" I ask, trying to focus. But God, it's hard, with his finger flexing deeper, and his palm pressing just right against my clit. Pleasure ripples, but it's still too far, just out of reach.

"How many fingers?" Saint thrusts a second inside me, curling them to rub, high against my inner walls.

Oh ...

I start to move with his hand, chasing the sweet rush of friction every time his palm brushes my clit. "There ..." I gasp as he starts to fuck me with his fingers, thrusting deep. "Oh God, right *there.*"

Saint eases a third finger inside me, making me tense at the stretch. "Saint—" I grip his arm, feeling too tight, too *full*—

"Shh ... You can take it."

He pumps his fingers, thrusting deep, and *fuck*, I feel my body stretch to accommodate him. Opening, blossoming with pleasure, the shivers starting to rise from the base of my spine.

"That's right ..." he breathes, eyes glittering on mine. Still gripping my jaw, he presses his thumb into my mouth, and I instinctively suck. "*Fuck.* That's a good girl."

Oh God.

I feel my body rising, cresting—

"Now come."

I can't resist him even if I tried. My orgasm slams into me, a wave of pure, wild pleasure. I cry out his name, forgetting that there are people downstairs. It doesn't matter. All that I care about for just a moment is the feeling of ecstasy washing over me.

It's so. Damn. Good.

Saint holds me through it, until I'm sprawled back against the desk, flushed and giddy, feeling the pleasure recede.

Then he withdraws his hand—lifting it to his mouth.

Slowly, he licks his fingers clean.

"Just as I thought," he says, looking smug. "You taste delicious."

I let out a breathless burst of laughter. "Did anyone ever tell you it's not attractive to be so damn cocky?"

Saint grins back at me, still perfectly groomed with not a hair out of place, despite just giving me an epic orgasm. "You seem to like it well enough," he retorts.

I pull my dress down and get to my unsteady feet again. "The jury's still out," I lie, giving him an arch look—even as my legs feel shaky, and my body hums with pleasure. "I might need some more evidence to decide."

"Just say the word." Saint gives me a smoldering look, then chivalrously holds out his arm. "Shall we?"

I take it, my heart still racing. He's a man of contradictions, alright. Standing there so dapper, with perfect manners, just moments after he was knuckles-deep inside me, ordering me to come.

But just as we're leaving the room, I notice something on one of the black-and-white photographs on the wall, the one with him and his buddies, from years ago.

Except it's not their faces I'm looking at this time, but the hand-written line I see scrawled on the corner of the photo matting.

Legacy is a gift, and our sworn bond.

Chapter Thirteen
TESSA

I keep a low profile for the rest of the evening, and then give some excuses about early study to make a polite exit.

Heading home, my head is spinning.

Not just from the words on that photograph, the same as the note at the party, but from my encounter with Saint, too. The way he knew exactly what I liked—what I *needed*—and how effortlessly he drew my pleasure from my body, until I didn't care about the risk of discovery or what his guests might think.

There's something about the man that seems to unlock a side of me I've never explored. The part of me that's wild, passionate, wanton. Who moans with need, and greedily arches against his hands. Who throws caution to the wind, just to feel that sharp, wicked rush of pleasure.

Who is that woman? I wonder as I let myself into the apartment and go sit at my dresser, gazing at my reflection in the mirror. I've never seen myself like this before. I can still see the flush of my orgasm on my cheeks, and the liquid heat in my eyes, just remembering how it felt, pinned there against the desk, with his fingers stretching me open and his dark gaze watching my every gasp . . .

I shiver. I like it, this new, sensual version of myself. I want more.

But I can't let myself forget for a moment why I'm really here. Even Saint's expert fingers and wicked tongue shouldn't distract me from my true mission, tracing Wren's footsteps until I find what really happened to her.

And something tells me that Saint is my passport to the truth. The secret society.

I should have guessed that Saint would be connected somehow. After all, if there really is some secret society here at Oxford, Professor Anthony St. Clair and his illustrious friends seem like the most obvious members. They're rich, aristocratic, connected . . . exactly the kind of people to belong to a group like that. Saint wasn't here at Oxford at the same time as Wren, so I can thankfully rule him out of being involved, but Max Lancaster . . . ?

He knew Wren, maybe even dated her, or was secretly hooking up behind Annabelle's back. Wren hated cheaters, she would never be the "other woman" and sneak around, but what if she didn't know he had a girlfriend? Max is a charming guy, I saw that for myself tonight, and if he turned the full force of his dashing good looks and playboy routine on my nerdy, play-it-safe sister . . . ?

Well, maybe she wanted to let go and live a little. Have a wild British fling.

Not realizing there might be consequences.

* * *

THE QUESTIONS WHIRL in my mind over the next few days. Questions, and sensual memories of Saint . . . but it turns out, I have to put a pause on any extracurriculars, because the semester kicks into high gear, with lectures and assignments demanding all of my time, until I feel just about brain-dead trying to keep up. Still, Saint texts me. Small, flirty messages, and invitations to have another date.

Another? I text back from my regular study spot, deep in the Ashford library stacks. *I must have missed the first one . . .*

You came, that makes it a date, the reply says, making me smile. *In fact, that makes it two now. Third time's a charm?*

Your charm will have to wait, I type, ignoring the butterflies of anticipation in my stomach. *I have two essays due, and a seminar to prepare for. And my professor is a real piece of work.*

I tuck my phone away and focus on my never-ending reading list of weighty eighteenth-century thinkers. But I'm not sure whether I'm keeping my distance from Saint because I really am snowed under with academic work . . .

Or because I know that just a few moments alone with him will make me forget about it all: my course load, my investigations.

My self-control.

It's safer to just ignore his charming messages—and the lavish basket of gourmet snacks he has delivered to the apartment, along with a note.

"Brain fuel," Jia reads aloud, as we all poke through the goodies on Friday night. "Study hard."

"Ooh, these are the fancy chocolates," Kris celebrates, biting into a truffle. "And is that . . . Dom Perignon?" He plucks the bottle of champagne out of the basket. "I wish a rich duke would try and seduce *me.*"

"He's not seducing me," I argue automatically. Then I pause. "Well, kind of . . . Is that bad?" I ask, sampling a truffle. They are delicious. "Against the rules of the college or something."

"I mean, it's frowned upon, but what are they going to do?" Jia replies. "You're both consenting adults. If you want to bang like bunnies all over Ashford, nobody can stop you."

"We're not banging," I say quickly.

"Yet." Kris gives me a smirk. "You know what? We should have a picnic, put all this fancy food to good use. It's your birthday to-morrow," he says to Jia—and keeps talking over her protests. "And yes, I know you don't want to do anything big to celebrate the impending march toward death, so we'll keep it small. The three of us, this Italian pistachio *foie gras,* and all the chocolate you can eat."

Jia relents. "Fine," she says, rolling her eyes. "But there better not be any balloons!"

Saturday dawns bright and blue-skied, a perfect September day. I squeeze in a couple of hours at the library, then stop by the gatehouse to subtly quiz one of the porters if they have any security cameras around.

"Why, you get something nicked from your mailbox?" he asks, sorting through packages.

"Yes," I fib. "My friend swears they dropped it off for me last Friday night. I thought if we could take a look at the security footage, we could see who took it. Or if my friend is lying," I add with a little laugh.

I haven't forgotten about that mysterious party invitation—or the scribbled note on the back.

I know what happened to Wren.

Whoever wrote it hasn't been in touch again, and I'm getting impatient, wondering who it is who's pointing me toward the secret society. I figure if I can get a glimpse of them dropping off the envelope . . .

But the porter just gives me an apologetic smile. "Sorry, love," he says. "We only store our video for three days—and just between us, the camera in the mailroom's been out for a month. Keep meaning to get it fixed but . . . anyway, your best bet is to have them leave things with us at the front desk here. We'll make sure you get it."

"Oh." My hopes fall. "Thanks all the same."

It looks like there's nothing I can do to find them out. At least, not today. So, I pick up a box of Jia's favorite cookies and go to meet my roommates by the river, at the Oxford Botanical Gardens. I'm looking forward to unwinding, and soaking in some of the rare English sun, but when I spot them on the riverbanks, I realize, it's not the low-key affair Kris promised. Not at all.

"Tessa!" Jia whoops in greeting, already pink-cheeked with a cup of something bubbly in her hand. "Come, sit. This is Klaus and Eric." She gestures to the hunky Nordic guys sitting with them on the picnic blanket. "We met them at the deli."

"Locked eyes over the fine salamis," Kris adds with a wink.

"Oh. Hi, nice to meet you." I give a little wave and try to find a space to sit. But with everyone else sprawled out, I wind up cross-legged on the grass. "Happy birthday, Jia," I add, passing her the card and gift I brought.

"Thanks!" She sets them aside and turns back to Klaus. Or Eric. "More champagne? Wait, we're already out!" she giggles, setting aside the empty bottle of Dom from Saint.

"Time to start on the cheap stuff," Kris declares, cracking another bottle. He leans in close as he refills Klaus-or-Eric's plastic cup, and murmurs something flirty. The guy laughs, his hand resting on Kris's thigh. "Don't worry," Kris adds to me. "We brought plenty. The day is young!"

I sit back, trying to get comfortable on the grass as the others drink and flirt. The riverbanks are full of students and locals enjoying the good weather, and I can even see people gliding past on low gondolas called punts, picnicking on the water.

But still, despite the lovely scenery, it's not long before I'm feeling like a fifth wheel.

"Anyone want more strawberries?" I ask, reaching for the container.

Nobody replies. Jia and her guy are laughing over something on his phone, and the other pair are murmuring sweet nothings to each other, looking like they're about to start rolling around right here on the blanket.

I'm just wondering when I can make a polite escape—and if they'd even notice—when a shadow falls over me. I look up to find Saint standing there, dressed down in jeans and another button-down, the sun forming a halo around his dark hair.

"Saint," I blurt, surprised. "I mean, Professor."

"Ms. Peterson," he replies, equally formal, although there's a teasing grin on the edge of his lips. "Enjoying yourself?"

"Yes," I lie, shooting a glance to my roommates. They're exchanging smirks. "Thanks for the snacks, by the way."

"Looks like you made good use of them." He smiles at the trail of empty wrappers littering the blanket. I nod again.

At least, the others did.

"Do you mind if I steal Tessa for a moment?" Saint asks Jia and Kris. "We need to chat about her contribution to my seminar last week."

"Sure."

"Go ahead."

My roomies can hardly keep a straight face as Saint offers me his hand and helps me to my feet. As we walk away from the picnic, I hear them explode in laughter.

"Sorry," I apologize. "They're feeling . . . merry."

Saint smiles. "It's fine. You looked like you needed some rescuing," he adds.

"So you don't want to debate my essay on libertine poetry?" I ask lightly, noticing Saint's hand is lingering in mine. "Gee, what a shame."

"I mean, if that's how you'd like to spend the afternoon—" Saint offers, and I quickly stop him.

"No, please! My brain feels like cotton wool. And it's so gorgeous out," I add, looking around at the lush grass and calm river. "I've been hiding out in the library all week. I need a change of scene."

"Then that's exactly what you'll get." Saint squeezes my hand, darkly irresistible. "Trust me?"

"Not at all," I reply, smiling.

He laughs. "Smart woman. Let's get out of here."

* * *

HE'S PARKED ON a street nearby, and we pile in. I don't ask where we're going as he starts the engine and drives through town, I just roll down the window and enjoy the feel of the sun on my skin and the breeze whipping around us. Saint turns on some music, and soon, the charming Oxford city streets give way to suburban sprawl, and then the wide, green expanse of open countryside.

I relax with every mile. It's gorgeous out here, as we pass by small villages, fields and woodlands. It's like something out of a postcard, the perfect English scene—especially when Saint pulls off the main road, beside an old water mill that's been turned into a charming pub, right on the riverbanks.

Saint orders us food and a couple of pints of beer, and we settle at a picnic table outside, with the sound of the water rushing nearby.

"Where did you grow up?" I ask curiously, taking a sip of beer. "Is it nearby?"

Saint shakes his head. "I mean, everything's near compared to the distances you go in America," he says with a grin. "But my family's place is South of London. A few hours away."

"Your estate," I say, slightly mocking. "*Duke.*"

Saint groans. "Don't call me that. That's my father's title, not mine. And if I had my way . . ." He trails off. "The Ashford name is more trouble than it's worth."

"Sure," I can't help teasing. "Wealth . . . privilege . . . noble blood . . . It must be such a drag."

Saint gives a self-deprecating laugh. "OK, OK, I get it. Don't worry, I know I'm fortunate. What about you?"

"No noble blood here."

"Come on, where did you grow up?" he asks. "Is your family still back in the States?"

I nod. "I grew up outside of Chicago. Suburbs. But we would go to a cabin on Lake Michigan every summer. Me and Wren would run around on the beach all day . . ." I trail off.

Saint reaches over and squeezes my hand. "I hope Max didn't put you on the spot the other night, about your sister."

I manage a smile. "It's fine."

"It's not fine," he says quietly. "Losing someone like that . . ."

I exhale. "You're right. That's just what I say, so people don't feel awkward."

"You don't have to pretend with me, Tessa."

I glance up. There's something in his eyes, something aching and raw, that makes me believe it's not just a platitude.

Somehow, he understands.

"It was awful at first. I couldn't even say her name without breaking down," I admit, letting myself reveal just a little of the truth to him. "But everyone says it just takes time, and I guess they're right. It's easier to talk about her now."

"When my brother died, it took me a year before I could even look at his photograph," Saint says quietly, and I widen my eyes in surprise.

"I . . . didn't know."

He gives a rueful shrug. "It's been ten years now. I don't like to talk about it. Clearly, I need some more time."

I think of that photo in his library, of the older blonde guy, and the similarities in their features, but before I can ask anything more, Saint suddenly gets to his feet. "Our food should be here by now," he says quickly. "I'll go check on it."

He quickly strides back to the pub, leaving me alone.

I exhale, listening to the river as I try to process this new revelation. It turns out Saint hasn't led the charmed life I thought. He knows what it's like to lose someone he loves, just like I lost Wren.

I wonder, is this the reason for the connection I feel with him? It turns out that under the charged chemistry and quick banter, both of us are hiding a deep, heartbreaking grief.

Maybe we're chasing after this chemistry—the passion, the excitement, this new hopeful spark—as a way to move on from tragedy.

But whether it's a fresh start or a mindless escape, I'm not sure yet.

Both might be just as dangerous.

By the time Saint returns, with our server right behind him, I've pulled myself together. Delving too deeply into the past is risky business, considering my mission.

And the fact that I still don't know if Saint's friends are connected to Wren's attack.

"You came back." I flash a breezy smile once we're set up with our lunch spread: a classic beer-battered fish and chips for me, and Saint's rustic pie. "I would have bet good money on you fleeing for the hills to get away from my weeping woman routine."

"I don't remember you weeping," Saint says wryly, reaching across to steal a fry—sorry, chip—from me.

I playfully slap his hand away. "You know what I mean. But let's lighten the mood. Tell me more about you. Family, hopes, dreams, . . ."

"And you said you wanted a lighter topic." Saint smirks.

I arch an eyebrow. "Well, now I'm intrigued. Go ahead, share your deep, dark secrets."

Saint grins. "Not exactly first date talk, is it?"

"I thought this was our third, by your counting." I remind him, smiling.

"Ah, but only if you come."

I flush at his brazen banter. I look around, but there's nobody seated close enough to hear him, just a couple of families by the riverbanks, kids trying to chase the ducks.

"I'm just trying to find out who you are, outside of the most popular professor in Oxford," I say.

Saint grins. "I don't know. Professor Montague gives me a run for my money."

I think back to our welcome sessions and vaguely recall a short, teddy bear of a man with wild Einstein-like gray hair. "He's got to be eighty, at least!"

"Some girls like an older man," Saint jokes, and I shudder.

"Eww, no thank you."

"So you don't have a taste for authority figures?" Saint gives me a smoldering look.

"I guess it depends on who's giving me instruction," I reply lightly, and take a bite of food, enjoying the brief flash of heat in his gaze. "But enough deflecting. You still haven't told me anything about yourself. Libertine, rake, seducer . . . what they say about you can't *all* be true."

Saint gives a wry smile. "It depends on who you ask. I've always been more of a sinner than a saint," he says. "So if you have any ideas about reforming me . . ."

I snort with laughter. "You mean, trying to save you from your wayward, decadent ways? No thank you," I say firmly. "That's not a good use of either of our time. Besides, the women of Oxford would never forgive me," I add, and he pauses.

"I'm not seeing anyone else right now. In case you were wondering."

I was, but I'm not going to let him see the glow of satisfaction I feel at that news. I shrug, instead. "Seeing, or fucking?"

"Neither. You have my undivided attention."

"Except when you have another woman on her knees," I remind him with a sultry look.

Saint's mouth curls in a wicked smile. "You enjoyed that?" he asks, his voice dropping.

My pulse kicks. "You know I did," I murmur, just as flirty. Our eyes lock, and the air turns charged between us, sizzling with promise and—

"Saint!"

A voice from across the beer garden breaks the heated moment. I look up to see a younger tow-haired man with a group of friends. He waves, then makes his way over to us, smiling broadly at Saint. "Fancy seeing you here," he says, with the same cut-glass English accent that would put Colin Firth to shame. "I thought this place was too rustic for your sophisticated tastes."

"I contain multitudes, little brother." Saint gives him a smile, then gestures between us. "Tessa, meet the baby of the St. Clair family, Robert."

"Hi." I smile, surprised. Up close, I can see a few similarities in their features, but while Saint is all dark, brooding good looks, his younger brother has a hearty, athletic vibe and cheerful good looks.

Robert reaches to enthusiastically shake my hand. "Great to meet you, Tessa. Keeping this guy out of trouble, I hope?"

"I wouldn't dream of it," I reply, and he chuckles.

"She's got your number there, Saint."

"What brings you to town?" Saint asks him, taking a gulp of beer. "I thought you'd be chained to your desk down at HQ."

"Just up to oversee some things at the Oxford lab," Robert explains. "Dad needs a steady hand on site, especially with the big launch coming up. You know, things would go a lot smoother if you could pitch in at the office," he adds, looking hopeful.

Saint sighs. "Come on, Rob, I told you—"

"I know, I know!" Robert holds his hands up. "Be warned, this one is about as stubborn as they come," he warns me, friendly.

"Noted," I reply, watching Saint's body language. He seems friendly enough with his brother, but I can feel a tense vibe just beneath the surface.

"You will be coming to the Lancaster party though, won't you?" Robert asks him. "Dad said I need to drag you there myself. Full family showing and all."

"I'm not sure." Saint gives a casual shrug. "I'll have to check my schedule."

"I know a stuffy garden party isn't your scene, but can you please do this one thing for the family?" Robert asks. "Dad's already stressed enough from work, and this is a big deal. Everyone will be there, and the last thing they need is—"

"I get it," Saint cuts him off with a sigh. "You don't have to give me the lecture, believe me, I've got it memorized by now. Duty, honor, the future of the Ashford line . . ."

"Well, as long as we're on the same page." Robert grins, slaps Saint's back, and gives me another smile. "Lovely meeting you, Tessa. See you soon, I hope."

He strides off to rejoin his friends, and I sneak a look at Saint. He drains his pint of beer, looking tense from the interruption.

"Lancaster . . . that's Max's family, right?" I ask innocently. If they're throwing a big party, then that could be a chance for me to get closer and find out more.

Saint nods, looking resigned. "They're hosting a couple hundred of their closest friends at the family pile. Teacups and croquet, a real wild time," he says.

"Like in *Bridgerton*, with the little hoops and mallets?" I ask. "That looks like so much fun!"

"It's not," Saint replies dryly.

"You just haven't played with the right person," I say, acting flirty again. I feel a small stab of unease, manipulating him like this, but it's for the greater good. Anything that gets me closer to the truth is worth it. "Every game can be fun, if the stakes are high enough . . ." I give him a sultry look.

"You want to join me then, to keep things interesting?" Saint asks, and I feel a rush of victory.

"Sure, why not?" I reply, still casual, but inside, I'm celebrating. If Max has any answers, I'm going to find them.

Chapter Fourteen
TESSA

A quick google for pictures from past Lancaster shindigs tells me that my normal student wardrobe isn't going to cut it for the big party. This isn't just some backyard cookout, but one of the social events of the season. I don't want to draw any attention or look out of place in the aristocratic crowd, but my budget doesn't stretch to designer, so I spend the day trawling through the vintage thrift stores of Oxford instead, looking for an outfit that screams *of course I have a trust fund, darling.*

"What do you think about this one?" I ask, emerging from the tiny dressing room for Jia to see. She had a spare hour between lectures and offered to help me shop. I spin around in the vintage silk floral sundress, assessing my reflection in the chipping, gilt-edged mirror. "Cute, right? Or would wearing it in the fall be breaking some 'don't wear white after Labor Day'-type rule?"

"It's kind of old-fashioned, isn't it?" she asks, examining the high-cut neckline and knee-length skirt.

"I know, but I'd prefer to be too buttoned-up instead of causing a scandal by flashing my shoulders. Isn't that what all those TikToks about 'old money' vibes say? When in doubt, dress like a snooty grandma." I duck back into the changing room and try another outfit from my pile of potentials. I've hit paydirt in my third stop of the day, a cute vintage store on a back street packed to the rafters with old designer goodies, like some eccentric society matron's dressing room.

"I don't know why you're so stressed," Jia comments through the curtain. "It's just a party."

"A super-fancy garden party, attended by every VIP in England," I explain, wriggling into the next outfit, a cream 60s shift dress with bold sequin appliqué on the hem. "I was looking at the photos from last year's event, and Princess Kate showed up. Makes sense. Cyrus Lancaster has a serious reputation . . . I feel like I should rewatch *Succession* just to prepare!" I joke, emerging from the dressing room again, but Jia just checks her phone, looking impassive.

"Is it really a good thing, trying to impress these people?"

I pause, surprised at her tone. "I thought you were all for me seeing Saint? You and Kris practically ordered me to go have hot sex with the man!"

"A sexy hookup, sure," she replies. "Everyone wants to be Professor St. Clair's new favorite plaything, but I didn't expect him to, you know . . ."

She trails off, and I frown. "Date me?" I finish, feeling a sting. "Why not?"

Jia looks away. "I mean, he's a total man-whore, you know that. So is Max Lancaster, according to all the tabloids. Just another trust fund kid running around, spending Daddy's money. And now you're trying to get all dolled up to impress them." She gives a shrug. "I'm just saying, seems like a lot of effort. I mean, you don't want to be friends with them, do you? Those assholes waltz around town like they own the place."

"Because they probably do," I reply, trying to keep my tone light. I'm not sure what Jia's problem is. "Anyway, it's just one party. I think it'll be fun, seeing how the other half lives. I'll see if I can steal some caviar," I add, joking, but Jia doesn't laugh.

"That one's too short," she says, nodding at the dress I'm wearing. "You don't want them thinking you're a slut."

I blink. *Okaaay.*

"Good point," I say brightly, and go to try another outfit, but after another half-hour of Jia's passive-aggressive comments, I wish I hadn't invited her along. Finally, she has to get to her next lecture, leaving me to shop alone.

I take a deep breath, trying to assess my reflection in the mirror. This one is understated: a two-piece set in sky-blue silk, with a boxy top and a longer, full skirt that nips in at my waist. It looks great, like something from a 1950s *Vogue*, but is it good enough for the St. Clairs and Lancasters of the world?

Jia's comments have rattled me. I try not to let her words get to me, but I have to admit that I felt out of place at Saint's dinner party, listening to all their exploits. The world they've grown up in is a million miles from my own modest, middle-class background. Will the Lancaster party be the same?

My phone buzzes. Saint is calling. I answer, still studying my reflection.

"Let's skip the party," he says immediately.

"Who is this?" I ask teasingly.

"Very funny." I can hear the smile in his voice. "But I'm serious. To hell with boring small talk and stuffy canapes. Let's have dinner instead, just the two of us. I know a great French bistro on the banks of the Seine."

I laugh at the suggestion. "Paris for dinner? Oh yeah, sure."

"Why not? Eurostar takes an hour, we could be eating our body weight in fine steak and eclairs by tonight."

I blink. "You're serious?"

"I never joke about French patisserie," Saint replies, and I have to laugh. A whirlwind trip to Paris . . . ? I would say yes in a heartbeat—if I wasn't on a mission.

"It sounds wonderful," I tell him. "But would we actually relax and have a good time, or would your family try calling every five minutes to guilt-trip you for not showing up?"

Saint sighs, sounding reluctant. "You've clearly met my mother, the queen of guilt."

"So, wouldn't it be easier just to keep them happy and drop

by the party, just for a little while?" I suggest gently. "I promise, you can whisk me away for some ridiculously over-the-top dinner date some other time."

"Count on it," Saint says. "But you're right, I suppose. See you later. I'll pick you up at three."

I hang up and take a deep breath. My plan for the Lancasters is still on track.

"What do you think?" the shop assistant asks, poking her head back.

"I think this is the one," I nod, smoothing down the silk. "I'll take it."

* * *

WHEN SAINT PICKS me up from the apartment in the afternoon, I can tell that I made the right choice. His gaze devours me, hungrily, and I feel my stomach turn over in a flip of awareness.

I spin for him in a pirouette. "Like it?" I ask playfully.

He pulls me into his arms for a slow, heated kiss. *Oh.* I melt against him, feeling the rush of electricity through every cell in my body.

Finally, he pulls away. "Let's go before I decide to blow off the party and just ravish you right here." Saint gives me a wolfish look.

"Ravishing? I think that's a new one for me," I say with a smirk, then neatly sidestep him to collect my coat. As much as I want to find out exactly what that would involve, I need to stay focused. This party is about research and gathering info, not the liquid ache Saint sends through my body.

"You know, Paris is still on the table . . ." Saint says as he holds the passenger door to his sportscar open for me. "Or Rome, Seville . . . take your pick. We could probably borrow a jet if you want to go further afield. Morocco is lovely this time of year."

I laugh, even though it's still wild to me that he's not even kidding. I can't imagine the kind of life that involves spontaneous trips and private jets. "Another time," I tell him, as he slides in behind the wheel. I pat his thigh. "You're forgetting, a classic English garden party is wildly exotic to me. If there are cucumber sandwiches and big hats . . . I might just swoon."

"I can think of better ways to make you melt." Saint takes my hand and lifts it to his lips, giving me a wolfish look as his lips brush my knuckles.

"Like what?" I ask, feeling breathless as we start the drive.

He keeps his eyes on the road, slowly tracing along my bare arm. "It involves much less clothing, for a start."

"Why?" I tease. "I thought you liked my outfit."

"I'd like you more naked, so I can see those pretty nipples of yours tighten up when I touch you."

I feel a rush of heat. Saint knows just the way to talk dirty to me, and his crisp accent makes the filthy words seem even more shocking.

I wriggle in my seat, and he gives a low chuckle. "You like it when I tell you what I want to do."

"Yes," I admit, breathing faster. Then, boldly, I take my hand from him and slowly trail it down his torso, until it's resting in his lap. "But you like it, too."

He's hard, his cock stiff and straining beneath his pants.

Saint sounds a low groan, and I give him the briefest nudging stroke before withdrawing my hand. "Eyes on the road, mister," I say, flirty. "You have precious cargo here."

"Yes, I do." Saint flashes me a brief smile before turning his attention back to the road ahead, gripping the steering wheel tightly. "But my God, I'm going to enjoy taking you apart."

Yes, please.

I crack the window wider, breathing in the afternoon air to cool my flushed body. Any more of this dangerously seductive banter and I might make him pull over and show me that ravishing, right in the nearest lay-by. So, I turn on the music, and change the subject, asking about his love of jazz and teaching work at Ashford, until we finally arrive at the famous Lancaster house.

"House?" I ask, peering out the window as we speed up the drive, past a gatehouse, riding stables, and a long stretch of ornamental elm trees. "This is more of an estate. A small kingdom!" I can see tennis courts in the distance, and then the main house rises up in front of us, imposing and grand.

Saint chuckles. "But just you try keeping the place heated through a damp winter. These old country piles are all the same: Pretty to look at, but wracked with draught and rot."

He pulls up beside a row of old, expensive cars, and I get out for a closer look. The sandstone is crumbled, covered with ivy in places, and there are statues and gargoyles along every roofline, and even a couple of turrets, too.

Turrets . . .

I pause, getting a flash of recognition. The photo in the Ashford yearbook, the one of Wren spinning around at a party . . . I quickly get out my phone and check the pic I snapped of the page.

It's the same building in the background: unmistakable ivy and sandstone.

Wren was here. The mysterious party, the night it happened.

This is where she was taken.

"Ready to face the boredom and small talk?" Saint asks, coming around the car and offering me his arm.

I quickly tuck my phone away. "And cucumber sandwiches," I remind him, my mind still racing.

"How could I forget?"

Impeccably uniformed staff direct us around the side of the house, along walkways lined with elaborate topiary, to the lush back lawn where hundreds of people are mingling with a perfect view of the countryside.

I look around, wide-eyed. I planned to pay careful attention to everything here, but it turns out, I won't even have to try. There are silk canopies, plush seating areas, and tables set with elaborate floral displays and incredible-looking foods. A live band plays soft-rock hits on the patio as the chicly dressed crowd chats, laughs, and challenges each other to croquet.

"Is that . . . Agatha Mays?" I whisper to Saint as I spot the legendary actress holding court with some dapper gentlemen. "She's an icon!"

"Don't let her hit the sherry though," Saint says, steering me past them. "She'll commandeer the piano and sing showtunes until dawn."

"Of course," I say faintly. Checking out the clothing of the women around us, I'm relieved to find that I blend right in. Some ladies have gone for elaborate patterns and wild headpieces like it's the first day at the races, but generally, the vibe is understated wealth—with a serious collection of jewelry on display. "So what's this event for again?"

"The official reason is to celebrate the anniversary of Lancaster Press," Saint explains, naming the newspaper publishing business that is the crown jewel in the Lancaster Media crown. "But they find a new theme every year. Nobody turns down an invite, not when every power player in British media and politics will be here. Handshake deals around every corner," he adds, smiling. "Look, over there," he whispers, pointing to two older men in designer pinstripes, murmuring intently by the rose bushes. "They could be dividing up British industry as we speak."

"*You* wanted to bail," I point out, and he laughs.

"That's because I have zero ambition," Saint says, lifting a couple of glasses of champagne from a passing waiter's tray. "I'm perfectly happy toiling at Oxford in obscurity."

"You mean, basking in adoration," I correct him. "And giving the occasional seminar. It's hardly backbreaking work."

"Now you're beginning to sound like my parents." Saint grins. "Who are around here somewhere, unfortunately."

"They are?" I feel a shot of nerves, which is crazy, I know. I'm not some eager girlfriend, anxious to meet the parents, I remind myself. This thing with Saint is just . . . fun. A welcome distraction, while I dig to find out what happened to Wren here that night.

"Does Max ever have parties here?" I ask carefully. "It seems like a great place to throw a rager."

"Sometimes," Saint begins to reply, but before he can say anything else, we're interrupted by a tall, elegant woman in her fifties with a long, aquiline nose and a massive pair of diamond earrings.

"Anthony! Darling."

"Bitsy." Saint politely accepts her air kisses. "You're looking lovely as ever. Henry better be wielding that croquet mallet to beat away your admirers."

Bitsy titters with laughter. "Aren't you sweet?" She looks to me, curious, and Saint introduces us. "Charmed. Is your mummy around?" Bitsy asks him. "We need to start planning the horticultural society events for spring."

"I'm sure she's around here somewhere," Saint says. "But you'll have to work to top last year's Salute to the Tulip. The displays were stunning."

"Thank you." She beams, before moving off.

"Friend of yours?" I ask, amused.

"One of my godmothers," he replies. "And if you think she didn't spend all my college years trying to set me up with her drippy daughters, you weren't the one sitting through a dozen bad dates. Luckily they're all married off by now," he adds, nodding to where three women with matching noses and loud floral prints are going to war on the croquet field. "And Bitsy's accepted that I'm the last man on earth anyone should be marrying."

"You are getting old," I say, teasing. "What's the male word for spinster?"

"Eligible bachelor," Saint quips, and I laugh.

But it turns out not to be a joke. As we move through the party,

Saint is intercepted a dozen times, by attractive women, and older people too. And every one of them looks disappointed to find out that he brought me as a date. But Saint doesn't skip a beat, he schmoozes like a pro, making small talk and in-jokes with everyone and keeping a polite smile on his face. Despite talking like he can't stand these society events, he seems a natural.

"Nobody would ever guess you hate these things," I comment as we browse a groaning dessert table for snacks. "I hardly recognize you without all the seductive flirting."

"Oh, I'm just storing it up for later," he promises, resting his hand low on my back. He leans in to murmur in my ear. "Like the fact I'm desperate to know what kind of panties you're wearing under that skirt."

"Who says I'm wearing any?" I reply with a smirk.

He sounds a low noise of frustration as we're intercepted— again. This time, it's an older gentleman in pale linen, with a slim wisp of a woman on his arm. "Saint, how are you?" the man says, taking Saint's outstretched hand and pumping it vigorously. "Exciting stuff afoot with Ashford Pharma, I hear. I might just have to buy some more stock, if the rumors about your new miracle drug are to be believed."

"You'll have to talk to my father about that," Saint says smoothly. "Or my brother, Robert. He's around here somewhere."

"Did you hear about Arnold Pottinger's new disaster?" the man continues, barely giving me a glance. But his partner does, looking me up and down with a thin-lipped smile, like she's been sucking on lemons.

"What did you say your name was?" she asks, as the men keep talking.

"Tessa Peterson, hi."

"Peterson." The smile warms for a moment. "Is that the Rhode Island shipping Petersons?"

"Nope," I say brightly. "The Bolingbridge Petersons."

"Oh."

Luckily, I'm rescued by Imogen, appearing suddenly at my side. She's looking polished as ever in a chic lilac shift dress, with her blonde hair pinned back in a French braid. "Lucille," she coos to the woman. "You don't mind if I steal Tessa here for a moment? Lovely to see you!"

With a firm hand on my arm, she steers me away.

"Thank you," I breathe, relieved. "I was about to give her a heart attack explaining that my parents are public school teachers."

Imogen laughs. "This crowd can be . . . traditional. Everyone knows everyone else," she explains. "And to gain entry into this world, you have to be massively wealthy, well-connected, or a fashion model third wife," she adds, dropping her voice as we pass two men who must be pushing seventy, braying loudly as their stunning twentysomething wives stand around, looking bored.

"And I'm none of the above," I agree.

She looks at me thoughtfully. "I wouldn't be so sure about that just yet. You know, Saint never brings dates to these things."

"I'm surprised he ever shows up," I say, watching him mingle. It may look effortless to an outsider, but I can already tell from the stiff line of his shoulders, he's hating every minute of it.

"Oh, Saint likes to act the rebel, but he knows what's expected of him. We all do," Imogen says, with a faint twist in her voice that makes me wonder what else is going on with her. "So, how are you enjoying meeting everyone?" she asks, smoothly changing the subject.

"It's . . . interesting," I reply, still on guard. Imogen seems like the ultimate society princess, polished and sophisticated, and I'm bracing myself for some dismissive comments to make it clear that I don't belong.

But, surprisingly, she grins. "It's OK, I know we seem like a bunch of rich assholes. And most of us are—me included." Imogen laughs. "But I'll say one thing about Cyrus and Juniper Lancaster. They know how to hire a good party planner."

"It is a gorgeous event," I agree, looking around.

"Why, thank you."

I pause. "Wait, you planned it?"

Imogen nods. "I have an event company," she says. "Tea parties, birthday bashes, the occasional wedding, when I can bring myself to deal with all the Bridezilla drama. And no, I'm not planning Annabelle and Max's big day," she adds. "You couldn't pay me to touch that explosion of ego and tears."

I smile, relaxing. "What's the story there?" I ask, curious for more information. I haven't seen Max yet, but I've spotted Annabelle across the lawn, wearing a hot-pink headpiece with feathers sprouting from the brim.

"Well, Annabelle's a few years younger than us," Imogen explains, plucking us martinis from a server without pausing for breath. "So she's adored Max forever. Her family, the deWessops, goes way back, too. A very old, aristocratic family. Her aunt was rumored to be one of the Prince's bit on the side."

"Which prince?" I ask, loving the gossip.

"My lips are sealed. But I will say, there's a deWessops offspring out there who's losing his hair very early," Imogen says with a wink, and I laugh.

"What other scandals are going on?"

"Well . . ." Imogen draws me closer and begins to point out people in the crowd as we sample desserts from the spread. The artist having a secret fling with the tech mogul's new wife . . . the man who just inherited a massive fortune from his aristocratic parents, despite having the same flaming red hair as his "father's" business partner . . . the mousy daughter of an earl who just shocked everyone by eloping with her riding instructor. It's like a soap opera. "Oh, and you know about the Ambroses, don't you?" Imogen asks.

The name is familiar. "Saint's friend, Hugh?"

She nods. "His father, Lionel, is a bigwig politician, running to be leader of the party. When he wins the ballot of members next month, he'll become the new Prime Minister—without even needing to compete in a general election. You've got to love the British system of government," she adds, rolling her eyes.

"Don't you mean *if* he wins?" I ask. Imogen smirks.

"Lionel and Cyrus Lancaster are thick as thieves. With the Lancaster Media empire behind him, there's no way he's going to lose. I mean, look." She points out a tall, friendly-looking man with Hugh's tow hair and broad smile, shaking hands and posing for photos. "It's no coincidence that it was a Lancaster paper that published the exclusive about the old PM's groping habit. They brought him down so Lionel could move up and take the top spot."

Watching Lionel Ambrose circulate, I can't help feeling a little bit in awe of the powerful people in attendance. It's like being at a party with the President of the United States. And maybe a few congressmen and celebrities, too.

"Have you met Saint's parents?" Imogen asks, nibbling on a cookie.

I shake my head. "Not yet."

"That might be for the best," Imogen says, giving a wince.

"Why?"

"No reason," Imogen says quickly, but her smile looks more forced. There's something she's not saying, but I decide not to push it. I need to focus on my own mystery. With that in mind, I look pointedly around.

"Is there a bathroom for us regular civilians to use?"

She laughs. "Just head inside, there are a dozen to choose from."

"True luxury!"

I head back toward the house. Inside, it's just as impressive, with huge, grand hallways, polished marble floors, and ancient antiques around every corner, like something out of a BBC period show. I wander through the rooms, taking it all in. Wren would have loved this place, I know. *Pride & Prejudice* was her comfort watch, and every holiday like clockwork we'd settle in to admire the costumes and scenery.

Did Max lure her away from the party here, promising a private tour? Did one of his fancy friends pull her away from the party, casually offering a spiked drink?

I pause, puzzling over the connection. Wren never once mentioned Max, or the Lancasters, or hanging out in such an exclusive crowd.

But why not?

She shared everything else about her time in Oxford before the attack, sending late-night texts full of exclamations and photos, FaceTiming to catch me up on all her fun tourist activities. And even after coming clean about what happened, she never mentioned Max as a suspect, or someone who might have known what happened to her.

Unless it was some kind of secret she was mixed up in . . .

Unless she was trying to protect me, somehow.

"This area is off-limits to guests." A rich, heavy voice interrupts my thoughts.

I startle, whirling around with a yelp. "Sorry, you scared me," I blurt, my heart pounding. It's an older man with thick graying hair and steely gray eyes. He's about my height, but there's something imposing about him, a stout figure full of authority.

"Were you looking for something?" he continues, assessing me.

"Oh, no. I was just looking around. All the art, it's an impressive collection," I add, unnerved. The grand salon we're standing in is lined with oil paintings in heavy gilt frames, classical landscapes and religious scenes that clearly are worth a fortune. I've been keeping an eye out for anything that looks like the crown and serpent Wren drew—the tattoo on the thigh of her attacker—but nothing has seemed familiar.

"Impressive . . ." the man echoes. "That's a word people use to be tactful, when they don't actually like something."

I blink. "Well, I guess I have to wonder where it came from. All of this." I nod around us, at the house clearly built by generations of wealth and luxury. "Like Balzac said, behind every great fortune is an even greater crime."

As soon as the words are out of my mouth, I regret them. After all, this guy doesn't exactly look like an outsider plus-one . . . which means he's probably just as wealthy and well-connected as the rest of them.

But the man doesn't react, just stands there, watching me, until my skin prickles. "But you're right," I say brightly. "I shouldn't be here. Nice meeting you!"

I quickly make my escape, heading back outside to the party before anyone else can bust me for trespassing where I shouldn't be. I look around for Saint and spot him chatting to Hugh, so I go to join them.

"There you are," Saint greets me with a smile—and a light kiss on my lips. "I was worried you'd made a run for it."

"You're the flight risk, not me," I say, teasing, and Hugh chuckles, wearing a preppy salmon pink shirt with his navy suit jacket.

"When we were younger, he climbed out a window to escape a particularly boring dinner," he confides, grinning. "And it was on the third floor, too!"

"I'm an expert tree climber," Saint says. "I was always sneaking out at boarding school after curfew."

"To go seduce the local girls?" I ask, and he smiles.

"A gentleman doesn't kiss and tell."

I catch sight of the stern man from inside, joining Max by the bar area. "Who's that man with Max?" I ask, pointing them out. Saint turns.

"You mean his father?"

"Cyrus Lancaster?" I gape. *Shit.* I just insulted the most powerful man in the Western hemisphere.

"Yes. Why?"

"Oh, no reason." I steal Saint's drink and take a gulp, cringing, as the guys keep talking. It's a good thing I'm never going to cross paths with these people after my time in Oxford, because I'm not exactly making the best first impression.

". . . we have so many applications for grants, I hate turning anyone down," Hugh is saying.

"Hugh runs the Ambrose family foundation," Saint explains to me. "They do a lot of nonprofit and charity work."

"That's great," I say, perking up. Before Wren's death sent me spiraling off-track, I was working in the field, helping an arts foundation back in Philadelphia raise funds for local organizations and education. "The advantage of a foundation is you're working with a set budget from the endowment, not scrambling to find fresh donors every quarter."

Hugh looks interested. "You have some experience?"

I nod. It doesn't contradict anything in my official backstory, and it's a relief to finally be talking about something I know instead of bluffing through studies and lectures.

"I did some work with an arts organization, back in the States," I tell him. "It was a great project, but the board had very particular ideas about fundraising. Lots of fancy thousand-dollar a plate dinners and gala events that cost almost as much to host as what they brought in," I say, rolling my eyes. "I mean, I get that it's all PR, getting word out, but we wound up wasting so much money on those red-carpet events. It could have been better spent on our programs. Do you do any fundraising?" I ask, and Hugh grins.

"Sometimes. Mainly fancy dinners and gala events," he replies.

"Shit, I'm sorry," I reply, blushing. I'm really on a roll here when it comes to insulting my hosts. But Hugh just chuckles good-naturedly.

"No, I agree, it's a real challenge. The big donors like to be wined and dined, get their photos in the society pages."

"Because if someone writes a check, and nobody's there to see it, did they even donate at all?" I quip. Saint laughs along with us—and then stiffens at my side as we're joined by a distinguished-looking couple.

"There you are." The woman coolly kisses Saint on the cheek. "I was beginning to think you wouldn't make an appearance."

"I was told my attendance was mandatory," Saint replies dryly, but there's a new edge of tension in his voice. Which begins to make sense, when he places a hand around my waist and introduces me.

"Mother, Father, this is Tessa. Tessa, my parents, Alexander and Lillian St. Clair."

His parents. *OK*.

"It's great to meet you," I say, managing a big smile as I take them in. Saint's mother, Lillian, is a tall, aristocratic blonde with elegantly graying hair, wearing a conservative shift dress and cream Chanel jacket. Tasteful diamonds twinkle at her throat and wrists, and she gives me a cool, assessing smile as she politely shakes my hand.

"Well, look at this," his father says jovially, greeting me with more enthusiasm. He's like an older, slightly paunchier version of Robert, with the same ruddy complexion and broad smile. "Finally, we get to meet one of Saint's lady friends."

"Dad . . ." Saint tries to interrupt, but his father just chortles.

"No, no, don't worry, I'm not going to interrogate the girl. He's secretive, this one," he adds, giving me a confidential wink. "Usually, I just have to read about it in the papers."

"So, what brings you to Oxford?" Lillian says. "I assume you're one of Saint's students?"

Excuse me? I blink at the subtle burn.

"Tessa is in the graduate studies program at Ashford," Saint answers for me. "She's keeping me on my toes."

"Clearly." Lillian's response is dry, and again, just on the right side of insulting.

Saint narrows his eyes. "Actually, she's the reason I'm here tonight at all. I would have ditched the whole thing, but she wouldn't hear of it."

"Well . . ." His father looks back and forth between us all, finally clocking his wife's cool tone. "Then you have our thanks, Tessa. We don't see Saint often enough, with him staying up in Oxford. Maybe we'll see you down in London soon. The both of you."

Lillian doesn't look thrilled with that plan. "We should go say hello to the Davenports," she says, tugging on Alexander's arm. "Lovely to meet you," she adds faintly, before steering him away.

I exhale.

Saint sees. "Yeah, they have that effect on people."

"No, I didn't mean—" I start to protest, but he cuts me off with a kiss.

"I need a drink, how about you?" he asks, and I nod immediately.

"Yes, please!"

Chapter Fifteen
SAINT

" . . . **N**ow, when are you going to knuckle down and join the family business?"

One of my parents' friends chuckles over his champagne, and I try not to scowl.

"Where would the fun be in that?" I ask instead. All evening, I've been getting the same tired jokes about growing up and settling down, and I've just about hit my limit. "Besides, Cyrus would never forgive me, I'm keeping the Lancaster gossip columnists in business, after all."

"Oh, you devil you!" The crowd all chortle, and I grit my teeth. Usually, I can laugh it off, but for some reason, it's like a weight is pressing down on me this evening: the expectations, the way they all look at me.

I can tell, they're comparing me to Edward. The brother who was supposed to be the heir.

And I'll never live up to him. Not even if I tried.

My temper burns, hotter. Then I feel Tessa's arm slip through mine.

"I nearly forgot," she says suddenly. "Leonora Fortesque-Smith was just dying to chat before she had to fly back to Monte Carlo."

What? I stare at Tessa, confused, before I catch the glint of mischief in her eyes. "Right," I say slowly, playing along. "Dear Leonora. And Freddie."

"No, Freddie passed in that polo accident, remember?" Tessa

adds, clearly trying not to laugh. "She's with Frederico now, the racing car heir. I guess it makes it easier," she adds to the other guests. "Less likely to blurt the wrong name at a sticky moment. Anyway, lovely meeting you all!"

We walk fast away from the group and make it around the corner and out of earshot before Tessa breaks out laughing. "Monte Carlo?" I ask, watching her body shake with mirth.

"Where else is she going to meet the racing driver?" she replies, through giggles.

"The Fortesque-Smiths are going to be so confused, they have a new member," I remark, still wound too tight.

Tessa blinks. "Wait, that's a real name?"

"Unfortunately. They're probably around here somewhere."

Chatting to my parents about what a disappointment I am.

"Sorry, that was rude, cutting out like that," Tessa adds, looking bashful. "But you looked like you'd just about had it with the small talk."

"You were right," I say, moving closer. "I owe you one."

I put her back against the wall, and claim her lips in a slow, deep kiss.

Damn. This is what I've been needing, the intoxication only she can provide. Tessa makes a breathy moan, pressing closer so her body is hot against mine, and just like that, all the stifling social bullshit seems to melt away under the surge of heat between us, and her wet, pliant mouth, already parting to invite my tongue deeper.

"Saint . . ." She gasps as I grow hard as a rock against her hip. I nip her lower lip and thrust my tongue deep again, feeling her whole body shudder in anticipation, thighs parting to accommodate me between them.

All evening, I've been wanting her, searching her out in the crowd. Burning with impatience for the moment when I can put my hands on her again. Touch her. Taste her.

Claim her.

When I draw back, she's pink-cheeked and breathless—but it's not enough. I remember the way she looked right after she came for me in my library: salty on my fingertips, her body arching and wild.

I want to see her tremble like that again.

I need it, before I go out of my goddamn mind.

Yeah, there's no way I'm making it back to Oxford before I make this woman come.

"Wait here," I instruct her, looking around. It's getting dark out now, and the party is turning raucous, with the music playing louder, and everyone halfway to drunk, or more. I've done my dutiful son routine. Nobody will notice if we slip away. "I'll be right back."

I leave Tessa and head inside, cutting through the house. I know it well, so it's easy to navigate to the huge mudroom out back and retrieve a woolen picnic blanket. Then I detour past the catering set-up and nab a bottle of champagne, before heading back to meet Tessa.

"I told you, I can't talk here!"

A familiar voice makes me pause in the hallway. It's my father, sounding stressed and urgent. I move closer to an open door, and glance inside. He's there, half-hidden in the shadows with a brunette woman I don't recognize. They're talking in low voices, and it's clear from the body language that this is a private conversation.

"You're ignoring my calls," the woman hisses furiously. She has a French accent, wearing a designer pantsuit and a gold rope necklace, her hair cut in a sharp bob. "Where else are we supposed to talk?"

"Now is not a good time, Valerie," my father growls. "If people saw us . . ."

He leans closer, and their voices drop, too quiet for me to hear anymore—but I don't need to. Clearly, they're having some kind of affair.

What the fuck is he playing at?

I back away, disgusted, before either of them can see me. Not that my father would think he needs to explain anything. I have no idea what he and my mother get up to these days. This would be just another topic to avoid, but we've got ten years of practice.

My God, the things the St. Clair family doesn't discuss could fill an ocean—or keep a therapist flying first class for life.

That tense weight returns, pressing down on my collarbone. Making it hard to breathe.

Fuck it.

I find Tessa waiting where I left her, grab her hand, and pull her after me, steaming away from the party and into the dark of the gardens.

"Slow down!" she protests, laughing. "Where are we going? Saint?"

"You'll see," I tell her, frustration driving me on. I need an escape, a distraction from all this bullshit, and God, if Tessa isn't the perfect release. "I've been going crazy all night. Do you know what you've been doing to me, in that outfit?" I look at her, hungry.

"But . . . I'm not showing any skin," Tessa says, confused, following after me.

"Exactly," I growl. "I can't see a damn inch of your body, so I've been remembering it instead. But my imagination isn't good enough. I need to see you. All of you."

Fuck, I could lay her down right here in the damp grass and make her scream loud enough for the whole party to hear, but I know she won't relax and unleash that incredible passion unless it's just the two of us.

I keep my grip tightly on her hand, finally spotting my destination up ahead. A maze, carved into the hedgerows, and lit with flickering torches. When we were younger, Max and my buddies used to sneak in and get high, so nobody could find us.

Now, I want the privacy for a very different reason.

"This way." I lead her into the first dim passageway. Tessa laughs in delight, looking around.

"They have a maze? An actual maze, in their grounds? You better know the way through this," she adds teasingly. "I have a terrible sense of direction, we'll never make it out."

"And that would be a bad thing?" I ask. My frustration is easing with every moment alone with her, but I still need more distance from the insufferable party.

"Not at first," Tessa agrees, flashing me a smile in the moonlight. "But sooner or later, it would be time for breakfast. And you don't want to see me when I'm hangry."

"You have a big appetite?" I ask, with a small smirk.

"For all kinds of things . . ." Tessa grins, playful, and my lust burns hotter than ever. Just when I think I have a handle on this woman, she shows I haven't even scratched the surface.

"I'll remember that," I say, finally pulling her around the last bend, to the center of the maze.

"Oh." Tessa lets out a breath of surprise. It's a small, round opening in the middle of the greenery, with a fountain lit up, and crumbling angelic statues dotted around. "This is lovely."

And worth the few extra minutes of my precious self-control.

But now, alone, I can't wait any longer. And judging from the flush in Tessa's cheeks and the heat in her eyes, she doesn't want me to.

I drop the blanket and bottle to the ground and yank her into my arms. "Take it off," I order her, hungrily kissing the curve of her neck, tasting her skin. I run my hands over the prim, voluminous silk, gripping her hips beneath it. "Strip for me, right now."

Tessa's breath hitches, but she steps back, fixing me with a sultry smile. "Here, Professor?" she asks, looking up at me from below her lashes. "But what if someone sees us . . . ?"

"Then they'll be the luckiest bastard around." I reach for the hem of her boxy top. "Off."

"Yes, *sir*."

She lifts the hem, and shimmies it over her head, revealing lush breasts encased in black silk, her nipples already tight and straining against the lace.

"Fuck." I groan aloud, reaching for her, but Tessa skips back, scolding me with a wink.

"I'm not done yet. You said everything. And I pay attention to detail," she adds, unfastening her skirt. It falls over her hips, leaving her long legs naked, topped with a scrap of matching black between her thighs.

Jesus Christ.

She stands there in the moonlight, a work of art. "More," I growl, my pulse thundering in my ears.

"You mean . . . this too?" Tessa gives me a teasing look, lifting her hands to her breasts, tracing over the fabric of her bra.

I snap, lunging to her and yanking her hard against my body. Our mouths find each other in an instant, hot and wild, as my hands rove over her, exploring every perfect curve and dip. Tessa whimpers as I palm her breasts, teasing her through the silk before I impatiently tear it away from her body, leaving her bare for me.

"Fucking magnificent," I breathe, taking in the sight of her firm tits and peaked, pink nipples. She's like a walking fantasy, but just as hot as her incredible body is the look in her eyes: Unashamed and hungry as she arches her back, presenting herself to me.

I reach for her, bending my head to lick, hot across the swell of her tits, and lap at her stiff nipples. She lets out a gasp, and then moans as I suck, hard. "That's right," I growl, fire raging through me now. "Make all the noise you like, sweetheart. Nobody's going to hear."

"Saint!" she cries again, as I turn my attention to her other breast, lapping and sucking in a frenzy until she sinks against me, clawing at my arms for balance. And when I slide a hand between her thighs, I feel her wet, even through her panties.

So fucking wet for me.

I lay her down on the blanket and kneel above her naked body. Tessa smiles up at me, eyes already glazed in pleasure, hair spilled in a wild halo around her head.

"You look like a fallen angel," she says, reaching up like she's tracing my outline against the night. "A sinner, through and through."

"That's me," I agree, even as I feel a hollow ache in my chest. "Here to corrupt you and lead you into temptation."

"You're forgetting, I don't need leading anywhere," Tessa replies, rising up. Reaching for me. Her mouth hot against my neck as she kisses and tastes me. "Maybe I'm the one corrupting you . . ."

Her hands slide over my trousers, feeling my hard, engorged cock. Making me groan, bucking against her hand. "You see?" Tessa whispers, her lips grazing my skin. She squeezes me through the wool, teasing. "I know a thing or two about sin . . ."

I catch her wrists before she can stroke me again and pin them behind her back, panting. Because if this woman touches me again with those nimble fingers . . .

I won't last a heartbeat.

"Down," I order her, firm. "Spread for me."

She gives a shiver at the filthy instruction, and does as I say, her body laid out like an offering, a sacrifice to the gods.

But she's the one who demands worship.

I settle on the blanket between her thighs and peel her panties away.

Suddenly, Tessa's body stiffens. "Did you hear that?" she asks, lifting her head.

I can't hear a damn thing over the thunder of my own heartbeat. I keep stroking, higher, and she bites back a moan as my thumbs graze across the damp apex of her thighs.

"I thought I heard something," she says again, sounding breathless.

"Nobody's here," I mutter, as I drop a kiss on the inside of her knee. "And if there is . . . let them watch. I thought you liked that," I remind her as Tessa's body rises to my touch.

I nip the delicate skin of her inner thigh, and then kiss higher. Higher . . .

"I thought you liked performing for a crowd," I murmur, feeling her tense in pleasure at the memory. "All those eyes, watching you be wicked. Watching you moan for more . . ."

"Saint!" Tessa lets out a shocked whimper as I finally lick against her core. Her thighs clench, and she clutches a hand against the back of my head as I lap at her again, teasing her clit in slow, wet strokes. "Oh . . . *Oh!*"

I scoop her legs over my shoulders and yank her closer, burying my head between her thighs, hungry for more. I've been craving this, fuck, ever since I got a taste of her, and now the whole damn county could be watching, and I still wouldn't stop.

I lick faster, flattening my tongue against her; flicking, swirling, dipping it to nudge inside her hot, clenching cunt.

Tessa mewls against me, twisting against my grip. "*Please . . .*" she gasps, panting. "Oh God, right there. *Fuck*, don't stop!"

Her cries drive me on, until I'm lost in the fucking tornado of lust, ravenous for her, consumed. I shift my grip, moving to ease one finger into her tight cunt, and then another, pulsing deep inside her in time with my laps.

Tessa screams.

Her head is thrown back, her body writhing. She's perfectly wild, uninhibited in her pleasure, urging me on, and fuck, I've never seen a more beautiful sight.

"This is what you need, isn't it, darling?" I growl, pumping my fingers, stretching her out. Tessa moans and trembles, desperately bucking against my hand to take me even deeper. "You like it wild, and dirty, and rough."

"Yes!" she cries. "God, yes!"

"That's it," I urge her on, drunk on the taste of her. The sight of her spread in the moonlight. "That's my filthy, reckless girl."

I withdraw my fingers and slap her clit lightly, making her scream. But right away, I'm soothing her with my mouth again, sliding my tongue over the swollen bud as I thrust my fingers back inside her, pumping fast as I feel her start to clench.

Dear God, this woman is going to wreck me.

I ease a third finger inside her, making her stretch at the thick intrusion. Then I close my lips around her clit and suck.

She comes like an avalanche, a low shudder rolling through her body before her pleasure takes her over with a scream, her body rising up, quaking with the force of it, leaving her gasping and mindless.

And then I lick again.

"Saint—" she mumbles in protest, but it melts into a moan before the word has even left her lips. "I can't . . ."

"You will."

I flex my fingers again, rubbing high inside her walls as I tongue her clit, and Tessa breaks apart again.

"*Fuck* . . ." Her wail echoes as her body shakes and I feel a surge of pure masculine pride, more intoxicating than any drug I've tried.

"My name," I growl, still lapping at her. "Tell them who's making you scream."

"*Saint!*"

I watch her tremble in the aftermath of pleasure, eyes rolled back and her hair a glorious mess. I can't keep my hands off her—or my mouth. Christ, I could do this all night.

But Tessa lifts her head, fixing me with a bright, reckless look. "It's your turn," she breathes, reaching for me. "Now I want to know how you taste."

Fuck.

Her hands find my belt and unsnap it before starting on my fly. I groan, my cock already so goddamn hard, my briefs feel like a vice. But before she can slide her hands to feel me, my phone sounds loudly from my jacket, beside us on the ground.

Tessa pauses.

"Ignore it," I growl, impatient, but the ringing doesn't stop. She gives me a look.

"Goddamn it," I mutter, yanking the thing out. It's Robert. I decline the call and set it to silent, but it just starts buzzing in my hand.

Tessa reaches over and plucks the handset from me. "Hello?" she answers sweetly, as if she's not sprawled naked in the moonlight. "Oh, hi Robert, he's just here. Uh-huh, I'll tell him."

She hangs up. "You're needed, back at the party."

"I don't care," I growl.

The phone starts buzzing again, and this time, it's my mother's number on the screen.

Tessa smirks. "They're persistent."

"They're a few other things besides," I mutter, dragging a hand through my hair. Clearly, the gods have conspired to cockblock me tonight, and already I feel my foul mood return.

I may have to put up with this shit, but Tessa shouldn't have to.

I lean in and drop a soft kiss on her mouth. "You should head back to Oxford," I say regretfully. "I don't know how much longer this is going to last. I'll call a car for you."

Tessa looks at me, clearly taken aback. "Just to recap," she says, with a smirk. "I'm literally naked in front of you right now, planning all kinds of wicked things, and you want me to . . . go?"

"I don't want it," I say immediately, running a hand over her hip. "It's the last thing on earth I want right now. But I have to go play the dutiful Ashford heir, and trust me, once these people get started on the port, things get ugly. I wouldn't subject you to it."

I get to my feet and offer her my hand. Tessa stares up at me for a moment, then, shaking her head in clear disbelief, she rises.

"I'll call a car for you," I repeat, tapping a few instructions on my phone. Tessa dresses and smooths down her tangled hair.

"How do I look?" she asks.

"Like you just came your brains out," I reply, and she laughs.

"Twice," she says with a wink, and then takes my hand. I lead her out of the maze and back to the party, which is raging full steam now.

"You were right," Tessa says with a laugh, pointing to where Agatha has grabbed the singer's microphone and is entertaining the crowd.

I put her in the car out front, pausing to steal one last kiss. Tessa's mouth is sweet and warm against me, and I find myself wishing I could take her back to Oxford myself. Slide into bed beside her.

Wake with her curled in my arms.

I pull back, unnerved by the vision of simple domesticity. "Have dinner with me," I find myself asking. "I'll make us a reservation. Somewhere romantic. A real date."

"Our fourth date," she points out, smiling. "Unless this one counts double . . ."

"Is that a yes?" I ask, as she slides into the backseat.

"It's a maybe." Tessa gives me an arch, teasing smile, and flutters a wave. "I'll think about it."

The door slams, and she drives away, leaving me on the front steps, alone.

And seriously unsatisfied.

But I'm beginning to wonder if I'll ever get enough of this woman. The way she surrenders to pleasure, offering herself up to me—but still, holding so much back . . .

It's irresistible.

I want to know this woman. I want *more.*

Chapter Sixteen
TESSA

I wake the next morning with pleasure still sweet and thick in my veins. It turns out, Saint's filthy mouth is good for more than just talking. Not just good, *spectacular* . . .

I lay back against my pillows, reliving the sinful scene: lying there in the middle of the maze, gazing up at the stars as Saint drove me wild. His hands . . . his fingers . . .

His skilled, sensual tongue.

I shiver, unable to keep the smile from my face. I know that the event was technically a bust—besides insulting Cyrus Lancaster and horrifying Saint's mom, I only have more questions about Wren's attack—but after that delicious time with Saint in the gardens, I can't even be frustrated.

No, Saint took care of that.

I sigh with satisfaction. All his talk about expertise and experience wasn't just a big game. The man really is gifted. *Although* . . . I remember his tension, talking to his parents, and the grim resignation that settled over him when our sexy fun was interrupted by those calls. Every family has its drama, but clearly, there's something going on with the St. Clairs that puts Saint on edge.

I can hear the sound of Kris and Jia talking out in the kitchen, so I pull on my cozy bathrobe and go join them, in search of coffee.

"Morning," I greet them brightly, heading for the coffeepot.

"How was the party?" Jia asks, sitting at the table, eating cereal.

"Great." I beam. "I mean, ridiculous, but kind of fun. I felt like someone on a nature show, touring a foreign world. I mean, there were all kinds of celebrities there and politicians, it was wild!"

"Huh" is all Jia says in response. She takes a spoonful and chews, looking at me coolly.

I blink, confused by the cold treatment. Kris is also keeping quiet, leaning against the countertop with his hands wrapped around a mug of coffee.

"I didn't wake anyone, did I, coming back?" I check as I go to pour my coffee. "It was still pretty early; I didn't know if you were home."

"We were just at the college bar," Kris replies. "It was a fun night. I mean, not packed with celebrities, and politicians . . ." His voice has a sarcastic edge as he mimics me.

I look between them. "Is everything OK?"

"Just peachy," Jia replies. "You're famous, by the way," she adds, moving past me to leave her bowl in the sink with a clatter. "All over the gossip blogs. You and your fancy new friends."

"What?" I ask, even more confused.

"Show her," Kris says, and Jia holds out her phone. There's a picture on some society page, showing me with Saint, Imogen, Hugh, and a couple of other people last night. The photographer captured us mid-conversation, and Hugh's cracked some joke. We're all laughing, looking like we're having the best time.

"You fit right in," Jia comments. "Listen. *'Britain's bright young things mingle at the Lancaster Press anniversary bash,'*" she reads. *"'Anthony St. Clair couldn't keep his eyes off his glamorous date. Might we be meeting the future Duchess of Ashford, perhaps?'"*

"Duchess?" I repeat, and give a snort of laughter. "That's insane. And that photo doesn't tell half the story. I was just about ready to gouge my eyes out with boredom from all the stuffy aristos," I promise, even though that's not exactly true.

Sure, meeting all those strangers was pretty intimidating, but Imogen was a ton of fun, and Hugh seems really nice, too.

Not that I'm going to tell my roommate that. I can already see spending time with Saint and his friends is driving a wedge between us.

"It was just one party," I add, reassuring. But Jia just gives a sharp shrug.

"So you don't have plans to see Saint again?"

Shit.

"I mean, he mentioned maybe us going to dinner," I fib again. There was already a text message waiting on my phone this morning when I woke:

Thank you for making the evening bearable.

And no, that isn't faint praise.

"But it's not like we're really *dating*," I say quickly. Even though Saint is being pretty persistent about that dinner date.

"Good. I mean, you know his reputation," Kris says with a smirk. "The man likes them young and fresh."

"No offense," Jia adds, seeing my face fall. "But you need to be careful you don't get hurt. He'll move on by the end of the semester."

"The end of the week," Kris adds.

"Right," I say, deflating slightly. "Of course he will."

"Sorry, I don't mean to be a bitch about it," Jia adds, giving me a little hug. "You should have fun and everything. We just don't want you getting hurt, that's all."

"Being swept up in all the glitz and glamor," Kris agrees. "Saint and his friends . . . they're not like us. It's like all the Greek myths, we're just mere mortals, and they're the gods who come down from the mountain to toy with us."

I nod slowly. They're still looking at me for a reaction, so I force a smile. "Don't worry, my feet are planted firmly on solid ground. I'm just going to enjoy the champagne and amazing buffet table as long as I can."

I grab my coffee and head back to my bedroom. So much for the thrilling morning afterglow. Now I've come back down to earth with a bump with my roomies' oh-so-helpful reminders that Saint does this all the time. He may not take his coeds to fancy family events, but I can bet plenty of them know all about his skilled, wicked tongue . . .

I feel a stab of insecurity—and immediately stop it in its tracks.

Nope. I'm not going to think about him like that, like a potential boyfriend or future partner. I'm not even looking for a serious relationship! Saint's experience is exactly what makes him perfect for a wild, reckless fling. Passionate. Breathless.

Temporary.

Feelings aren't part of the equation . . . which means that I need to be careful not to mistake our sizzling sexual connection for anything deeper. Kris and Jia's "advice" might have been wrapped up in a package of passive-aggressive envy, but they're right. I can't afford to be swept up in emotions, not with so much at stake.

Which means maybe I should cool it with Saint, just a little . . . let him chase me if he wants, but I'm a busy woman with things to do, I don't need to dive for my phone every time he messages me.

BUZZ. BUZZ.

Sure enough, my phone sounds on the nightstand. I coolly stretch and then leisurely stroll over to check it . . . only to find out that it's not Saint, after all.

It's a text from Lara, Wren's old college friend.

Sorry, things have been crazy at work. But I talked to Phil, and he's happy to meet!

She's shared a contact, too, for Phillip McAllister, the guy who worked with Wren at her lab here in Oxford.

A new lead.

Brightening, I send Phillip a quick text. He says he has some time to chat at lunch today, so I jump in the shower and make a valiant effort to look at some of my reading for the week before taking a bus across town to Phillip's work. It's located in a more modern part of the city, with ugly office buildings and regular chain stores, and I realize how much of a bubble we are in at Ashford, all the students tucked away in the historic old part of the city, rarely venturing out of the crumbling ivy-covered walls into the real world.

Now, I climb off the bus and follow Phillip's directions to a gleaming new building: two wide stories of chrome and glass, arranged around a central courtyard. When I step inside the sprawling, modern lobby area, the sign above reception reads The Ashford Neurobiology Research Laboratory.

Ashford.

I stop, blinking up at the letters in surprise. That's Saint's family name. I knew his dad's company was in pharmaceuticals, but he's never mentioned anything else.

"Tessa?"

I turn. A studious-looking man in his early thirties is approaching, dressed in battered corduroy pants and a white lab coat.

"Hi, I'm Phillip," he says, greeting me with a friendly smile. "It's great to meet you. I mean, not under the circumstances," he adds, the smile slipping. "But Wren talked about you all the time. It's nice to finally put a face to the name."

"You too." I smile back. Phillip is nerdy and faintly awkward, just like Wren described her work husband. I glance back at the sign. "Ashford . . ." I say casually. "Is that the company that you work for?"

"Kind of." Phillip makes a face. "We're technically independent scientists, but they're the ones funding our research."

"That's generous."

Phillip laughs. "Not at all. They'll own everything we discover. It could be worth billions, if these trials turn out a success."

"Phil?"

We're interrupted by a voice calling from across the lobby. It's a slim woman in a chic navy pantsuit, her hair shining in a sharp bob. She walks over, her heels echoing on the polished concrete floors. "Did you review the data I sent you?" she asks in a French accent, barely glancing at me—or Phillip, tapping on her phone.

"It'll be done by end of day," he says immediately. "This is Dr. Valerie DeJonge," he adds, introducing us. "She's our lead researcher on the project. This is Tessa Peterson, Wren's sister."

"Oh." Valerie finally looks up and fixes me with a sympathetic smile. "I was so sorry to hear about your sister. It's a great loss, she was a promising young woman, an excellent mind."

"Thank you." I nod.

"Phillip?" she asks, looking brisk again. "The data? We can't afford to fall behind."

"End of day, Valerie, I promise," he replies.

"Good." With a nod, she walks off.

"She seems . . . wildly intimidating," I say, watching Valerie breeze past security and into the main part of the building.

Phillip chuckles. "I wish I could say that she's just a softie, underneath it all, but . . . nope. But she's a brilliant woman," he adds. "Ashford poached her from some bigwig drug company to spearhead our work. She and Wren got along great," he adds. "Valerie was mentoring her."

"Oh." I nod, steeling myself to talk about Wren more. It hurts, but I'm curious, too, about her work here at the lab, and the projects she was so passionate about.

I wait until Phillip and I are settled with our lunches at a cute café down the block from the lab, then I admit: "I never actually followed much of what Wren was working on. She tried to explain it to me, but, well, she would get carried away and go into full scientist mode, and it would all go way over my head."

Phillip laughs. "That sounds like Wren. It's actually pretty straightforward, as far as neuro-biochemistry goes."

"Well, sure," I quip, munching my sandwich. "But why don't you explain it to me like . . . well, like I'm a woman who barely scraped through high school biology."

He smiles. "OK, so the human brain is made up of millions of neurons, they're special cells that communicate with each other, and the whole body," he explains. "Like when you lift your sandwich, or blink your eyes, or even think about the last time you had tuna salad. That's your neurons firing, millions of them, forming thoughts and actions."

"OK." I nod. "I'm with you so far."

"Well, our research is focused on how abnormal levels of proteins in the brain clump together and form plaques," he continues. "They disrupt those basic neuron functions, leading to conditions like Alzheimer's, where memory and identity are damaged. We've been testing a new drug that acts to stop the protein clumps, and even reverse the early damage. It could be revolutionary for treatment of the disease."

"Oh, wow." I feel a pang. "Wren always did want to save the world, or cure cancer."

"Well, if the trials continue the way they've been going . . . *Shit*." Phillip seems to realize something. He makes a face. "I'm not supposed to even talk about them, we all signed iron-clad nondisclosure agreements, everything's top-secret, under pain of death."

I smile. "Talk about what?" I ask, with an innocent smile.

"Thanks." He looks relieved. "I'm just sorry Wren isn't here to see it through with us. She worked on an early version of the drug," he explains. "Back when we were in animal trials. Now we've progressed to human clinical trials. None of this would be possible without her work."

I nod slowly. "You know, that helps, in a way. That her work will live on," I add, feeling a little better. "Help people, change their lives for the better, the way she always wanted."

Phillip nods, and picks at his food. "Lara mentioned you're studying at Ashford College?"

"I'm not sure my professors would agree," I say wryly, thinking of my half-assed essays and skimmed reading lists.

"How do you like it?" he asks. "I only moved here after university, but Oxford seems like a fun place to study."

"It is . . ." I reply, spotting a way to turn the conversation back to my investigation. "Wren always told me so much about her time here. Did you hang out much, outside of work?"

"Oh, yeah." Phillip smiles. "She was always trying to drag the lab off on some tourist activity on the weekends. We all went punting down the River Cherwell . . . toured Christ Church college—you know, the *Harry Potter* one."

"I remember, she sent like a billion photos." I pause. "Did she ever mention anything about secret societies?" I ask, trying to sound casual.

Phillip looks puzzled. "I don't think so. I know she was interested in local history . . ."

"No, it's not that." I decide to reveal a little more of the truth. "Wren had a . . . bad experience at a party," I explain, staying vague.

"And she thought it was connected to a secret society?" He frowns.

"Maybe. I don't know." I look down, painfully aware of how crazy it sounds. "I just wondered. You hear rumors," I add. "Rich and powerful people, up to all kinds of things . . ."

Phillip looks at me sympathetically. "Look, you don't need a secret society for bad things to happen. It's a university town. There are plenty of creeps around."

"Right," I agree. But I can't tell him about Wren's memories, and the tattoo, and the cryptic notes. I know *I'd* think I was clutching at straws if I was listening to me right now. "It's probably nothing."

Phillip's phone buzzes. And again. He glances at the screen, and winces. "It's my boss, Valerie. She's waiting on some materials from me, and . . ."

"Isn't exactly the most patient woman?" I finish for him. "It's fine. Thank you for even taking the time to get together," I add, as he scoffs down the last of his food and gets to his feet, clearly eager to get back to work. "It's nice to hear about the parts of Wren's life I didn't get to see. Or understand," I add wryly, and he smiles.

"Anytime. How much longer are you in Oxford?"

"My fellowship is for the year," I reply, even though I'm hoping it won't take me that long to get to the truth and find Wren's attacker.

"Then let's keep in touch," Phillip says. "Get a drink sometime, reminisce."

I smile. "I'd like that," I say honestly. His phone buzzes again.

"Shit, I've really got to run. Nice meeting you!"

* * *

I LINGER OVER my lunch and the stroll back toward the bus stop, feeling a new wistfulness. My sister wanted to make a difference with her work: save lives and change the face of medicine. I wish she was around to see her efforts pay off now. Phillip was cagey about the specifics of these big clinical trials, but he's clearly excited about the results they're seeing.

Results my sister contributed to.

It's bittersweet that she's not here to share in the excitement, but it's true, what I told him: I love the idea that her ideas and dedication are living on in the world, and maybe one day soon even helping millions of people. After she died, one of the hardest things was just her *absence*. Picking up my phone to call her or send a dumb video over text . . . and then remembering she wouldn't be on the other end of the line. Seeing a face in the crowd, and for a split second thinking it might be her . . . before my brain caught up and remembered that it couldn't be.

Listening to Phillip talk about their work today with that same spark of excitement in his eyes, it feels like a piece of Wren's spirit is still alive.

My phone rings as I'm walking, and an English number flashes up on-screen.

"Hello?" I answer, wondering for a moment if Saint is getting impatient about the texts I've left unanswered.

"Tessa, hi, it's Hugh. Hugh Ambrose."

"Oh, hi," I say, surprised.

"Saint gave me your number," he explains. "Do you have a moment to chat? I have a proposition for you."

"Uh-oh," I reply, only half-joking, and he chuckles.

"Nothing bad, I promise. It's really more of an opportunity. You see, we have an opening here at the Ambrose Foundation, fundraising and outreach, and I think you'd be perfect for it."

I stop dead in the street. "You mean, like a job?" I check, confused. "But, I haven't even applied for anything. I'm a student here, at Ashford."

"It wouldn't have to be a full-time gig," he replies easily. "You could come by a couple days a week or work remotely from Oxford. To tell the truth, I was really impressed by what you said the other night at the party. You seem to have experience in this world, and an outsider's perspective. That's what we need right now, some fresh blood in the organization, to shake things up. It is for a good cause," he adds, sounding tempting. "Just think of all the good we could do if you steer us away from those stuffy old fundraising dinners . . ."

I can't help but smile, even though I'm still seriously confused by where this is coming from. "Did Saint put you up to this?" I ask, even though I can't think why.

"Besides vouching for your general brilliance when I asked,

no," Hugh replies. "I told you, I like your perspective. How about you come by the office, and I can talk you into it in person? See what we're doing—and how desperately we need your help. Say, tomorrow?"

I think quickly over my schedule. I should be buckled down, writing essays and studying nonstop, but . . .

My work at the nonprofit was so rewarding compared to these dry, academic essays. Real people, real problems—and real solutions, too. The thought of another day locked in the library, wading through old texts gives me a headache just imagining it.

"OK," I agree. "But just to take a look at things. No promises that I can actually take the gig. I have a lot on my plate right now."

"I totally understand," Hugh reassures me. "I'll send all the details. Do you need me to send a car? The office is in London."

I smile at the idea of being driven around in a chauffeured car, like some kind of VIP. "That's OK," I tell him. "I'll manage."

I hang up. I have to admit, I'm curious. Thinking about how Wren wanted to make a difference in the world, I'd love to be able to do the same. And even if this Ambrose Foundation gig isn't for me, it's the perfect opportunity to find out more about Hugh. After all, he's buddies with Max, well-connected, and clearly part of the exclusive crowd.

Maybe he has some answers about this secret society . . .

Chapter Seventeen
TESSA

S aint texts again. And calls. And sends another lavish study-snack gift basket to the apartment. It's taking all my self-control, but I'm still playing it cool, responding with a casual, *Sorry, buried with work! Talk soon* message, and going to bed alone.

I may spend all night replaying the hot pleasure of our sexy encounters, but I'm determined not to lose my head and let him know I'm biting back moans, thinking about him as I touch myself in the dark.

A little mystery never hurt anyone.

Besides, I have plenty of academic work to be busy with, and Hugh's intriguing new offer to explore. The next day, I spend the morning cramming my reading in the library, then take the train down to London again and follow his directions to the Ambrose Foundation offices, which, to my surprise, are housed in a funky warehouse in Shoreditch, a buzzing neighborhood on the East side of the city.

"Not what you were expecting, huh?" Hugh greets me in the large, open-plan lower level, giving a friendly smile and a kiss on my cheek.

"Well . . . nope," I admit, looking around. I was planning to smile and nod through whatever pitch he had while scoping for information about Max Lancaster and any potential secret society, but now, I'm paying attention for a different reason. There are concrete floors, bare brick walls, and the old vent system and piping running all across the walls and ceiling. A few dozen people work on open desks and in glass-walled rooms. There's a buzz of pleasant activity in the air.

"We used to be over in Mayfair," Hugh explains, "but when the lease was up, I thought the change would be good for us. I'm trying to shake things up," he adds. He's dressed casually in jeans and a button-down, his blond hair curling over his collar, in need of a trim. "Come on, let me give you a tour."

He takes me around the sweeping space, pointing out different meetings and hubs of activity. "It's all hands on deck right now," he explains, enthusiastic. "We're juggling a bunch of projects: logistics for vaccine distribution in South Sudan, a scholarship program for girls in Pakistan, plus our work right here in the UK with food banks and the cost-of-living crisis . . ."

I take it all in, impressed.

"You see, I took over as chairman a few years ago, and it was clear to me right away, we could be doing so much more," Hugh adds, looking enthused. "My aunt was in charge before then, and don't get me wrong, she did a wonderful job, but she very much was part of the old school brigade." Hugh gives me a look. "Those thousand-pound a plate fundraising dinners, sending money to the historical preservation society to buy a new Roman bust. I want to do things differently. I've been bringing in new faces, new ideas . . . I think you'd be a great fit."

"Doing what, exactly?" I venture. The Foundation offices are great, and I love the vibe here, but I'm still fuzzy about what this job would even be.

"All of this takes money," he says simply. "And yes, our endowment is great, but I want more. Our fundraising team could always use fresh ideas, and it seems like you have experience in that area."

"I wouldn't say that—" I start, but he cuts me off.

"But new ideas are more important than experience. And you definitely have them."

"I just don't think I have time for an internship right now," I say, feeling a pang of regret.

"Internship?" Hugh frowns. "No, it would be a real job. Our salary is competitive, whether you want to be part-time or otherwise. Listen, I have to jump on a call now, but the team is getting together for a meeting. Why don't you sit in, and see how you like it?"

Before I can object, Hugh is steering me up a wrought-iron staircase to the mezzanine level, where there are more gleaming, glass-walled rooms. The meeting room has comfy couches, and views over the bustling street below, with bold abstract art and photos from some of their charitable causes. "This is Priya, our head of fundraising," he says, introducing a dark-haired woman in her forties, with amazing fuchsia lipstick. "This is Tessa, the woman I was telling you about. She's going to sit in and get a feel for things."

"Great." Priya shakes my hand. "Take a seat, grab some snacks and coffee. We finally got Ambrose here to spring for the good stuff," she adds with a wink. "I've been telling him, great cold brew is essential for team morale."

I laugh, liking her immediately. "Just pretend I'm not here," I say, grabbing a can of coffee and taking a seat in the corner. The meeting gets underway, and I can see that Priya is a natural leader: steering everyone through their upcoming schedule, brainstorming new fundraising ideas, and taking the time to give everyone praise and feedback over their work.

"We need to be thinking outside of the box," she urges them. "Our older patrons are inundated with requests, and frankly, the way the markets are performing right now, many of them will be pulling back on their charitable giving. We need to be finding new ways to bring attention—and money—to our work."

She wraps things up, and everyone heads back downstairs, but I linger, hesitant. "Priya?" I venture.

She looks up from her tablet with a smile. "Yes, Tessa, what did you think?"

"I think you're doing great work here. But . . . I did have an idea," I say shyly. All the brainstorming in the meeting got my wheels turning in my mind, but I didn't want to speak up, out of turn. "You talked about finding new avenues for fundraising and raising awareness. Have you looked much into social media influencer outreach?"

"It's been on my to-do list," Priya says, looking frazzled. "But to be honest, I don't know enough to get started. We talked to an agency once, but the fees they would charge were atrocious . . ."

"You wouldn't need a middleman," I say immediately. "You could go directly to the influencers themselves. I'm sure there would be a ton of them interested in promoting some of your projects, and it would get you attention from a different generation. The dollar amounts donated might be smaller than their parents could give, but—"

"—it would get us a whole new audience," Priya finishes for me. "Sounds great. Get it done."

I blink. "Excuse me?" I ask.

"Initiate the project." She smiles. "Make the lists, contact the influencers, go ahead and run with it."

I open my mouth to argue and tell her that I don't even work here, but I bite my tongue. Because a flash of excitement runs through me at the idea of doing this.

Maybe it's selfish, when I'm supposed to be working 24/7 to find Wren's attacker and bring them to justice, but after weeks now of feeling out of place, like I'm playing a part and faking enthusiasm for my studies, this feels real. Like *me*. The woman I was before Wren's death changed everything.

And I haven't felt this way in a long time.

* * *

PRIYA SETS ME up with a spare laptop and workstation, and I get started researching the project. I tell myself it's just for a little while, until Hugh finishes his call and I can say my goodbyes and head back to Oxford, but the hours fly by, and I'm surprised when I hear my name being called.

"Look at you, so official."

I glance up from my screen to find Max's fiancé, Annabelle, is planted in front of me, wearing a chic shearling jacket over designer jeans with a megawatt smile on her face. "Annabelle." I blink, surprised. "Hi, what are you doing here? You don't work here, too?"

"Me? No," she giggles. "I heard you'd been conscripted and decided to swing by and take you to lunch. I know the cutest little place nearby," she adds. "The fried courgette chips will change your life. Come on," she beckons, "I already told Hugh I'm stealing you for an hour."

She waves across the room at Hugh, who waves back at us, even though he's on the phone. He gestures to go, giving a thumbs-up.

"I guess, if it's OK with him . . ." I reply, realizing it's a great chance to get some gossip about Max and the group. Annabelle seems like a social butterfly—and chatty. And if there is some secret society lurking in the shadows of Oxford, Lady Annabelle deWessops seems like a prime candidate for membership.

"Good! Because I don't take no for an answer," she adds, beaming, as I collect my things and follow her out. "Just ask Max. He said there was no way I was having a horse-drawn carriage to take me to the cathedral, but now it's all arranged. If you close one eye and sort of squint, it's just like the one Meghan rode in when she married H—Harry," she adds, seeing my blank expression. "But all his friends call him H."

"You know Prince Harry?" I blink, as we stroll the busy street toward a small park area.

"Obviously." Annabelle says, breezy. "One of my cousins hooked up with him. Before Megs, of course. She looked so gorgeous on her wedding day. I wish we could have booked St. George's Chapel too, but even the Lancasters couldn't swing that. Royals only."

"I thought Cyrus Lancaster was more powerful than any of them," I say, remembering his stony stare. I shiver.

"You've met him then?" Annabelle says, seeing my reaction. "He gave me the willies, too, but he's a sweetheart, really." She pauses. "OK, maybe not a sweetheart, but he's not as scary as he makes himself out to be. If you just forget about all that power and his ruthless reputation, it's fine! The man plays a mean game of tennis."

I try not to laugh, imagining a situation where I might wind up trading backhands with the most powerful man in media.

"Good to know," I manage to say through my smile.

"Ooh, here we are," Annabelle exclaims, coming to a stop outside a restaurant with a shady patio right off the park. "They have amazing vegan food. I'm in fittings right now, and I need to keep my measurements for my dress!"

She launches into an excited monologue about the wedding plans as we're shown to a table, and barely pauses for breath right up until I'm halfway through my salad. ". . . of course, the hen-do will be nothing compared to the stag. That's the bachelorette and bachelor parties," she translates for me. "Although God knows what Max and his boys will get up to. That man can find a wild scandal on a sleepy Wednesday afternoon, never mind when it's his final night of freedom."

Finally, I see an opening for my investigations.

"It seems like they get up to some crazy things," I agree, fibbing now. "Saint was telling me about some of the parties Max hosts at Lancaster Manor . . ."

"Oh my God, right?" Annabelle laughs, sipping her mimosa. "Just the best time."

"And then there's the secret society events . . ." I add impulsively. I give her a knowing look, like I'm in on the secret already. "Those sound pretty scandalous, too."

I mentally cross my fingers, hoping she takes the bait.

"Secret society?" Annabelle asks, freezing.

"Whoops." I give a little laugh. "Sorry, I know it's supposed to be a secret." I drop my voice to a confidential whisper. "Don't worry, I won't tell."

Annabelle gives a nervous little giggle. "Well, obviously I don't know anything about a secret society."

"Obviously," I agree, still acting like I know everything already. "It's just that Saint said you . . . no, never mind."

"What did he say?" Annabelle leans in, curious.

"No, you were right," I insist. "I shouldn't have mentioned it. What you guys all get up to, it's none of my business." I smile, and take a sip of my drink, watching carefully for her reaction.

Annabelle pauses and picks at her food, and then looks over at me. "Things must be getting serious with Saint," she says slowly, as if assessing me with fresh eyes. "It sounds like the two of you are getting close."

"Oh, you know . . ." I give a vague shrug. "That man is an enigma. And I'm pretty sure he likes it that way," I add.

Annabelle smiles. "Typical Saint," she agrees. "I suppose legacy is a gift to him. A gift, and a sworn bond."

She says the cryptic words slowly, deliberately, meeting my eyes.

I blink. "Right," I answer, shivers spreading through me. There they are again: the words on the mysterious note, "Legacy is a gift, and our sworn bond." Scribbled in the corner of Saint's photograph. A motto, Lara said. And now Annabelle's repeating it in answer to my questions about the secret society. It's all connected.

Holy shit!

I take another drink of my mimosa, trying not to let my reaction show, but inside, I feel a stab of victory. Is Annabelle trying to send me a message, or just confirm what she thinks I already know?

Either way, I have it now: The first solid confirmation that this secret society exists. And that Annabelle, Max, and the rest of them are members.

"Anyway, you won't believe the trouble I've gone to in order to find trained doves for the ceremony . . ."

Just like that, we're back to talking about her wedding, as if nothing happened.

* * *

AFTER LUNCH, ANNABELLE walks me back to the Ambrose Foundation office, before smothering me with air-kisses and insisting we "simply must" do a girly spa day ASAP. I can't help but be charmed by her. We have exactly nothing in common, but she's right: she doesn't take no for an answer, and it's impossible to withstand her avalanche of enthusiasm—and hot gossip.

I make my way back to my desk, my roommates' warning echoing in my ears. Are Saint and his friends just toying with me as their latest amusement? I don't for a moment believe that Annabelle would seek me out for friendship, or Hugh would suddenly call me up and offer me my dream job if I wasn't showing up at events on Saint's arm. But still, I have to admit, I like being included like this, and having a window on their glamorous, fun world. After a long, lonely year of grief and rage mourning Wren, it's a relief to just be swept up in simple, normal things like gossiping over lunch or planning a social media outreach campaign for a good cause.

Although, there's not much "normal" about Lady Annabelle, or Anthony St. Clair, the future Duke of Ashford.

Arriving back at the desk I've been using, I stop. The workstation is covered with an extravagant bouquet of roses, and not just the simple red drugstore kind. No, these are blush-pink antique roses, dozens of them, rich with fragrance, in a stunning arrangement.

I inhale the incredible scent as I check the card.

Congratulations on your new job

—Saint

I smile. Maybe I've played it cool for long enough . . .

I call him, and he answers on the first ring.

"A lesser man would be feeling deeply insecure about your silent treatment," he says, picking up.

"Hello to you, too." I trace the velvety petals of the roses. "The flowers are beautiful, thank you. But I haven't agreed to take any job."

"You will. It's perfect for you, and Hugh says you've already hit the ground running."

"Did he?" I ask, looking around. Hugh is in a meeting, talking enthusiastically with his team. "Well . . . I don't know. It's been hard enough keeping my head above water with all my academic work. Especially with all the distractions I've had . . ."

Saint chuckles, wicked. "Are you calling me a distraction?"

"You're certainly not helping me focus on my studies, *Professor*," I mock-scold him. "Whisking me out of Oxford, recommending me for extracurricular gigs . . ."

"You're having fun, aren't you?"

I pause, biting my lip. "I am," I admit.

That's the dangerous thing.

"So, about this dinner you owe me," Saint says, and I can hear the filthy promise in his voice. "I've waited long enough. I'm taking you out, tonight."

"I'm in London," I point out, even though my pulse kicks at the thought of getting him alone again.

"How convenient, so am I," he replies. "I have a place here, so you don't even need to worry about that train."

"Because I can sleep in your guest room?" I ask meaningfully.

He chuckles. "If that's what you choose. Meet me after you're done at work? Don't make a grown man beg," he adds, and I can't help feeling bold.

"I don't know . . ." I muse softly, feeling a shiver of anticipation. "I rather like you on your knees."

And then I hang up, before he can reply.

Chapter Eighteen
TESSA

After I finish up my work at the Foundation, Saint sends a car to meet me and deliver me to a gorgeous, romantic restaurant in Notting Hill.

"I'm underdressed," I tell him, glancing around at the other stylish diners having intimate conversations in the dim, candlelit corners. It's clearly some kind of hotspot, with a mismatched, Parisian feel: crystal chandeliers twinkling overhead, and lots of white linen and fresh flowers. "I didn't plan for a date."

"You look beautiful," he corrects me, getting up to greet me with a kiss. His lips graze mine softly, and I shiver, remembering the last time they were on my body . . .

"So, you just *happened* to be in London?" I blurt, taking a seat. He's looking casually devastating as usual, all in black, with his hair tousled over his eyes.

Saint gives a smirk. "Well, it seems like everyone else was. And if you won't come to me . . ."

"I don't recall that coming was my problem," I quip flirtatiously.

He laughs, clearly surprised by my boldness. And so am I. But there's something about the heat that sizzles between us just sitting across the man: it's tempting, already making me feel freer. More myself.

"So, tell me how it went at the Foundation today," Saint says, taking my hand across the table.

"Aren't we going to order first?"

He gives a dismissive gesture. "The chef knows me. He'll send something wonderful. I'm more interested in your new job."

"It's not a job!" I insist.

"But it could be," Saint points out, as a sommelier delivers a bottle of wine to the table. "Didn't you enjoy it?"

I sigh, reluctant. "I did."

"So why do you look like you just spent the afternoon reading Horsely?" He references one of the driest, most dull writers on the reading list, and I give a smile.

"No, it was great," I admit. "They have great resources, and the projects they're working to fund could really resonate with a younger audience . . ." I start telling Saint about my ideas for social media outreach, getting carried away explaining the plans. ". . . I've already drawn up a list of a dozen influencers who would be the perfect partners on this. And the great thing is, they would all love to be associated with charity work and giving back, so they'll probably do it for free. We get their audience exposed to the Foundation, a new fundraising drive, and they get to look like thoughtful citizens. Everybody wins!"

I finally stop to draw breath—and to sample some of the amazing appetizers that have been delivered to the table: tangy, fresh crudo, little cheese puffs, and some delicious, marinated vegetables. When I glance up from the food, I find Saint looking at me with a puzzled expression.

"What is it?" I ask.

"Nothing, really. I just . . . It's obvious that this kind of work is your passion. What are you even doing at Oxford, studying literature, if this is what you really love?"

I pause. *Shit.* I can't tell him the real reason for coming to Ashford. Stalling, I take a sip of my wine.

"Why does anyone stay in academia?" I asked, my voice bright. Maybe too bright. "To delay the real world, of course."

He gives a wry chuckle. "That's what people think about me. That I'm up in Oxford to avoid reality, and my responsibilities."

"Are you?" I ask, glad to deflect his questions back to him.

Now he's the one taking a slow sip of wine. "Yes," he replies simply. "The life my parents planned for me, the one I'm supposed to lead as son and heir . . . I don't want any part of it."

I pause, suddenly realizing something for the first time. "Your brother was older than you, wasn't he? He was supposed to inherit the title and be the next Duke of Ashford."

Saint nods, giving a rueful sigh. "Edward was made for it. Solid, dependable, a born leader. He actually liked all the family responsibility; he couldn't wait to take his position at the company with my father. Carry on the good St. Clair name. Nobody expected anything of me—and I liked it that way. I could do whatever I wanted—and I did." He gives me a familiar smirk. "But all that changed when he died."

"What happened?" I ask softly. "If you don't mind telling me."

He shakes his head. "It's alright. It was ten years ago. Edward went to volunteer with Doctors Without Borders, in Afghanistan. It was his day off, he was at a café with friends . . . there was an explosion. Suicide bomb."

"Oh my God," I breathe, stunned.

"I guess they were targeting foreigners." Saint gives a shrug. "Even though my brother never hurt anyone in his life. We were told it was quick." He looks away. "That he didn't feel anything."

I reach over and squeeze his hand. "I'm so sorry," I say, and he nods.

"After that . . . well, it was suddenly down to me. The future of the duchy, the great Ashford line. And I was nobody's first choice."

"So, Oxford."

He nods. "Far enough from my parents that I don't have to see the disappointment in their eyes." He says it archly, like a joke, then tips back the rest of his wine, draining the glass dry. "But enough about the past."

"Saint—" I start softly, but he shakes his head.

"I mean it. The only thing my brother's death taught me—besides the cruel lack of reason or justice in the world—is that we have to enjoy life while we can. Suck the marrow from the bones of fate," he adds, nodding to the food on the table. "So I mean to savor every moment of pleasure I can. How about you? Can I interest you in a little adventure tonight?"

He holds my gaze. An invitation.

A temptation.

I think of Wren, and all the adventures she'll never get to experience. The places she'll never travel to, the men she'll never kiss.

I'm the one left to do it all, for the both of us.

I give him a determined nod. "I'm in."

* * *

WE TAKE A cab from the restaurant across the city, to what looks like an upscale residential neighborhood. Saint holds my hand in the back seat, keeping up a casual conversation with the driver about sports and the latest soccer results, but his thumb strokes a slow circle on my palm, over and over, caressing the sensitive skin until I'm breathless from the light, tempting touch.

By the time he helps me out of the car, I'm burning up with curiosity about this adventure we have in store. Saint leads me to a discreet town house, marked only with a bulky bouncer on the door. "Nico," Saint greets him, friendly, and the man smiles, stepping aside to open the door for us immediately.

"Enjoy your night, sir."

I follow Saint inside. It looks like some kind of private members club, with an understated entrance area, and a gorgeous hostess in a severe black dress. Again, she knows Saint on sight, and is all smiles, cooing at him to have a great time and let her know if he needs anything.

"You're a regular, then?" I ask, as Saint leads me down a long, dimly lit hallway.

He gives me a wicked smile. "You could say that. When I've had a stressful time of it, I like to come here and . . . unwind."

We emerge into a bar area, designed like an old-fashioned speakeasy, with Art Deco gilt edgings and brocade wallpaper. The entire wall behind the bar is mirrored and backlit, with exotic bottles of liquor lined up, casting the room in a multicolored glow, like stained glass. Around the room, booths and tables are already occupied by chic, sophisticated guests, enjoying conversation, laughter, and—

I pause. A couple in the corner is kissing, but not just a casual peck on the lips. The woman is backed up against the wall, her elegant silk dress hiked up and her long legs wrapped around her partner's waist as he thrusts against her.

Thrusts . . . *into her*?

I blink. *They couldn't be* . . . But they are. There's no mistaking the glaze of pleasure in the woman's eyes, head falling back, diamonds glittering at her neck as the man's thrusts increase in fever and tempo. Her moans begin to echo, loud enough for the people nearby to turn and watch.

Nobody seems surprised that they're fucking, right here in front of everyone.

My cheeks heat in a rush of realization.

"This is a . . . sex club?" I ask Saint, keeping my voice low.

He looks amused. "That's one way of putting it."

"I think it's the only way," I say, noticing the other illicit details all around us.

The woman lounging back in a booth, sipping her cocktail as a man waits patiently on his knees beside her, a finely crafted leather collar at his neck . . .

The female couple across the bar, taking turns lavishing each other in kisses, before turning their attention to the younger man sitting between them, his hands resting lightly on the back of their heads as they start to peel open his shirt and lick their way down his body, sucking his cock in turn . . .

The handsome older man who strolls over to the first couple, just as the woman's moans reach a fever pitch. The man fucking her comes with a loud groan, sinking briefly against her body— before setting her down and stepping aside, so the other man moves to take his place, fucking her in slow, deep strokes, drawing new cries of pleasure from her lips.

I watch it all, enthralled. My blood is suddenly running hotter, my whole body tingling with a fiery anticipation. It's like the Midnight party all over again, but somehow even more tempting and explicit. At the party, I was in a state of giddy disbelief, totally out of my element.

But now . . .

Now the heat in my veins is thick with awareness, already knowing that whatever happens, I'm going to love every filthy minute of it.

Already wondering what particular pleasures Saint will show me and how far I'll go; what lines I'll happily cross tonight.

Saint takes my hand and leads me to the bar. He orders us drinks, and then turns to me, smiling when he sees me still watching the room, enthralled. "You like it," he says, pleased.

"I've never seen anything like it," I reply.

He looks surprised. "Not even back in the States? There are places like this all over, if you know where to look."

I shake my head. "I don't. Know where, I mean. And even if I did, I don't think I ever would have gone . . ."

Not before Saint fixed me with that seductive look across the party and led me into temptation. Freed me to indulge my wildest fantasies for the first time in my life.

"So you've never experimented, explored your own kinks and desires?" Saint asks, sliding an arm casually around my waist as he leans in closer to talk.

"No. I mean, I've read plenty, and mentioned things to old boyfriends, hoping that maybe we could try . . ." I add, thinking back to those blushing encounters, full of embarrassment—only to discover to my disappointment that nothing came close to the heady fantasies lurking on my Kindle.

At least, not until Saint.

"But I never felt like I could ask out loud for what I wanted," I continue, meeting his eyes. "What I've fantasized about. It always felt . . . I don't know, shameful and dirty."

Saint nods. "Shame can be erotic," he says thoughtfully. "The idea that you're breaking the rules, transgressing with the taboo. It's why it's bound so closely to pleasure, in art and literature."

"Is this one of your famous libertine lectures?" I tease, and he laughs.

"No, it's just interesting to realize how universal this all is." He gestures around the room, to the low groans of pleasure; hungry mouths and searching hands. "It might feel novel, or illicit, but that's only because society has been set up to make us think so. In fact, people have had these desires for thousands of years—and found every opportunity to indulge them."

He's right. It's a new way of looking at it, one that feels more honest than everyone just pretending like there isn't a part of them that's craving pleasure and release.

"I think that's why I feel so free with you," I find myself saying. "You've probably seen it all. I know there's nothing I can do or say that will make you judge me."

Except that I've been lying since the day we met.

The voice whispers in the back of my mind, but I push it aside. Tonight is about pleasure, what *I* want, where no lies or faking are required. And already, Saint is stroking me softly through my clothes, a slow rub of his fingertips against the curve of my hip, back and forth.

Back and forth.

I inhale in a rush, feeling the heat spiral from his touch. Saint shifts closer. "These fantasies of yours," he murmurs, breath warm against my cheek. "Tell me about them."

Despite everything I've just said, I flush. "I . . . I don't know. What do you mean?"

"I mean, when you close your eyes at night, alone, and you reach under the covers and play with that sweet, wet cunt . . . what do you imagine?" Saint's voice is low and hypnotic, his hands shifting, stroking over my body now, tracing over my breasts and ass. "Are you on your knees, waiting for an order, or on your back, commanding someone to pleasure you?" he continues, his touch turning possessive, plucking at my nipples and delving between my thighs. "Are you taking one man, or many? Being feasted on, or swallowing his cock while a woman licks you out? Are you begging, or screaming out in pleasure? Are you being used, fucked mercilessly, or taken slow, until you're mindless and shaking for release?"

Oh God.

I exhale, shivering at the rush of filthy images—and the promise in his voice. "Yes," I breathe, dazzled by the possibilities.

"To what?"

"All of it," I reply with a moan, as his grip tightens.

Saint sounds a low, approving groan. "Fuck, baby. We're going to have fun together."

I turn my head to face him and claim a hot, pulse-racing kiss. Saint pulls me closer against the heat of his body, and I feel him harden, his cock stiff against me, as his tongue sensuously explores my mouth.

Finally, he draws back, eyes glittering in the dim light. "You liked watching, at the party?"

I nod, already unsteady as my body shivers with lust.

"We could find a show to enjoy tonight . . ." he murmurs, dipping his mouth to lick along my collarbone. "Or, perhaps, you'd like to be the main attraction."

People watching me?

My body tightens at the idea. Saint notices my reaction and lifts his head, fixing me with a smoldering look. "Oh, that's how it is." His mouth curls in a wicked grin. "You want to be watched. To have their eyes on you . . . seeing just how you like to take it."

I moan, I can't help it. My body floods with a hot rush of need, just imagining it.

"Come with me," he says, taking my hand. He leads me deeper into the building, past open doorways and the sounds of animal pleasure. I glance around, glimpsing flashes of explicit scenes and the luxurious surroundings before we arrive in an open lounge area, lit by the romantic glow of lamps on the wall, and lined with low couches. There are maybe a dozen people here already, relaxed, heads bent in leisurely conversation—and more.

But when Saint steps into the room, the energy changes.

People turn to look at us, assessing. I can see interest and attraction on the women's faces—and some of the men, too. And unlike the Midnight party, nobody is wearing a mask.

I feel a fresh edge to my thrill. I'm not hidden here, the way I was there. People can see me, know me. Whatever I do here tonight, they'll know exactly who is participating.

There's no hiding from my desires.

Saint draws me over to one of the chaises, positioned in the middle of the room. I pause, suddenly nervous. "Saint . . ." I whisper, glancing around. Everybody's looking now. I want this, God, I do, but still . . .

"Shhh . . ." Saint seems to read my mind. He tugs off his tie and ties it over my eyes in a makeshift blindfold. "There," he whispers, his voice seeming more intimate in the darkness that suddenly settles over me. "They're all watching you, darling. But I just want you to focus on me. Can you do that?"

I exhale in relief. Enfolded in this velvet darkness, with nothing but the sound of Saint's voice, my nerves melt away, and I feel bold again.

"Yes," I whisper.

Yes to whatever happens next.

I feel Saint's hands on my body, undressing me. He peels away my blouse and jeans, skimming over my breasts before unfastening my bra and letting them fall free, already heavy and aching. He palms them roughly, and I shudder under his possessive touch. Every one of my senses feels heightened, now that I'm blindfolded, and every caress seems to spark through my taut, craving body.

And when I picture everyone in the room watching us . . .

My heart races, beating wildly in my chest.

Saint tugs down my panties too, and when I'm naked, he guides me back until I'm lying down, spread there on the chaise. "God, you're so beautiful," his voice murmurs hoarsely, and then his mouth is skimming over my body, lavishing my breasts and sucking my nipples into two wet, aching peaks.

"Saint . . ." I whimper, arching against his mouth.

He chuckles against my bare skin. "You have such perfect tits. Maybe I should have one of our audience come lick them, while I'm occupied elsewhere . . ."

My body clenches with shocked lust. Saint dips a hand between my legs, softly stroking my core. "Getting wetter, baby?"

I moan, writhing against him. Here in the darkness, every pleasure is intensified. And when he eases one finger inside me, and then another, thickly pulsing, I feel it everywhere. I arch against his hand, chasing the staccato rhythm as he thrusts, fucking me with his fingers until I'm gasping for more.

"Another, darling?" Saint muses. I moan my assent. "Say it," he orders me softly. "Tell everyone what you need."

Our audience.

Again, the realization that I'm spread for him, naked and moaning in front of everyone, sends new heat spiraling through my body.

Heat, and a bold recklessness.

"I need another finger," I gasp, hearing my own voice ring out, clear and loud in the hushed room. "Please, fill me up. Fuck me deep."

God.

Just saying it out loud thrills me. Asking for what I want. Begging, so everyone knows my deepest desires.

"Good girl." Saint thrusts another finger into me, and *fuck*, it's almost too much. Stretching me wider, making me grip the chaise for balance, but oh, it feels so fucking good. Saint is thrusting now in a filthy rhythm, and I can hear the sound of my wetness mingling with my own breathy moans as the shivers start, low in the base of my spine.

I whimper.

"Are you close, baby?"

I moan, louder, arching against his hand. I can feel it, so close, so fucking good—

Saint stops. He moves his hands away, leaving me gasping and dizzy in the darkness. "What . . . ?" I start to ask, disoriented by the sudden end to my pleasure.

Then I hear the unmistakable sound of a zip.

"We were interrupted, in the maze." Saint's voice is low and commanding. "I think it's time we picked up where you left off . . ."

Oh.

"Get on your knees," he instructs me softly. "Let's see that smart mouth of yours wrapped around my cock."

I shiver in excitement, sitting up. I'm clumsy in the blindfold, but Saint carefully helps guide me to the floor, where I kneel, my body still trembling in unreleased pleasure.

I feel his hands settle on the back of my head, and then he's guiding me closer, until his cock is hard and heavy against my cheek.

"Open wide, darling," Saint says, lacing his hands in my hair. "Show them all you can take it nice and deep."

Fuck.

Surrounded by darkness, I can only imagine the people watching as I obediently part my lips and lick him, running my tongue from root to tip.

Saint gives a groan above me. The sound of his pleasure emboldens me, and I use my hands to guide me, gripping the thick base as I swirl my tongue over the fat head.

"Fuck . . . Tessa . . . Don't tease me, baby. Swallow that dick."

I part my lips, and take him into my mouth, sucking him as deep as I can. Saint growls, pushing even deeper, almost making me choke at the girth of him. I try to pull back, but he holds me in place.

"Don't stop, baby. You can take it. That's right . . . *Good girl.*"

I shift my angle, glowing at the praise, and take him deeper than ever.

"Fuck . . ."

His groan floods my body with fire, as slowly, I find my rhythm, struggling to accommodate the hard, straining length of him.

"You look so pretty on your knees," he urges me on. "Everyone's watching, baby. They can all see you take me so well."

I moan around him, picturing it: their eyes on me as I suck his cock.

It's thrilling and erotic, and I find myself taking him deeper, breathless as my own body responds to the wild scene. My nipples stiffen, and my core aches, still needing release.

I slip a hand between my thighs and stroke myself, in time with Saint's thrusts.

"You're touching yourself?" His groans of pleasure turn fevered. "Oh fuck, baby. Spread your knees wider, let me see how you like to play with my cock in your mouth."

I do as he says, lost in the haze now, consumed with passion. His pace quickens and he thrusts faster. Deeper. Holding me in place there until it's all I can do to frantically rub my swollen clit and not to choke as he mercilessly fucks my mouth.

But God, it's the hottest thing I've ever felt. My senses working overtime, every touch making me sob in pleasure, moaning around his cock.

I'm close. Oh God, I'm close.

"Tessa . . ." His groans echo, a roar of pure animal need. "Don't stop. Don't stop. *Fuck* . . ."

He pulls out of my mouth, but his groans don't stop. I hear the slap of flesh on flesh, and then suddenly, Saint sounds a roar, and I feel a rush of hot liquid, sticky on my breasts.

He's coming on me.

Fuck.

The knowledge that I'm on my knees, blindfolded, with Saint spilling his climax all over my naked body for everyone to see . . .

It's too much. *Too good.* My orgasm slams through me, blotting out everything but the sweet, intense rush of pleasure, and the sound of Saint's praise.

I sink back against the chaise, dizzy with one of the most intense orgasms of my life. I can't move. I can't even lift my hands to remove the blindfold, I just lay there, stunned and gasping.

Holy shit.

As if from far away, I hear the sound of Saint's zipper, and then his hands are on me, wiping my body down with some kind of cool, damp cloth. I sigh, worn out, happy to be tended to, as I float here in a blissful cloud.

Because what just happened? Even my wildest fantasy could never come close.

Chapter Nineteen
TESSA

T he next morning, I wake in an unfamiliar bed, made with
the softest linens I've ever felt against my skin. I stretch,
still lost in the haze of sleep, until I finally open my eyes to
sunlight filtering through the airy drapes and pooling on the polished wooden floors.

Saint's house.

I sit up and look around, memories from last night flooding
back to me. After the scene at the club, I felt like I was floating,
blissed out on an intense sexual high. Saint brought me back
here, and put me to bed in the luxurious guest room, every inch
the gentleman—despite being so dominant and adventurous just
moments before. He still surprises me, and every time I peel
back a layer, I find there's something unexpected waiting to be
discovered.

Like the fact he didn't just take me to bed and fuck me senseless last night, the way my body so obviously craved.

But as I slowly stretch, yawning, I realize I'm glad he called it
a night when he did. Every encounter we share is wilder, more
thrilling than the last. It's overwhelming to experience a desire
like this, for the first time in my life, and as much as I should
be pushing my investigation right now, I want to take things slow.

And keep a firm grip on my self-control.

Because I can't deny that the connection between us is growing
deeper now. Stronger. Talking about our families over dinner, the

shoes his brother left him to fill . . . I understand, because I've felt the same way, wondering if I can ever live up to Wren. And learning more about what he's been going through . . . it makes me see him in a whole new light.

Except he's still the same man, I remind myself sternly, as I finally get out of bed. Reckless, seductive. A full-on rake, as my historical romance novels would say. Who else would have me on my knees in front of a room full of strangers, shamelessly swallowing his cock and moaning for more?

Connection means nothing. I'm just here to investigate his friends and have some more mind-blowingly seductive fun.

Aren't I?

* * *

I FIND A fluffy bathrobe hanging on the en suite bathroom door, plus all the high-end toiletries a woman could want. After freshening up, I head downstairs, in search of Saint—and the delicious bacon smell that's wafting through the house.

On my way to the kitchen, I look around, curious. I was still in my orgasmic haze last night, and didn't really take it in, but now I realize I'm in another historic town house. This one has been recently renovated, opening up the narrow hallways and small rooms to form a modern, expansive space. The staircase is metal and glass, and everywhere is warm sunlight and clean lines, which makes a dramatic contrast to the vintage furniture, moody artwork, and heavy antique rugs.

I find Saint in an airy kitchen/diner with black-and-white checkerboard marble floors and a massive Aga stove dominating one corner. He's barefoot in jeans and an unbuttoned shirt, hair still wet from the shower as he whisks eggs at the huge farmhouse table island in the middle of the room.

I can't deny the way my stomach turns a slow loop at the sight of him.

God, this man is beautiful.

"Good morning," I say finally, and he looks up, smiling at the sight of me.

"It is now." Saint beckons me over, then draws me against him for a lazy kiss. I inhale the scent of him, clean and citrusy, and feel a dangerous sense of peace.

Like I belong here.

"Let me guess, the caterers just left," I tease as he returns to the breakfast prep. Bacon is sizzling on a grill pan, and there's fresh bread, jams, and the scent of coffee in the air. I steal a sip from the mug he has poured already, and immediately, he goes to fix me a fresh mug.

"Don't believe Imogen, I can manage a good English fry-up," he promises, handing me the coffee. "How did you sleep?"

I sigh happily. "Like I was on a cloud."

"Good."

He returns to the stove, and I perch on a stool by the table, watching him at work as he pours the eggs into a buttery pan, and expertly folds them, nudging the bacon pan off the heat before it burns. "You're spoiling me," I say. "I usually just grab cold cereal or toast for breakfast."

"Haven't you heard? It's the most important meal of the day."

"Well, I did eat late last night," I can't resist quipping. Then I laugh. "Sorry, terrible pun. I couldn't resist."

"That makes two of us."

Saint deposits a plate in front of me with a flourish, before tilting my chin up and kissing me, deeper this time. I sigh, melting into the feel of his mouth, and the slow, sensuous way his tongue explores my mouth. By the time he draws back and goes to fix his own plate, I'm just about ready to shove the breakfast dishes aside and demand he devour me, instead.

But the bacon smells too good to waste.

"This is delicious, thank you," I say, biting into the first crispy piece. "And for being such a gentleman last night."

"Always." Saint pulls up a seat beside me, and we dig into

the food. Jazz is playing low from another room, and with the morning sun gleaming through the windows, and leafy green backyard beyond, I find myself relaxing completely, just enjoying the simple pleasure of the meal and Saint's easy company.

"Where are we, exactly?" I ask. "The neighborhood, I mean."

"South Kensington," Saint replies, drinking his coffee. "Hyde Park is nearby, if you fancy a walk. Or we could hit Harrods for a spot of shopping."

I try not to laugh. As if my meager savings would stretch to that luxury hotspot. "Is there a train station nearby?" I ask instead. "I should really be getting back to Oxford."

"Now, why would you want to do that?" Saint asks, with a playful sigh.

"Because I have a pesky thing called studying to do?" I smile. "Lectures to attend, work to catch up on before my classes this week. Some of my professors can be real assholes if you're not caught up," I remind him with a smirk.

"Or," Saint suggests, "just as an alternative option, you blow all that off and stay here with me, naked in bed all day?"

I laugh. "Not this time."

"Damn, I must be losing my touch," Saint says, still playful. He gets up and takes his empty plate to the sink. "Don't tell me you've already grown tired of my charms?"

I pretend to think about it. "Hmmm . . . well, you are a pretty predictable man," I joke, "Same old, same old, that's Saint for you."

In an instant, he has me up against the kitchen counter, his hands hot on my waist and his mouth blazing a path along my collarbone. "Predictable, huh?" Saint breathes on my bare skin, peeling my bathrobe wider to kiss and nip at the sensitive flesh of my throat.

"Boring. Bland. *Old*," I tease breathlessly, even as I arch eagerly against his hands. "I mean, you can't help it, losing your spark. You're practically middle-aged—*Ah!*" I let out a shriek as

Saint's cool fingers slide under the bathrobe and pluck one nipple, making me shudder in a heady mix of pleasure and pain.

"Old?" Saint echoes, laughter rumbling against my skin. "You'll pay for that . . ." His hands slide lower—and then withdraw. ". . . Another time."

I blink, breathless, as he steps back, regarding me with an arrogant smirk. "I'd hate to be boring and predictable, after all," Saint says with a grin. "And ravishing you on the kitchen counter . . . well, that's just old hat."

* * *

I GET DRESSED in yesterday's clothes, and head back to Oxford. Saint insists on having a driver take me back, and I don't put up much of a fight. After all, would I rather spend a couple of hours crammed in coach class on the train, or relaxing in the air-conditioned comfort of a luxury car? The countryside glides by the windows, and in no time at all, I'm deposited directly outside my apartment building—just as Kris and Jia emerge from inside.

"Hey guys," I greet them, smiling. "What's up?"

Jia's eyes flick over my wrinkled clothing and the departing car. "Let me guess, another fabulous date with the professor?"

"We had dinner," I admit. "Down in London."

Kris looks annoyed. "So that's why you didn't make it to my show."

His show? *Shit.* I completely forgot that Kris was doing an open mic night at a comedy club in town. He'd asked us both to come to support him.

"I'm so sorry," I blurt. "How did it go?"

"Fine." He gives a little shrug. There's silence.

"Well, I want to hear all about it!" I say brightly, trying to cover the awkward vibe. "How about we all go out tonight, my treat? Get some drinks, have some fun. You can tell me all the details."

They exchange a look. "OK," Kris says finally. "We could go to Llewelyn's, in town."

I wince. I've heard them talking about it, and it's one of the most expensive cocktail bars around. But I know I've got some serious making up to do for missing the show. "Great," I declare. "See you there tonight at nine?"

"See you."

They head off together, while I go let myself up to the apartment, and quickly shower and change for the day ahead. I race over to catch my first lecture of the day, and then manage to get in a few hours of study at a café before heading back to Ashford College.

I stop by the mailroom, and find Bates is on duty in the main lodge. "Anything fun?" he asks, nodding to the stack of junk mail and student flyers in my hand.

I shake my head. I've been holding out hope that whoever sent me the invitation to the Midnights party might reach out again, but there's still nothing from them. "Not unless you think a Tarts and Vicars costume party is fun," I offer, and he chuckles, sorting packages behind the desk. It's a lull, and we're the only ones here, surrounded by packing crates and Ashford merchandise.

"And how are you finding the rest of it?" he asks, his weathered face looking friendly. "Finding your feet yet?"

I flash back to the club last night, how thrilling it felt to be blindfolded and on display like that. Like I belonged.

I cough. "Kind of," I say vaguely, lingering by the desk. "It's a lot to get my head around, all the classes and lectures," I add. "It feels like no matter what I do, I'm still running late, or playing catch-up."

Especially when my mind is still back in London, sitting in the calm morning sunlight with Saint.

"You'll find your way," Bates reassures me. "I've been here long enough to know."

"And you don't see blind panic in my eyes just yet?" I joke, and he laughs. Then I get a thought. "How long have you been at Ashford?" I ask.

"Going on twenty years now," he replies.

"Then you must have seen everything," I say, still acting casual. "All the wild student pranks and parties . . ."

"Oh yes," he chuckles. "High spirits and alcohol, it's a recipe for something alright."

"My friend was telling me about all the clubs here," I continue, carefully getting to my point. "Drinking clubs, secret societies . . . she swears they're still around," I add. "You know, elites getting up to all kinds of things, hazing rituals and bonding ceremonies. But I said she was crazy. People don't do things like that anymore . . . do they?"

I fix Bates with an inquisitive look. He smiles, still methodically sorting packages. "Well, I can't say that I know anything about that," he replies. "And even if I did, they'd have sworn me to secrecy, wouldn't they?"

I give a laugh. "Right. Make sure you didn't spill their secrets."

"But if you're curious about that sort of thing, I remember there was an article a few years back, in the *Oxford Student*." He names one of the student newspapers. "It caused quite the kerfuffle at the time."

"About secret societies, here at Ashford?" I ask, remembering to hide my excitement.

Bates nods. "'Course, it was all probably rumors. Someone caused a stink, and the whole thing got retracted, but I'll tell you, that was a fun week, watching everyone buzz around like ants who lost their queen!"

I smile and change the subject, chatting a while longer about the cricket scores in case Bates thinks I'm too curious about the one thing. But as soon as I say goodbye and go get settled in the college library, I pull out my phone, and start to search.

I find the *Oxford Student* website easily enough, full of events and local reporting, but when I try to search anything about secret societies, the results come back empty.

No articles found.

I frown. Looks like Bates was right, and someone managed to get the story completely scrubbed. There's nothing on the newspaper's site, or when I try using a search engine instead. The only thing I can find is a cryptic, vague editor's letter from May three years ago:

The *Oxford Student* editorial board apologizes un-reservedly for the article published last week. We regret that it did not meet our usual high standards of accuracy and fact checking. We accept complete responsibility, and disavow all claims, statements, and conclusions made therein. The journalist responsible shall no longer be printed in these pages.

Wow. Now, I'm really curious.

If the story hit a little too close to home, and revealed something about this secret society . . . what don't they want us knowing?

On a hunch, I get up and go to the front desk, where my favorite clerk, Maeve, is working. She's got immaculately coiffed grey hair, a collection of bright, modern spectacles, and knows every inch of this place. "Tessa," she greets me, smiling. "I managed to tuck away that essay collection you ordered. Half your class came in to try and find it," she adds. "But I know you needed it."

"Thanks," I exclaim, as she hands me the slim volume. "I'll try and be quick. I hate how the minute the reading lists get sent out, it's like *The Hunger Games*, every man for himself."

Maeve chuckles. "Anything else I can help you find?"

"Well, actually, does the library keep old newspaper copies?" I ask hopefully. "There's an article I'm looking for. The *Oxford Student*, from three years ago. May 6th edition."

Maeve checks her computer. "We've got most of our periodical collection digitized, but . . . oh yes, we haven't gotten around to those just yet. You should find them in the basement, Room D, far back wall. Boxes are labeled."

"Thanks!"

I head down the creaking spiral staircase to the basement. Upstairs, the main library is all vaulted ceilings and stained glass, with carved wooden study carrells and leather-bound books on towering shelves, but things couldn't be more different down here, out of view. Strip lights flicker overhead, and squat metal shelves fill a rabbit warren-like mess of rooms and hallways, all crammed with books.

I follow Maeve's directions to a stuffy, low-ceilinged room, and find stacks of boxes shoved against the wall. They're filed in no particular order, so I have to dig through three different crates before I finally find the year I'm looking for. April . . . May . . .

There it is.

I pull out the crumpled, yellow pages. *"Oxford's Secret Societies: Revealed!"* the headline reads.

The light flickers overhead, and I pause, glancing around at the dim, dusty stacks. For some reason, it feels like I'm doing something illicit here, but I tell myself I'm just being paranoid. I turn back to the newspaper and open it wide.

Inside, there's a double-page spread, an exposé of the most popular societies, past and present. There are details of scandalous initiation ceremonies, and lists of members, with grainy black-and-white photos of groups posing for the camera. "By far the most notorious—and secretive—organization is the famed Blackthorn Society," the article reads. "Members are tight-lipped, but are thought to include media mogul Cyrus Lancaster and Member of Parliament Lionel Ambrose."

The Blackthorn Society.

I inhale in a rush. There it is, in grainy black and white. Another clue that the society is real.

And if Cyrus and Lionel were members back in their day . . . then Max and Hugh have got to be, too, just like I thought.

And Saint, too . . .

I eagerly read the rest of the article, but to my disappointment, there's nothing particularly shocking. Details about a hazing ritual involving a dead pig's head, like Jia joked, and some speculation about the Blackthorn Society influencing student elections.

Nothing important. Nothing I can use.

Still, it's the closest I've come to anyone confirming that the society actually exists. The article was written by a Jamie Richmond, so I snap a few photos to copy the article, then pack up the boxes and head upstairs to daylight again. After a quick internet search, I find a social media profile that seems to fit for Jamie, so I send a message, saying I'm interested in his research, and would love to talk. Fingers crossed he gets back to me soon.

Right now, he's the best lead I've got.

* * *

BY THE TIME I finish up my studying, racing to get another essay finished before my deadline, I'm tired out. I'm doing the bare minimum of my studies to keep up with my classmates, but still, the past couple of days have been nonstop, and I want nothing more than to change into my comfiest sweatpants and collapse on the couch. But I know I can't blow my roommates off, *again*. I'm walking on seriously thin ice right now, and they already have a weird chip on their shoulders about all the time I'm spending with Saint and his friends. So, I change into jeans and a basic black tank top, grab my jacket, and head out across the city to meet them for drinks.

The bar they picked is in a classy neighborhood of upscale stores and restaurants, about a twenty-minute walk from Ashford. It's in a converted church, with soaring ceilings and a long, polished bar running in front of the original stone statues. When I arrive, the place is already buzzing, with some of the more elite students and local twentysomethings, all sipping expensive cocktails as upbeat music plays.

And I mean, *expensive*. When I catch a glimpse of the prices on the menu, I wince.

"You're buying, right?" Jia greets me with a hug, and I'm relieved to see that Kris seems to be in a good mood, too.

"Sure!" I say, pulling out my credit card. I'm determined to put the awkwardness behind us and smooth things over—even if it is going to cost me. Literally.

"Then let's have martinis," Jia decides.

"Ooh, and lemon drop shots," Kris pitches in. "And some of those yummy olives to nibble, too."

I place the order, reminding myself that it's a small price to pay not to live in a war zone for the rest of the semester. "Keep the tab open!" Jia trills, as I hand over my card. "We're just getting started."

They down their shots—and then order another round and slam them back too. I blink. I guess they really are going hard tonight. "So, how's everyone's day?" I ask, determined to keep things upbeat.

"Ugh, don't ask." Jia sighs. "I was late turning in my thesis prep notes to my supervisor, and she was awful about it. I tried explaining that I'm working extra shifts at the bookstore to cover tuition, but she didn't want to listen."

"Bitch," Kris agrees.

"I didn't know you were working a job here, too," I say, taking a sip of my cocktail. It's strong, but the others are gulping theirs back like it's seltzer. "When did you start that?"

Jia pauses. "Well, I haven't actually started, I just picked up an application. But she doesn't know that! It's typical," she continues, glancing around. "This whole place is set up for people who can just snap their fingers and have Daddy pay for tuition, they can't even imagine we might need some extra time, because we have to work for a living, too."

I bite my tongue. Jia might have more time to study if she didn't hit the bars with Kris every other night, but I'm not about to point that out right now. "That's too bad," I say instead, murmuring sympathetically.

"If the bookstore doesn't work out, I heard they're hiring at the college bar," Kris offers, but Jia shakes her head.

"Are you kidding? Serving all the rich bastards like I'm some lowly paid member of staff? No way. I've seen the way they look down on everyone."

It sounds like Jia looks down enough on the staff herself, but again, I don't say anything, I just sip my drink.

"You have that scholarship covering all your fees, don't you?" Kris looks over at me.

I nod. "But it's still taking up all my savings, too," I add. "Although . . . I do have this job offer," I admit, thinking of Hugh's insistence. He emailed me an official offer, with all kinds of perks and benefits. "At the Ambrose Foundation? It's a part-time gig in their fundraising department, and I don't know how I'll manage to juggle it with my studies but . . . I think I'm going to take it."

I feel a buzz of excitement, saying the words out loud. I don't think I decided up until this moment, but now I feel it in my gut, it's an opportunity I want to take.

"That's awesome," Kris says, raising his glass in a toast. "Congrats!"

"Thanks." I beam, but Jia isn't smiling.

"Wait, when did this happen?" She frowns.

"Um, just yesterday," I reply. "That's why I was in London. Hugh asked me to come take a look around."

"Hugh *Ambrose*?" Jia's lips thin.

"Um, yes. We met at the Lancaster party the other week and got to talking. Why?" I ask, confused by her sudden icy reaction. "What's the problem?"

"Oh, no problem," she says sarcastically. "Only that my friend Lucy was on her third round of interviews for that position, and you just swept in and took it."

I gulp.

"She has her master's in public administration, and *years* of experience," Jia adds, glaring. "But I guess the old boys network strikes again. I bet Saint put in a good word to his pal, didn't he?" she says meanly. "I guess those extracurricular sessions are paying off for you, after all."

"Hey!" I protest sharply. "I didn't fuck my way into this job. I'm sorry about your friend," I add. "Really. But maybe she just wasn't a good fit for the position."

"And maybe she's not hanging out at the right VIP parties, sucking up to rich assholes to get a break."

I don't reply. I understand it's not fair that Hugh called me in and basically offered me the job on a silver platter, and I'm not naïve enough to think that dating Saint isn't a huge part of why, but still, I'm not going to grovel and apologize. I've been on the other side of a hundred missed opportunities, passed over for someone's niece or cousin or friend from school. If the scales have finally tipped in my favor, I'm going to make the most of it.

I'd be a fool not to.

Silence falls. Kris looks back and forth between us. "Another round!" he declares.

Jia smirks at me. "Let's make it champagne. To celebrate your *amazing* new job."

"I don't think that's a good idea," I say, before she can get the bartender's attention.

"Why not?"

"Because their champagne is like a hundred pounds a bottle," I point out.

"So?" Jia challenges me.

I take a deep breath. "So, we've already drunk plenty tonight. How about we just head home, stop at Ahmed's for some of those chili-cheese chips you love?"

"Are you saying I'm drunk?" Jia's voice rises.

"No." I try to calm her, but she gestures wildly.

"I can handle myself, you know. Maybe I'm not walking around with a stick up my arse, like the rest of your new friends, but that doesn't mean—"

CRASH.

Jia's elbow catches some cocktails on the bar, sending them careening to the ground with a smash.

Heads turn.

"Shit, I'm so sorry," I apologize to the guys who were standing right there. "She didn't mean to—"

"Don't apologize for me," Jia snorts. She slides down from the barstool, unsteady on her feet. "And especially not to *them*. Assholes," she adds.

They scowl. "What did you just say?" one of them demands.

I look to Kris for help, and thankfully, he takes Jia's arm. "Let's go get some air," he says, smoothly steering her to the door. "And ice cream."

They disappear, leaving me alone with the scowling guys. They look like they want to start something—

Until Max Lancaster materializes at my side. "Everything alright?" he asks them cheerfully. "Let me take care of that. Kevin!" He gestures the bartender over. "Another round for these gentlemen. And a couple of glasses of your finest scotch, too. You have to try it. There's no trouble here, is there?" he adds, giving the men a measured look.

They back off. "No trouble. Cheers, mate."

"Anytime!"

I exhale in relief. "Thank you," I mutter, when the guys move away with their fresh drinks. "My friend got kind of messy, then took off."

"Leaving you to clean up the mess?" Max says, raising his eyebrows. "Some friend."

I don't reply. Max is dressed impeccably in fine wool pants and a button-down shirt, an expensive watch gleaming on his wrist, and his blonde hair perfectly tousled. He looks every inch the handsome playboy, and I can't help wondering if Wren fell for his obvious charms.

He gestures for the bartender again. "I'll take a glass of that scotch myself, now," he says. "And a passionfruit martini."

"Thanks, but I shouldn't stay," I say reluctantly. I'd love to subtly quiz Max some more about Wren, but exhaustion is hitting hard, and I know I need to stay sharp around him. "I need to be getting home."

"It's not for you," Max replies, smiling. "Although, you're welcome to join us . . ."

His gaze moves past me, and I follow it to a curvy brunette at a corner table. She's poured into a figure-hugging dress, with sultry eye makeup.

She's gorgeous—and definitely *not* his fiancée, Annabelle.

"Oh," I blurt, before I can stop myself. "OK."

Max turns back to me. "Can I get you a cab?" he asks smoothly, showing absolutely no shame about being out on the town with some other woman.

"I'm good, thank you. And thanks again for stepping in there," I add. "I really appreciate it."

"Anything for a friend," he says, stressing the word, just a little. "Discretion is the better part of valor, after all," he adds with a wink, before taking his drinks to rejoin the brunette woman.

Maybe they're just friends, I wonder, heading for the doors. Then I see Max slide in to join her, his hand resting on her hip, leaning in to whisper in her ear in a not-so-platonic way.

OK then.

I shake my head, emerging into the cool night air. I'm not about to go wading into someone else's business—not when I need to keep Max close to try and uncover more about Wren. If Annabelle ever asks me about it, then sure, I'll tell her the truth. But right now, these people are still practically strangers to me.

I don't know what kind of games they like to play.

* * *

I SET OFF back toward Ashford. It's late, and the streets are dark and quiet, lit with the glow from the old-fashioned streetlamps. I walk, thinking about Jia's comments.

She's right, I know. I don't deserve the job at the Ambrose Foundation—but I want it all the same. Does that make me a bad person?

I sigh, torn. I understand why my roommates look at Saint and his friends with such suspicion and resentment. They're wealthy, privileged, and live in a different world to the rest of us. They don't ever have to do the mental math on whether they have enough cash to cover a bar tab or work extra hours just to pay rent.

But still, that doesn't mean they don't have struggles of their own.

Like Saint, losing his brother—and suddenly finding himself thrust into a role he never wanted. Heir to his family's title and business. I can see now how his reckless, libertine behavior is more than just a mindless pursuit of pleasure. To him, it must feel like a last-ditch statement of rebellion, to reject the life he should be leading—that his family is pressuring him to take up—and follow his own path instead. He likes to act as if it's all careless self-indulgence, but I caught the shadows in his eyes when he talked about Edward . . .

Deep down, he thinks he'll never live up to his brother—so why even try?

I feel an unfamiliar swell of emotion. Damn it. So much for keeping our connection purely sexual. Already, I'm finding how much I have in common with him, the past grief driving both of us on, and shaping our every choice. Just as Saint has defined himself against everything his brother stood for when Edward was alive, I've wound up defining myself by Wren's death. The blame for her suicide has haunted me, sharpening my anger and driving me on.

But now that I'm here in Oxford, closer than ever to the truth, it feels like that anger is . . . not softening, but easing its tight iron grip on my heart. I have a hundred new distractions pulling me away from my mission, and even though I've told myself the only reason I'm hanging out with Saint and his friends is to follow these clues toward this secret society and Wren's attacker, I know it's not the whole truth.

For the first time since Wren died, I'm feeling more than just blind rage and grief. The desire that Saint draws from me, the satisfaction of brainstorming those fundraising ideas at the Ambrose Foundation, even hanging out, chatting to Annabelle and Imogen at these events . . .

I'm having fun.

Guilt rises, bitter in my mouth. This isn't a field trip I'm on, I remind myself. And these people could know more than they're telling me. I can't let myself be seduced by the glitzy parties and wild, sensual nights with Saint, and forget what's really important here.

I need to see through the dazzling displays of wealth—to the dark truths that might be lurking beneath the surface. Because if I find that any one of them knows what happened to Wren . . .

I won't stop until I burn them to the ground.

I turn a corner and find myself on an empty street. The sound of footsteps comes, behind me.

Moving closer.

I glance back, but it's too dim to see who's there, just the dark outline of someone strolling, about thirty feet behind me.

I grip my shoulder bag more securely at my side. For all its historic charm, Oxford is still a big city, and I'm a woman walking home alone at night. I cross the street and speed up, my feet tapping on the cobblestones.

The person behind me crosses, too. Following me.

Shit.

I'm just a couple of blocks from my building, so I pull out my phone, and pretend to answer a call. "Yes, I'm right around the corner," I say loudly, my heart pounding now as I speed-walk down the empty street. "You're outside the building? Great. I'll meet you there. No, it was a fun night . . ."

I keep chatting to my imaginary friend, keeping one ear out

for my pursuer. Maybe I'm overreacting, and it's just someone else heading home, but my body is prickling with awareness, and there's nobody else around. *Just one more block*, I tell myself. *You're almost home.*

Then I hear the footsteps, closer, and I can't stop myself from turning to see.

They're just twenty feet away now, closing the distance between us, a tall male frame in a black jacket and joggers. He passes under a streetlight, and in the flash of illumination, I see that his whole face is covered with a black and white mask, like the one from the movie *Scream*.

He sees me looking. For a terrible moment, we're both frozen in place. Then he lunges, breaking into a run—straight for me.

Raw panic flashes through my entire body.

Fuck.

I flee, my boots clattering on the ground as I race desperately to the end of the street. I can see the lights of the main road up ahead, cars passing, even the sound of people nearby. But I don't even have time to scream for help before the masked man grabs my arm, yanking me back.

I whirl around, striking blindly, clawing at him. But with a single hard fist to my stomach, he sends me careening to the ground.

Fuck. The pain blossoms behind my rib cage and I gasp for air.

"Back the fuck off," my attacker growls from behind the mask. "Stop asking questions about Blackthorn—or you'll be sorry."

He looms above me, and I instinctively curl up in a ball, closing my eyes and bracing myself for the killer blow.

But it doesn't come. There's a rush of footsteps, and then someone arrives, panting.

"Hey, are you OK?"

I open my eyes. An older couple is leaning over me, concerned. "I . . . He was . . ." I gasp, still winded. I look around, but there's no sign of my attacker.

He's gone.

Chapter Twenty
SAINT

"More tea?"

"I think we're covered, Mother," I say dryly, eyeing the table already covered in a full tea set and various scones and sandwiches. "But I would like a glass of whiskey, when you get a moment, thanks," I tell the waiter.

My mother waits until he's departed before tutting at me disapprovingly. "It's not even noon, Anthony."

"Well, I figure I'll need it for this little get-together." I look around the fussy, upscale hotel dining room she summoned me to. "What's on the agenda today?" I ask, sitting back and getting comfortable for what's sure to be an unpleasant hour. "The usual 'It's time you gave up this life of wanton debauchery and accepted your familial responsibilities'? It's a classic, to be sure," I add. "But getting rather old, don't you think?"

"I do." Lillian St. Clair presses her lips together. She's immaculately dressed in pale blue Chanel, with the Ashford family sapphires glittering at her earlobes. "But that's not why I invited you here today."

"Intriguing," I say, sampling some of the tiny pastries. "I'm all ears."

My mother sighs. "I do care about you," she says, sipping her tea. "I'm interested in what you're doing with your time. How are things at Oxford?"

"Fine," I reply, not believing for a moment that simple affection and curiosity is what's behind this lunch. My mother always has an ulterior motive. "Nothing new to report."

"And your book," she continues. "I heard your publisher wants a follow-up?"

I nod around a cream puff. "I'm thinking over some ideas, but I'm not sure I want to do another. Deadlines . . . pressure . . . it's not really my kind of thing."

"It was lovely seeing you at the Lancaster party," she says evenly. "Thank you for making an appearance."

"I was told it was mandatory."

"When has that ever made a difference?" Lillian says with a wry smile, and I smile back.

"True."

My mother takes another sip of tea. "And that Tessa girl seems . . . lovely."

I look up and catch the curl of distaste on her patrician face.

"Oh," I say flatly. "So that's what this is about."

"It's not *about* anything. Can't a mother want to know more about her son's life?" she asks. "And the people he's sharing it with?"

"You didn't seem that interested to know more about Tessa at the party," I point out, feeling a flicker of tension. I should have known this was coming from the moment they crossed paths. I usually keep my romantic exploits far away from my family, but I couldn't resist the temptation of having Tessa with me to dull the sting of yet another society party.

And she did. God, the sight of her spread naked in the moonlight in the middle of the maze will haunt my dreams forever.

But now it's time to pay for that reckless indulgence.

"What did you expect, for me to interrogate the girl in front of everyone?" my mother asks. "That would hardly have been polite. But I'm interested. I understand she's a student of yours."

"She's twenty-six," I reply, defensive. "It's hardly a scandal."

"Of course not. But Peterson . . ." she muses. "I can't say I'm familiar with her family."

"I wouldn't expect you to be." I fix her with a look. "They're public school teachers, in Illinois."

"Oh." She dabs her lips with a napkin. "How nice."

I sigh. My mother's snobbery runs deep. Her family can trace its lineage back to the court of Henry the Eighth, and now, as Duchess of Ashford, she's determined that Robert and I will follow in her footsteps and make good, *appropriate* marriages.

"Did I tell you, I ran into the Chumleys at the opera last week?" Lillian changes the subject. "Their renovations at the Manor are exquisite."

"Uh-huh . . ." I start to tune her out, wondering if I can tempt Tessa away from her studies for another dinner.

Or dessert.

I haven't been able to stop thinking about her. Every night we spend together, every adventure is wilder and more passionate than the last. I'm still moving slow, not wanting to push her limits too far, but damn if she doesn't urge me on. I thought it would be easy to keep control, the way I always do, but there's something about her that makes *me* feel like the one who's discovering desire for the very first time. The way she begged for me at the club, the way she moaned and put on such a show, loving the thrill of being watched . . .

Lust tightens in my body, just remembering the look in her eyes when I finally removed that blindfold. She was blissed-out. Reeling.

The most beautiful woman I've ever seen.

". . . and of course, Lisbeth is a credit to them."

"Uh-huh." I try to banish thoughts of Tessa from my mind, because getting hard at lunch with my mother?

Not something I want to try.

"You remember Lisbeth, don't you?" My mother smiles at me, with suspicious warmth. "She just graduated with her history of art degree, she's interning at Sotheby's. Lovely girl, so well-spoken, and cultured. We were chatting about the Caravaggios almost all night!"

I try a slice of cake.

"The two of you should get together," she continues brightly. "Have dinner sometime and catch up. I told her you'd give her a call."

My head snaps up. "Now why would you do something like that?" I ask, my voice dropping dangerously.

"Why not?" Lillian replies, playing dumb.

"Because I'm otherwise engaged."

"Oh, I didn't realize."

I narrow my eyes. "With Tessa," I tell her slowly.

"But that's not serious," she says dismissively.

"It could be."

As I say the words, I'm surprised to realize that they're true. I was planning for it to be just another fun fling, but everything with Tessa feels different, somehow.

Every night I spend with her just makes me want another. Every kiss makes me hungry for more.

"Well, it's not like there's a ring on her finger," my mother continues, undeterred. "You're young, still waiting to find the right fit. And Lisbeth is from a wonderful family, of course. Their land holdings, the export business . . ."

"Do you want me to go out with Lisbeth, or the family accountant?"

Lillian flicks her eyes upward, impatient. "All I'm saying is that it wouldn't hurt to meet the girl for a date. A proper one," she adds with a warning look. "Somewhere nice, and respectable. She's not one of your students."

She says the word *student* like she's saying *whore*.

My tension grows. "I'm not going to date anyone else, Mother. Proper or otherwise. Things could be getting serious with Tessa. Who knows, there may be a ring on her finger soon enough," I add, more to wind her up than because I'm serious.

But then I remember making breakfast for Tessa after our night at the club. How simple and easy it was to sit with her in the sunlight, trading coffee cups and sections of the morning newspaper.

Like we belonged.

Lillian must see something in my expression, because her eyes widen. "You can't possibly be serious."

"I thought that's what you wanted," I reply, taunting. "For me to settle down and start facing my responsibilities. Well, getting married would be plenty settled, don't you think?"

I watch her take a deep breath, collecting herself. "Well, we'll just have to see, won't we? Perhaps we should all have dinner together soon," she suggests, calling my bluff. "You, me, your father, and Tessa. Get to know her properly."

No fucking way. I can just imagine how that would go: an evening of chilled soup and even chillier smiles.

"Perhaps," I reply vaguely. "I'll have to see about her schedule."

"And we'd love to see more of you," she adds, fixing me with a look. "Are you sure you can't stay in London any longer? It's all hands on deck at the company, getting ready to announce these trial results. Your father has been run off his feet. He could use your help. I've barely seen him in weeks."

"I have classes." I give a shrug. Although, I wonder if Dad's absence has anything to do with the French woman he was whispering with at the Lancaster party. Not that I'm about to mention their tête-à-tête to my mother.

Luckily, she spots someone across the restaurant and waves. "I'll be right back," she says, getting up to cross the room.

I finish my drink, still tense and wound way too tight. I don't know what it is about this particular lunch that's got me on edge;

I've sat through conversations like this a hundred times. I never let my parents get under my skin, but hearing Lillian talk so dismissively about Tessa . . .

I don't like it. And I certainly don't like the way she assumes I'll be moving on soon, to some other woman, some other fling.

Maybe I have done in the past, but this is different.

Tessa is different.

I haven't even begun to scratch the surface of that mysterious, surprising woman.

I pull out my phone, checking to see if she's responded to any of the messages I've sent over the past few days.

Nothing.

My thumb itches over my keyboard, but I restrain myself from sending another; even though I want to hear from her again. I don't want to seem desperate.

Christ, how the mighty have fallen.

I'm about to tuck my phone away when it buzzes with a new message. Not from Tessa, but my cousin Imogen.

I just heard what happened. Hope Tessa is OK.

I stare at the message, my whole body going cold.

What the fuck?

I call her back immediately. "What happened?" I demand, the moment Imogen picks up. "Where's Tessa? Why wouldn't she be OK?"

Imogen pauses. "You haven't heard?" she asks, with surprise in her voice.

"I wouldn't be calling you if I had," I reply through gritted teeth. "Imogen, tell me. Now."

"I don't know all the details," she says quickly. "But I heard she was attacked. A mugging, I think, outside the college."

I'm on my feet in a heartbeat, striding for the doors.

"Anthony? Saint?"

I hear my mother calling me, but I don't slow down.

I have to get to Tessa.

* * *

I DAMN WELL break the speed limit, driving up to Oxford, and by the time I arrive at Tessa's flat, I'm nearly going out of my mind imagining the worst. Somebody hurt her. She was scared.

And I wasn't there to protect her.

"Tessa?" I hammer on her door. "Tessa, it's me, Saint. Open up!"

The door cracks a couple of inches, and her cautious blue eyes peer out. When she confirms it's me, she removes the chain, and opens it wider.

"Hey," she whispers, stepping back to let me in.

I stop dead in the doorway. She looks like she's been through the wringer. Her face is pale and drawn, there are dark shadows under her eyes, and an ugly bruise on her forehead.

"My God, what happened to you?" I immediately go to her, tenderly cupping her cheek to examine the bruise.

"I'm fine." Tessa starts to pull away.

"Liar." I try to draw her closer to comfort her, but she winces in pain, and puts a protective hand to her stomach.

"Really," she insists again, even as I see the pain mar her delicate features. "I went to the hospital, they checked me out. Nothing but some scrapes, and a few bruised ribs from where he . . . he hit me."

Blood pounds in my ears. Rage strikes through me, but I force myself to stay calm.

"Who was he?" I ask, carefully leading her over to the couch. I tuck a blanket around her, and she curls up, looking more vulnerable than I thought possible. Tessa, who always has a smart retort; fearless and bold. Now she wraps her arms around herself protectively and gives a little shrug.

"I don't know, I didn't see his face. He was wearing this creepy mask. It was over quickly," she adds. "He just grabbed me, and knocked me down, and then some people came, and he ran off."

"But he didn't get your purse?" I ask, noticing her brown leather shoulder bag hanging on a chair.

Tessa blinks. "No. I, umm, I guess I held on to it instinctively. It was stupid," she adds, "I should have just let it go."

"This isn't your fault." I take her hand, holding it tightly. "It's Ashford's, for not having better lighting in the street. Or cameras. What the hell are they doing housing students here, outside the college walls?" I demand, shaken by what a near-miss it was. I'm gripped with an overwhelming sense of protectiveness, furious at the world—and myself—for allowing her to be hurt.

If somebody hadn't come . . .

"You're moving in with me," I decide suddenly.

"What? Saint, no," Tessa protests, clearly surprised.

It was an impulsive suggestion, but now I think about it, it's the perfect solution.

"It's clearly not safe here," I point out. "You'll be much more secure at mine. The streets are safe. I have a top-of-the-line security system, you can easily walk to class. And I'll be there to protect you."

Tessa gives me a tired smile. "I'm not a damsel in a tower, Saint, and I don't need you to play like a white knight. I can take care of myself."

"The bruise on your forehead says otherwise," I point out.

She lifts a hand, pressing it to the purple welt, and winces. "You couldn't have stopped it, even if you'd been there," she says. "He wanted . . ."

"What?" I ask. "What did he want?"

She looks away, evasive. "Nothing. Just some cash, I guess. Look, it's a very sweet offer," she adds, getting to her feet. "But come on, me moving in with you? We both know that's just crazy."

"Why?" I demand. The idea of her staying with me makes perfect sense. I can look out for her, take care of her. And more than that, it feels *right*.

But Tessa laughs, like she's not even taking it seriously. "Umm, because we've barely been dating a couple of weeks—if that's even what you can call this. Trust me, you're going to come to your senses in about five minutes and be seriously relieved that I'm the one thinking straight. Bruises heal. I'll be fine."

"But if you stayed with me, we would have more time together . . ." I draw her closer, more gently this time, and tilt her chin up to me for a slow, deep kiss. Tessa sighs, melting into my arms. "More time for me to ravish you," I whisper, sliding my hands over the curve of her hips. "To lay you down and make you come, over and over again . . ."

Tessa neatly ducks out of my embrace. "Using sex to manipulate me, Professor?" She gives me a knowing smirk. "Tempting, but that's not going to work on me. I know all your tricks. Now, I need to get to class."

Dammit.

I stifle my frustration, watching her collect her books. Tessa is stubborn and independent, acting like the attack was no big deal, but I can tell, she's shaken; her usual bold spark dimmed.

Why can't she see, she doesn't have to deal with this alone?

"Will you at least let me set this place up with groceries and supplies while you're in class?" I ask, getting a new idea. "You need to be resting and taking it easy. Mineral salt baths for the bruising. Chicken soup. Ridiculously expensive gelato and chocolates . . ."

Tessa finally smiles. "That sounds lovely," she says, exhaling. "And maybe you could come over later, watch a movie or something?" she adds, tentatively. "I know it sounds stupid but . . . I don't want to be alone."

Dammit.

"It's not stupid at all," I reassure her, even more certain she shouldn't be in this flat on her own.

"Thank you," she says with a pale smile. "Spare key's on the table."

"I'll call you later," I tell her, seeing her off with another kiss.

The door slams behind her, and I stand there a moment in the well-worn living room, looking around at the cheap furniture—and the pathetic excuse for a lock on the door.

She's scared.

The knowledge shakes me to my core—and fills me with determination. I don't know if it's just the after-effects of her attack, or something more, but it makes no fucking difference to me. Tessa thinks she has to be brave and handle this alone, but she's wrong.

I'm going to take care of her, and keep her safe, no matter what.

Even if she hates me for it.

Chapter Twenty-One
TESSA

I hate lying to Saint. Especially about this. But what could I tell him? *"Yeah, the creep in the mask was sent to warn me off my secret investigation into all your friends"*? So, I just told him the same story I told to the police and Ashford porter: that it was just a random attempted mugging, and he got scared off when he heard people coming.

But if they hadn't . . .

I shiver. I've been telling everyone I'm fine, but the truth is, I'm not. I couldn't sleep a wink last night, and even now, I flinch at every unexpected noise and passerby walking too close as I leave the apartment building and catch a bus across town. I'm still shaken up—from the blow that still hurts my ribs every time I make a sudden move, and the real reason behind the attack.

It wasn't so random. A stranger stalked me across the city and hunted me down to deliver his message.

Back off. Stop digging into the Blackthorn Society.

They know who I am, and what I'm doing, and they're willing to go to violent lengths to stop me.

Which only means one thing: I'm getting close to the truth.

* * *

"Jamie Richmond?"

I loiter in the classroom doorway as a horde of teenagers charge past me, joking and jostling. I have to step back fast to avoid being pushed over. I've tracked the author of the newspaper article to a high school on the outskirts of the city, and it couldn't be further away from the peaceful, ivy-clad walls of Ashford and the other Oxford colleges. Here, a nondescript concrete block building looks out over a parking lot, and the scuffed linoleum floors sit, dusty under strip neon lights.

"That's me." The guy wiping down the whiteboard looks over. He's in his mid-twenties, with tortoise-shell spectacles and a rumpled button-down that has an ink stain on the collar. "How can I help?" he asks, looking tired but cheerful. "If you're looking for the staff room, it's out of operation. Some kid trapped a skunk in there over the weekend, and, well, you can imagine the smell."

"I'm not a teacher here," I say, stepping into the room. "My name's Tessa Peterson? I emailed you a few days ago, about the article you wrote for the *Oxford Student*."

Jamie's smile disappears. "And I didn't reply," he says, turning back to the board.

"I know, but I really have to talk to you," I insist. "It's why I tracked you down and came here."

The attack made me realize that I couldn't just sit around and hope Jamie would reply. If the secret society is going to come after me, I need to be one step ahead of them.

I need to know exactly what I'm dealing with.

"It wasn't hard," I add, in case he's freaked out by my private investigator routine. "It says right on your website that you're teaching here."

Jamie sets down the eraser with a sigh. "I don't know what you expect me to say," he says, still eyeing me cautiously. "The paper retracted the article. Everyone agreed, it was libelous speculation."

"Except, we both know that's not true." I meet his eyes, making a last-ditch play. "Look, the Blackthorn Society exists. And I'm not stopping until I figure out the real story. So please, help me. You're a journalist, aren't you? It's your job to expose the truth."

Jamie snorts. "Look around," he says, bitterly nodding. "Does this look like a newsroom to you? That article cost me everything. My scholarship, my newspaper internships, my whole future. I wasn't born with a silver spoon in my mouth, I worked my whole life to get into Oxford, so I could make something of myself. And that was all taken from me. Gone."

"So, why not talk to me now?" I demand. "What have you got left to lose?"

Jamie pauses, and I cross my fingers. He's my only lead right now, and I have to know what happened. Finally, he sighs. "I don't have long," he says, warning.

"That's fine!" I swear, my hopes rising. "Anything you can tell me will help. No detail is too small."

He gives me a wry look. "When it comes to Blackthorn . . . nothing is small."

* * *

JAMIE LEADS ME to a quiet corner of the schoolyard, overlooking a dusty all-purpose play area where a Phys Ed class reluctantly runs laps.

"I thought the story was going to make my whole career," he says ruefully, unwrapping a homemade PB&J sandwich and taking a bite. "A big exclusive like that. We were all fighting to get attention from the big London newspapers, you see. If you could get a story in the national press while you were still a student . . . well, it opened all kinds of doors. I already had an internship lined up at a big news magazine, but I wanted more. And a story like that had everything: drama, secrets, famous names . . ."

"Like Cyrus Lancaster and Lionel Ambrose," I note.

He nods. "I didn't make it up," he says, looking over at me plaintively. "I know they painted me as a liar, fabricating sources, but every word of that article was the truth. I researched it for months, did dozens of interviews. The Blackthorn Society exits."

"I know," I reassure him. "I'm trying to find out more, but

there's nothing but dead ends. Everything's been scrubbed. I only found your article because there was a copy in the library basement," I add, and he chuckles.

"Yeah, the lawyers were thorough. But I guess Cyrus Lancaster can afford the best."

"That's who shut you down?" I ask, remembering his stony stare.

"It's just a guess, but yeah." Jamie shrugs. "Any one of them have the power and influence to do it. Pulling strings with the university, getting my internship pulled. I couldn't even find a job with the *Brighten & Hove Gazette*, once they were through with me. I was just a bug on the windscreen to them, and they crushed me."

"I'm sorry," I say quietly.

He shrugs. "It was my own fault. They warned me off, but I wanted to cause a splash."

"What do you mean, warnings?" I ask, feeling a chill.

"Once I started digging around, weird stuff started happening," Jamie explains. "Anonymous notes in my mailbox, a break-in at the dorms. One night, the newspaper office got trashed, they ransacked the computers, but nothing was taken. After that, I took my laptop with me everywhere. I didn't let it out of my sight."

I swallow hard. It sounds like threats and intimidation are just business as usual to the Blackthorn Society.

"Who was your source?" I ask.

Jamie looks cagey. "Who says I had one?"

"Come on," I sigh, impatient. "The details you published, about the initiation rituals and membership . . . something like that could only have come from the inside. Someone who'd seen things up close. Who was it?"

Jamie shakes his head. "I can't tell you."

"It's a little late for loyalty, don't you think?" I exclaim, frustrated. I'm so close to a breakthrough here, and if I could talk to a real-life member . . . "Your source didn't protect you from losing everything, having your name dragged through the mud. Everyone called you a liar. Why didn't you say who was feeding you information?"

"Because I don't know who it was!" Jamie finally admits. "They were anonymous. I got a note in my mailbox one day, saying they had information about the society. They would leave messages for me, behind the counter at this greasy café in the market that nobody ever went to," he continues. "Harry's, it was called. They sent all the information, about the initiation rituals, members . . . Even that photo, the one of Cyrus and all his powerful pals."

"And you never knew who it was?" I ask, my hopes sinking. "Not a name, or a clue?"

He shakes his head. "I tried staking out the place, fancied myself a real detective," he says wryly. "But I never figured it out. If it was one of the members themselves, who wanted to expose the group for some reason. Or someone who got close, who didn't think anyone would believe them. Either way, it didn't work. My story didn't make one jot of difference, to any of them. They're too powerful already," he says grimly. "Above scandal, above suspicion. Even above the law."

I feel a shiver again. Because Jamie's story hadn't contained anything really shocking—just the confirmation that the society existed. And still, they destroyed his life, as punishment for that one tiny truth.

And as a warning to anyone else who might be tempted to go public.

"Now it's my turn to ask you a question," Jamie says, sizing me up. "Why are you digging around in all of this? What's Blackthorn to you?"

I pause. "I think my sister may have been caught up in it, somehow," I say carefully. "She studied here, a year ago, and . . . something happened to her. I found out she was looking into secret societies at Oxford, and all the signs point to the Blackthorn Society being involved."

"What does she say?" Jamie asks, finishing his lunch.

"She died," I reply quietly. "That's why I came here, to find out more. I've been asking a lot of questions and last night . . ." I pause and swallow hard around the lump in my throat. "Last night, I was attacked. A guy in a mask, he warned me to stop digging around into Blackthorn."

Jamie looks concerned. "Maybe you should. There's no guessing how far these people will go."

I shake my head stubbornly. "I can't stop. I won't."

My determination must show, because he balls up his trash and tosses it in the dumpster. "I could ask around . . ." he says, getting a new spark in his eyes. "Go over some of my old notes, see if anything jumps out."

"Would you?" I ask, hopeful. "That would be great."

"Send me the information about your sister," he adds, and I can already see the journalistic wheels spinning in his mind. "Where she studied, what dates . . . but be careful," he warns me, serious. "Unravelling these people's secrets is a dangerous thing. You should know, you're asking for trouble."

"I know," I reply grimly. "But I've come this far. There's no turning back."

* * *

BY THE TIME I make it back to my apartment, I'm feeling exhausted and drained. The stakes of this investigation were always high, but things just escalated to a whole new level.

There's no guessing how far these people will go . . .

Jamie's words echo as I unlock the door and head straight for my bedroom, flopping down on my quilt with a sigh.

Except it's not there.

I sit up, confused, to find my room has been stripped bare. No clothes tossed over the back of the chair or hanging in the wardrobe, no study books piled on the desk. My laptop is gone, and all my makeup and toiletries, too.

Have we been robbed?

I rush into the living room, but it looks normal. Nothing out of place. I check my roommates' bedrooms, too, but there's nothing missing.

Only my things are gone.

Saint.

I realize in an instant what's happened here. He took my stuff. The bastard just packed up all my things and moved them out, without a single word.

Motherfucker.

I grab my jacket and storm out, heading straight over to his town house to hammer on the door.

Saint opens it immediately, barefoot and shirtless, wearing just a pair of washed-out jeans. Lust rolls through me at the sight of him—but my anger burns even hotter.

"Asshole," I scowl, jabbing my finger at his chest.

"Sweetheart," Saint replies, looking smug. "Come on in. I have a key cut for you," he adds, as he strolls down the hallway to the kitchen. "There's no need to knock."

"Asshole," I say again, louder this time. Fury beats through me—especially when I see a box of my things sitting on the table. "What the hell do you think you're playing at?" I demand. "I told you I wasn't moving in with you. N. O." I spell it out, spitting mad. "What part of that don't you understand?"

"The part where you're hurt, and shaken, and don't even want to spend the night alone in your own apartment!"

I step back, blinking. Saint looks just about as furious as I feel, practically shaking with tension.

"I . . . That's not the point." I frown, distracted by the fierce possession in his gaze.

"It's entirely the point," Saint roars. "Why do you have to be so goddamn stubborn?"

"By wanting to make decisions for myself?" I retort. "This is my life; you can't just bulldoze over me every time I don't agree with you!"

"Not every time," Saint replies grimly. "Just when you've been through a traumatic ordeal, and need someone to take care of you."

"I told you, I'm fine," I insist, even though it couldn't be further from the truth. "I don't need anyone—"

Saint curses, cutting me off.

"Would you give it a rest, for one minute?" he demands, face dark with fury. "You're not some superhero, you don't have to do this alone! Why won't you let me help you?" he demands. "Why won't you let your guard down for just one minute, and let me in? Christ, Tessa, when I heard that you'd been hurt . . ." Saint paces, dragging a hand through his unruly hair. "I goddamn near lost my mind! You think I like feeling this way?" he demands, moving closer to me. "No! But I'll be damned if anyone lays a finger on you from now on . . . except me."

Wow.

I'm frozen in place, stunned by the fierce passion in his gaze.

Stunned . . . and turned on. Because fuck, I've never seen Saint like this: desperate and undone. Out of control.

Because of me.

He stands there, just inches from me, breathing erratically. But despite the anger and frustration in his voice, his touch couldn't be gentler when he reaches out and tenderly cups my cheek. "Let me take care of you, Tessa," he says hoarsely, his eyes full of conflicted emotion. "Please . . . let me protect you. Just this once."

Emotion wells at his ragged plea, making me reach for him. Making me hold on tight.

Because I've been so alone in this.

I've taken care of myself, because I had to. Told myself everything will be OK because I've had no other choice. Trying so hard to reach Wren, to save her from herself—and failing.

Dealing with the heartbreaking aftermath of her death, hiding the truth from our parents and saving them the burden. Striking out on this mission to avenge her . . .

I've done it all by myself.

And now . . .

Now Saint is holding me tightly and telling me I don't have to be alone anymore. That I can depend on him. That he'll protect me, no matter what.

Something in me breaks wide open.

"Saint . . ." I whisper, lifting my face to his, needing to lose myself in his devastating kisses. To feel something other than the grief and rage and fear that are always haunting me.

Needing *him*. Like never before.

"Shh, darling, it's OK," Saint murmurs, kissing me softly. "I'm here now. I've got you. Everything's going to be OK."

His touch is reverent, slowly moving hair back from my eyes, and kissing me again, featherlight, as if I might break.

But I won't. I *can't*. I feel like all my defenses are crumbling down, and I don't know what I might reveal if Saint keeps gazing at me with that heartbreaking tenderness in his eyes.

I'll say too much.

I'll ruin everything.

So I squeeze my eyes tightly shut, and kiss him harder. Hungry and aching, needing the relief only he can provide.

Saint tries to draw back. "It's alright," he murmurs. "Slow down . . ."

"No!" I yank him back to me, holding on tight. Desperate to keep my secrets locked up where they belong.

Tenderness will be my undoing, but *passion* . . . ?

Passion will set me free, the way only he knows how.

I run my hands over his bare chest, down to the waistband of his jeans. "Saint, please . . . I want you," I demand breathlessly. "All of you. *Now*."

His eyes darken with lust, realizing that I mean it. And then he's kissing me again—not so gentle anymore, as hot and hungry as my own fevered embrace.

Yes.

I moan against his mouth as we stumble across the kitchen. I arch up, loving the feel of Saint's body, hot and hard against me, his hands already tearing at my clothes.

I help him, eagerly stripping off my T-shirt and shoving down my jeans.

"Upstairs," he tries to tell me, but I shake my head, already wet and aching for him.

"No," I insist, stubborn. "Here. *Now.*"

Saint groans, suddenly spinning me around and shoving me face-first against the wall. My pulse kicks with excitement, and I press my palms against the smooth surface, bracing myself for balance as Saint kisses and nips at the back of my neck. His hands move around to cup my breasts, squeezing and palming the tender flesh as he thrusts his hard-on against my ass.

I moan, head falling back against his shoulder.

"Is this what you want, baby?" Saint growls behind me, low in my ear. His expert fingers work me into a frenzy, pinching and plucking my aching nipples into two stiff peaks. "You need it fast and dirty?"

"Yes," I gasp, as he roughly shoves my underwear down. "God, yes. *Please . . .*"

My plaintive cry echoes as his fingers find my core, rubbing my clit swiftly, sending pleasure ricocheting through my trembling body. "Saint!" I cry out, bucking against his hand. He moves lower, dipping into my wetness, and I moan, trying to take his fingers deeper.

"Fuck, Tessa . . ."

I hear the sound of his zipper, and then Saint's hands are on my hips. He pushes my legs wider, positioning me there up against the wall.

Then I feel his cock nudging, hot and hard against my entrance.

I tense, remembering the thick girth of him, and how I struggled to fit him in my mouth. But Saint pets my clit again, rubbing swiftly until I'm gasping.

Then slowly, he sinks inside me.

Fuck.

My moan echoes, mingling with his low groan of pleasure as he sinks his thick cock deeper, pushing relentlessly until he's buried to the hilt.

"Christ, Tessa . . ." Saint's breath is hot in my ear. He grips my hips tightly from behind, his body shaking, coiled with tension. "You feel so good, so goddamn tight for me."

I gasp for air, stretched wide, filled completely with his cock. But before I can even adjust to the invasion, he snaps his hips back and thrusts into me again. Harder this time. Deeper. So deep. *Fuck . . .*

"Saint," I sob, thrusting back to meet him, pure animal instinct taking over as we find a filthy, groaning rhythm. The friction is incredible, the thick drag of his cock stroking my inner walls just right. Already, I can feel my body start to tense, driving higher with every sinful thrust. "Don't stop," I gasp, pushed up on my tiptoes now with the force of his strokes, cheek pressed to the wall, my whole body pinned there and trembling as I take his cock. Over and over again. I moan, lost in the heat of it, going out of my mind. "God, Saint . . . Don't you dare stop!"

Saint pauses at my words, still buried deep inside. "What was that, darling?" he murmurs, trailing his mouth over my bare shoulder, making me shudder and clench around his cock. "Giving me an order?"

He eases out of me, leaving me empty and panting. I wail in protest and try to turn, but Saint keeps me trapped there, at his mercy.

"You can't have it both ways, baby," he teases, nipping at my earlobe as I shake. "If you want me to take care of you . . ." He lazily strokes over my clit, making me moan. "Then you have to let me *take care* of you, too."

I suck in a breath of realization. "Bastard," I mutter, finally seeing his game.

Saint's chuckle sounds, low and smug. "Move in with me," he demands softly, sinking his cock into me again, just the tip. I whimper, struggling in his arms. Needing more. But he holds me in an iron grip, right there on the brink of pleasure. Waiting for me to submit. "Let me protect you. Say you'll stay."

He sinks another inch inside me, and I clench around him, sobbing with a desperate, raw need. Is it crazy that I love this, knowing he can control my pleasure so effortlessly? The low, steely tenor of his voice, the vice-like grip on my hips . . . it only adds to the inferno burning through my body, crying out for more.

"Is that a yes?" Saint demands, caressing my swollen clit. Shivers gather in my toes, racing through my bloodstream. Oh God, I'm close. So fucking close.

"Bastard," I pant again, writhing. But it's futile, I know. Saint is determined, and I . . .

I want nothing more than to fall.

"Yes," I blurt, my voice rising to a cry. "Yes, I'll stay!"

Saint groans in satisfaction. "Good girl," he praises me, finally thrusting deep to fill me in one wicked stroke. "That's my good fucking girl . . ."

Oh fuck.

My orgasm breaks through me like a tidal wave, fierce and relentless, drowning everything in its path. I throw back my head and wail, my legs giving way as my body shakes with ecstasy.

"Tessa . . ." Saint doesn't pause for breath, pinning me in place up against the wall with every thick, merciless thrust. His hips snap faster. Deeper. *Fuck.* "Tess—"

A second climax hits me, blinding, and I scream with the force of it as Saint lets out an animal roar, shuddering into me. I feel his body spasm with the force of his release, until we're both slumped and gasping, lost to the pleasure.

Oh my God.

* * *

MY MIND IS thick and hazy with bliss when Saint finally pulls out of me. He zips up his pants, then lifts me effortlessly and carries me upstairs to the dim bedroom, setting me gently on the bed. "Do you need anything?" he asks, passing me a glass of water, and then going to the dresser where, of course, my night things are already folded, neatly in place. He picks out my favorite comfortable pajamas and brings them over to me, as tender now as he was thrillingly merciless only moments ago. "You can take a nap, while I make dinner. Or we can order in. What would you like?"

He looks down at me, so considerate. Slowly, my senses come back to me, and I realize what just happened.

"Don't ever do that again."

Saint blinks, surprised by my words—and harsh, determined tone. "What's wrong? Did I hurt you?" he asks, concern flashing on his face.

"No." I shake my head. "It was . . . amazing. Mind-blowing, even. The best sex of my life!"

Saint relaxes, grinning.

"But you knew that," I continue. "And you used it to manipulate me and make me agree to something I already refused." I glare at him and fold my arms. Sure, I'm naked in his bed after coming my brains out—twice—but I need him to know I'm serious here. "I'll stay here with you, for a little while—because *I* want to," I emphasize. "But you can't ever use sex like that against me again. Fuck me because you want me, because this chemistry between us is off-the-charts hot. But don't you dare fuck me as some kind of power move, to make me submit to your plans."

I hold his gaze, determined. Saint nods, looking chastened.

"You're right," he says, exhaling. "I'm sorry. I just couldn't stand the thought of you alone and scared."

I soften. "Me either," I admit softly. "Which is why I'm going to shower, and put on my pajamas, and you're going to cook me something delicious, and we're going to watch a stupid movie until I fall asleep. Safely. Here with you. Because that's *my* choice, not yours."

"I'm sorry," Saint says again. He leans in and kisses me, and I finally relax in his arms. "But the sex part," he whispers, cheeky. "We're going to do that again?"

I laugh. "Oh, yes. Count on it."

Chapter Twenty-Two
TESSA

When I wake, Saint is sleeping in bed beside me, his naked body sprawled under the sheets.

I pause, admiring the sight of his toned back, and the muscular curve of his biceps. After all the drama, I've never slept better: passing out halfway through the movie so Saint wound up carrying me back upstairs and tucking me into bed with a tender goodnight kiss.

Now, I'm tempted to wake him, but I've been called to a meeting with my academic supervisor. The terse email told me to be waiting at her office at nine a.m. sharp. She didn't mention why.

A second round of blazing hot sex will just have to wait.

I slip out of bed and into the bathroom to take a long, luxurious shower. The list of perks being Saint's houseguest is growing by the hour; compared to the sputter of lukewarm water back at the student flat, the jets here are pure bliss, pummeling my tired limbs until I'm refreshed and wide awake. I towel off, then pause by the mirror, examining the ugly bruise that's bloomed on my rib cage. I trace the site of impact and wince. It's another reminder that I need to be more careful now.

My questions have consequences.

Still, I have to admit that I feel safer already, staying here with Saint. The town house is secure, with a modern security system. Dozens of people come and go at all hours of the day from the student apartment block, but here, we're located on a quiet street, and anyone hanging around will draw attention. At least, that's what Saint reassured me. And it's a relief to linger as long as I like, blow-drying my hair, without wondering if my roommates are whispering about me in the next room. I sent Jia a quick text last night, explaining that I've gone to stay with a friend.

She didn't respond. Not even to ask if I was doing OK.

Saint is out of bed when I return, already dressed and buttoning his shirt. He looks delicious, there in the morning light, and I feel a strange sense of warmth blossom in my chest.

Comforted, and calm.

"Good morning." He looks up, smiling when he sees me. "Am I going to wake up to a vision like this every day?"

I laugh, my hair still damp, and dark circles still lingering under my eyes. "Flattery will get you everywhere," I tease, pulling him down for another kiss, longer this time. Then, reluctantly, I break away. "I need to get to college," I say, sighing. "I've been summoned."

I show him the email. "Ouch," Saint says, then catches my nervous expression. "I'm sure it'll be fine. You can be very charming, when you like," he adds.

"Somehow, I don't think my charms will work half as well on Ms. Latimer as they do on you," I joke wryly.

"I don't know about that." Saint grins. "Maybe you're just her type. And I could always put in a call for you. I have some pull here," he adds, smirking. "The Ashford name and all . . ."

I shake my head. "Thanks, but I don't think that'll help."

"Then let's meet for breakfast, after. I have some time before my first class."

"Wait, you *teach* here?" I ask, teasing. "I just thought you hung around, hitting on sexy grad students."

"Hush you." Saint lands a light tap on my ass. "If I recall, you have a paper due."

I wince. And his assignment isn't the only one waiting for me.

"A quick breakfast," I agree. "Very quick. Because I'm going to have to spend the rest of the day in the library."

* * *

I FINISH DRESSING, and quickly walk over to Ashford. I can't stop glancing over my shoulder and wondering if that masked man is still on my trail. But it's bright and busy out in town, with plenty of people around, and I'm reassured that the porters are keeping a watchful eye on the front gate, checking student IDs of everyone who passes through.

Unless my attacker is a student here, too . . .

No. I shove that thought aside and try to focus on the problem right in front of me. Ms. Latimer, my supervisor, is waiting in her office with a stern look. "Good morning," I say brightly, as I enter the room.

"Miss Peterson. Take a seat."

Oh boy. I brace myself as I take a seat across from her desk. Ms. Latimer is an intimidating woman at the best of times, with a severe grey bob and matching tweed, but today, she's got an extra-disapproving look in her eyes.

"I assume you know why you're here?"

I gulp. Has she discovered I'm snooping around, here under false pretenses? "I . . . um . . . I'm not sure." I offer an innocent smile. "Is something wrong?"

She shuffles some papers in front of her. "I've heard concerning reports," she begins, and I sink a little lower in my seat. "Your tutors are worried you're falling behind. It's still early in the term, but you've been late with a number of your essays, and your performance in tutorials has left something to be desired."

This is about my academic performance? I let out a breath of relief. But no sooner have I relaxed than Ms. Latimer fixes me with a look.

"You understand, of course, that as an Ashford Scholar, we

have certain expectations. A commitment to your studies. Perhaps we were mistaken, extending the placement to you—"

"No!" I blurt, panicking. "I'm sorry, I know I'm a little behind, but . . . it's been an adjustment, I guess. I'll make it up, I swear," I add quickly.

Ms. Latimer gives me an assessing look. "Oxford is an exacting environment, and not everybody is suited to the rigors of Ashford's high academic standards. There would be no shame in deciding it wasn't the right place for you."

No shame, maybe. But it would stop my investigation dead in its tracks. My student visa is tied to this program. There's no way I can leave.

"I'll work harder," I vow. "Whatever it takes. I'm committed to this program, I promise."

Ms. Latimer arches an eyebrow. "I understand it's easy to be *distracted* . . . but I would hate to see a promising scholar sent off course by, let's say, certain extracurricular activities. However charming they may seem."

I blink. She's talking about Saint, I realize. Clearly, word travels fast in a place like this.

I fix her with an even smile. "I'm not distracted." Not just by him, anyway. "I'll get back on track, I promise."

"See that you do, Miss Peterson."

* * *

After a few more promises to get my shit together, I leave the office, grab some fruit from the commissary, and head straight to the library.

Can't do breakfast, I text Saint. *Got the riot act from Latimer. Will be at the library until the end of time.*

Good luck, he replies. *I'll see you tonight.*

I settle in to work, and my head is aching by the time my stomach rumbles loud enough to break me from my panicked studying.

I check my phone. It's four p.m. already—and I've missed a message from Jamie Richmond. He wants to meet.

I quickly text him back. He's in the city now, and sends me an address, a café in the center of town. I pause, glancing guiltily at my pile of books. But it's no competition. Anything that can lead me closer to this society and Wren's attacker will always be my first choice.

I grab my bag and walk quickly to meet him. The café is in the courtyard of an old, converted church, bustling with old folks fresh from choir practice taking tea and cake.

"Tessa." Jamie waves me over to a discreet corner, in the shadow of some trees.

"Hi," I say, breathless from my rushing. "Did you find something? What's going on?"

Jamie glances around, clearly nervous, and beckons me further from the crowds. "I may have something . . ." he says, looking jittery. "I went over my old notes, and the materials the anonymous source left for me."

"And?" I urge, trying to hide my impatience.

"And they mentioned something about an annual Blackthorn meeting. Some kind of big event, where they all gather and do . . . well, whatever powerful secret societies do," he says. "My source said it's traditionally on the same date every year. The second Sunday in October."

I quickly do the math. The weekend Wren was taken. "That's in a few days!"

He nods.

"So where's the event held?" I ask eagerly. "What are the details? How do I get in?"

"Woah." Jamie holds up his hand to stop me. "That's all I know. I don't have any more information, but even if I did . . . you can't just show up there, are you crazy? An event like that—even *if* it's happening—will have security for miles around. And what are you expecting to find, anyway?" he asks.

I pause. Dammit, he's right. What would my plan even be? I can't just waltz in and ask people point-blank if they're connected to Wren's attack?

I sigh in frustration. "Was there anything else?" I ask. "Any lead to current members who might be willing to talk?"

Jamie shakes his head. "Anyone I approached stonewalled me. They know better than to go spilling secrets and causing trouble. And you should too. These people don't fuck around," he adds, warning me.

"I know," I say, instinctively bringing a hand to my bruised ribs. "But I can't stop."

Jamie glances around again, nervous. "I have to go," he says. "But . . . maybe it would be best if you don't contact me again. At least, not for a while. Something feels off about this."

"Come on," I urge him. "Don't you want to find the truth, after everything they've done to you?"

"Yes, but I know when to quit." Jamie gives me a regretful smile. "Good luck."

He turns on his heel, and ducks into the crowd, weaving his way out of the courtyard past—

Saint.

I stop dead. He's standing by the gates, watching me. And he doesn't look happy. Clearly, he's just seen my conversation with Jamie.

Shit.

I put up my hand and force a cheerful wave. "Hey," I greet him, walking over. "What a nice surprise."

"Is it?" he asks, frowning. "I thought you said you were locked in the library all day. Who is that guy?"

"He's, um . . ." I wrack my brains desperately for a cover story, but Saint fixes me with a piercing look.

"You've been keeping secrets from me, Tessa. Now tell me, what's going on?"

Chapter Twenty-Three
TESSA

I stand there, frozen in place, my mind racing.

Saint folds his arms, glaring at me. "Well?" he prompts, and I hate it, but I have to lie to him. Again.

"I *was* studying," I say brightly. "That was Jamie. He's in one of my lectures, and I've been falling behind, so he agreed to meet and lend me his notes—"

"Bullshit." Saint cuts me off with a scornful look. "Come on, Tessa, I'm not an idiot, so don't treat me like one. What's going on? I know there's something you're not telling me. I think I've known it since the day we first met," he adds, studying me. "You hold back when we're talking, like you're deciding what you can say. You're evasive, you're keeping me at arm's length—"

"I just moved in with you!" I protest, trying to steer the conversation away from dangerous territory, but Saint stands firm.

"Yes, and I still feel like you're miles away, even when we're in the same room." He exhales a ragged breath. "Tessa, I've tried to be patient, and wait for you to open up at your own pace, but I'm sick of the lies and half-truths. I've been totally honest with you, about the good and the bad. I'm a goddamn open book. But I need to know, what is it that you're hiding from me?"

I open my mouth, but no words come out. It's ironic, this man makes me feel more bold and liberated than I've ever felt before, but when it comes to revealing this, I quake with insecurity.

Can I trust him? I wonder, searching his handsome face.

What will he think when he knows the real reason that brought us together?

"You can tell me anything." Saint moves closer, cupping my face in his hands. His eyes search mine, open and sincere. "I promise, there's nothing you can say that will shock me, or change the way I see you."

I shake my head, pulling away. "You don't understand."

"So try me," he challenges hotly. "Give me a chance to prove that this connection between us, it's real. It matters to me."

"It matters to me too," I whisper, feeling torn up inside. Caught in a battle between my secrets and the inexplicable instinct to confess it all. "And I want to be honest, I do, it's just . . ."

"What?" Saint demands. "For Christ's sake, Tessa. It can't be anything as bad as all the suspicions I have spinning in my head now. Are you seeing that guy?" he adds, nodding in the direction that Jamie fled. "If you have, it's OK. I mean, my pride will take quite a beating, but we never said this was exclusive—"

"No," I tell him right away. "It's not that. There's nobody else."

"Then *what*?" Saint throws up his hands, frustrated. I can tell he's on the brink of just walking away. Leaving me and my fucked-up secrets behind him. Washing his hands of me for good.

I don't want to lose him. And more than that, I don't want to lie to him anymore.

"I came to Oxford for a reason," I blurt, before I can overthink it. "Someone hurt my sister. I'm trying to find the man who attacked her. I'm going to make him pay!"

There's silence for a moment, as Saint looks at me in confusion. Whatever he expected to hear, it clearly wasn't this.

"That's what I've been hiding from you," I admit, my heart pounding. "The sneaking around, the lies . . . it's all because of Wren."

I wait, on edge, wondering if I just made a massive mistake. Saint's expression is unreadable as he stands there, processing my words.

Have I just ruined everything?

Then he takes a deep breath. "Tell me everything," he says. "Start at the beginning."

* * *

WE TAKE A walk from the town center out to a leafy area by the river, where there aren't so many people around. Saint listens patiently as I tell the whole story, from Wren's time at Oxford, to her attack and tragic suicide.

"That's why I came here," I say, feeling a tightness in my chest. We sit on a bench overlooking the water, as a group of ducks glide by. The scenery is so innocent and bright, it makes a sharp contrast to the dark story I'm telling. "My studies are just a cover, so I could get on the inside at Ashford College and figure out who might have done this. Because I have to find out who attacked her, and drove her to take her own life," I say fiercely. "They need to face justice for what they've done."

There's a long silence. Saint stares straight ahead, and I can see the flicker of tension in his jaw.

"Is this why you got close to me?" he asks finally, his voice cool. "So that I would introduce you to Max? Take you to the Lancaster party, so you could retrace Wren's steps?"

"No!" I cry immediately. "I didn't even know about them, not until after the Midnight party, when we'd already . . . when we were . . ." I trail off.

Having wild, mind-blowing sexual adventures that made my head spin and my body hum. Surrendering to the blazing hot chemistry I couldn't resist.

"When I thought there was something real between us," Saint finishes, icy. He turns to me, betrayal in his eyes. "You used me."

I shake my head. "You're the one who pursued me," I remind him. "You wouldn't quit, you sent all those texts, and gifts, showed up. I thought . . ."

"You thought you'd kill two birds with one stone," Saint says, getting to his feet. Hurt and anger mingle in his expression. "Have a little fun fucking the professor and pick up some clues about Wren at the same time."

"No!" I leap to my feet and start after him. "I didn't know what to think, OK? What happened between us took me by surprise. It wasn't part of my plan. All I had were these cryptic clues, about Wren and the Blackthorn Society—"

Saint flinches at the mention.

I stop, registering his reaction. Which can only mean . . .

"You know it," I breathe, moving closer. "*Legacy is a gift, and our sworn bond*," I quote, and I can tell he knows exactly what that means. "You're a member, aren't you? You're one of them!"

He pauses, unreadable emotions flashing on his face. And my heart sinks.

I suspected he was a part of it, but I didn't really consider what that meant.

"All this time I've been explaining and justifying my actions to you," I say, backing away from him. "Maybe it should have been the other way around."

"I don't know what you mean," Saint says quickly, and I give a bitter laugh.

"All that talk about being an open book was bullshit. You've got secrets, too. Only yours might wind up getting me hurt—or worse. It wasn't a random mugging," I add. "That was your friends in the Blackthorn Society, sending me a message. A warning, to stop digging in their business."

Saint looks shocked. "What the fuck, Tessa? You didn't say."

"And you wonder why?" I demand, furious. "I can't be sure where your loyalties lie!"

"You're saying I had something to do with that bastard hurting you? With what happened to Wren?" Saint asks, looking outraged.

"No." I glare. "But one of your fancy friends sure did."

"You don't know that," he protests, but I shake my head, feeling foolish. I thought coming clean to him would be a relief, a weight off my shoulders—but instead, it might have been my biggest mistake.

"You're part of the Blackthorn Society," I say accusingly. "Which means you're honor bound to protect them—no matter what their crimes."

"You don't have any evidence they're connected!" Saint retorts angrily. "Just some anonymous notes, and a vague motto. You're going around accusing people off nothing but rumors and conspiracies!"

"Yeah, well it's funny how those conspiracies have all turned out true so far," I say grimly. "You need to think about whose side you're on. Because if it turns out to be one of your friends who hurt my sister . . . I won't hesitate. I'll burn their entire fucking world to the ground. And I won't stop to see who else gets caught in the flames."

Saint face changes, turning cold again. "Well, thank you, Ms. Peterson," he says, all formal tones. "You've made it quite clear what you think of me. You should be proud," he adds bitterly. "Your investigation tactics have proven quite the success. Here I was, falling for you, and I never thought for a moment you were just fucking me for information about my friends."

Guilt strikes through me, but he's already walking away.

Fuck.

Saint leaves me standing on the riverbank, lost in a whirlwind of conflicted emotion.

I should have seen this coming.

The moment I realized that Saint was likely involved with the Blackthorn Society, I should have stayed the hell away from him. But instead, I couldn't resist his charms. Not just the wild, reckless sex, as unbelievable as it is, but the way he makes me feel—like the woman I was before tragedy turned my world dark and full of rage. He urged me on, made me laugh, encouraged me to follow my passion for the Ambrose Foundation job . . . unlocking a new direction I didn't know I wanted. Swearing to protect me, even when I insisted I didn't need him to.

My heart aches from the bitter words we just exchanged, but still, I find myself returning to his town house and using my key to let myself inside.

I pace, restless, conflicted about what to do next. Should I pack up my things and leave, or stay, and wait it out to talk some more? Not because I want whatever information he can give me about the Blackthorn Society, but because I need him to understand that I didn't set out to hurt or betray him.

I care about him. More than I've wanted to admit. And if there's even a chance he might feel the same way, despite all my lies . . . I have to take the risk. Otherwise, I know I'll always wonder. Did I give up on him too soon? Assume the worst about him, the way he accused me?

My gut tells me the connection between us is real. But real enough to weather this storm? I don't know just yet.

So I stay.

* * *

THE HOURS PASS, and still Saint doesn't return. The night darkens outside the windows, and my fears run riot. He could go straight to his friends in the society and tell them everything. Warn them about my investigation, and ensure that I'll never find the truth . . .

I try to calm my nerves by lighting some candles and running a bubble bath. I sink into the steamy water, wondering if I'm a fool for even thinking he might choose my side, when I hear a key in the door downstairs. Footsteps sound, and then Saint enters the bedroom. I see him throw his jacket on the bed, before he turns and notices me.

He moves to linger in the open doorway. He has a bottle of

whiskey and a glass in one hand, already worse for wear. "You're still here," he says, with a faint slur in his voice.

I nod, feeling self-conscious in the tub, naked save the bubbles up around my chest.

Saint leans against the wall, sliding down until he's sitting there, sprawled on the floor. He looks about as torn up inside as I feel, with his shirt rumpled, and his hair in disarray.

"What do you want to know?" he asks, finally looking at me from across the room.

I blink. "What?"

I was expecting more fighting and recrimination, not the low sincerity in his voice.

"What do you want to know about Blackthorn?" Saint asks me, point-blank and direct. "Because if you think it was somehow involved in your sister's attack . . . I'll help you. We'll find the answers. Together."

My heart leaps. Still, I fight to keep my head. "But . . . they're your friends." I venture, unsure. "What about your sworn loyalty and oaths? You've known all these guys for years."

Saint pours a measure of whiskey into his glass and knocks it back, looking grim. "If any one of them did this, hurt Wren, they're no friend of mine. Whoever this bastard is . . . they need to pay for what they've done. You can count on me to help."

He's on my side.

The realization rolls through me, and I exhale in a rush, relieved. "I'm sorry I didn't tell you sooner," I admit. "I just didn't know if I could trust you. Wren trusted the wrong people," I add, feeling an ache. "And look how that turned out."

Saint gets up. He crosses the room, kicks off his shoes, and then, before I can protest, he gets in the tub with me, fully clothed.

"Saint!" I exclaim, as water sloshes to the floor. "What are you doing?"

He sits opposite, facing me, and takes my hands. Soaked through all his clothes. "I won't let anyone hurt you again," he promises, gazing intently into my eyes. "I swear, Tessa, you can count on me. You don't have to carry this alone anymore."

His mouth covers mine in a searing kiss, heated and full of a passion that pulls me into its whirlwind. I sink into his embrace, kissing back hungrily, suddenly overwhelmed with emotion. I've been worried if he would even believe me, or just try to brush off what happened to Wren and close ranks with his buddies in the society. Boys being boys.

Loyalty over justice, just like it always is.

But Saint holds me tightly, promising that we'll uncover the truth, together. However uncomfortable that truth might be.

He's choosing me.

Saint dips his head to my collarbone, trailing fire through my bloodstream with every kiss. I moan as hands move to cup my wet breasts, caressing them, lifting to lavish them with his tongue.

"Saint . . ." I gasp in pleasure as he closes his lips around my nipple and sucks. I arch up against his mouth, writhing, not caring that my restless movements send more water sloshing out of the tub.

"God, look at you." Saint lifts his head long enough to sweep his gaze over me, half-masked by the bubbles, my hair falling wet into the water. "My sweet, dirty girl. I could worship you forever . . . that mouth of yours . . . these perfect tits . . . and *here*." He slips a hand between my thighs and strokes, curling his fingers up into my slick heat.

I shudder, clenching around him. "More," I gasp, and he chuckles.

"Oh, there's more for you, baby. You can have it all."

Saint shifts us, moving so that I'm the one on top now, rising up out of the bubbles, straddling his lap. He returns to my breasts, licking and sucking at my sensitive flesh until I'm gasping, grinding on him, seeking out the hard ridge of his cock.

He groans.

"Need you," I moan softly, dipping my head, biting down on his lower lip. "Inside me . . . *Please* . . ."

I reach down, fumbling with his soaked pants until Saint helps me undo his belt and zip, freeing his cock. The water moves, warm around us, bubbles clouding the surface as I position myself above him, and then sink down, slowly taking his hard length inside.

"Fuck, Tessa . . ."

Saint groans, gripping my hips tightly as I seat myself fully, clenching him all the way to the hilt.

Oh God.

It's different like this. Deeper. More intense. And straddling Saint, facing him this time, I can see the burning heat in his gaze, and every ripple of fierce self-control that crosses his face.

"That's right, baby," he growls, as I tremble there above him, trying to adjust to the incredible stretch. "Take every inch of this cock like you own it. Show me what you need."

I inhale a shuddering breath, and rise again, sinking back down on his cock in one swift motion. Friction shivers through me, hitting inside and out, so perfect, I toss my head back and whimper with pleasure. "Saint . . ." I moan, grinding deeper, rubbing against him as I start to move.

"You feel that?" Saint matches my rhythm, thrusting up, deep inside me as I ride him. "Feel how well you're taking me, how perfectly we fit."

He takes my palm and presses it to my lower abdomen, and *fuck*, I can feel the outline of his cock moving inside me, the pressure of our hands making the friction even more intense. "Ride it," he groans, slipping his hand lower, so his fingertips brush my swollen clit. I mewl at the added sensation, but he doesn't stop, just strokes again, toying with me, in time with every deep, thick thrust.

God, it's so good. *Too good.* Already, I can feel my body tremble. Stuttering, my movements slow, overwhelmed. "Saint," I whimper, gasping for air. Needing more but stranded here on the precipice. "Saint, *please . . .*"

"I've got you, darling. I've always got you."

With a growl, Saint pistons his hips, thrusting up into me, hitting just right. "You need that extra inch, don't you, sweet-heart?" he groans, pumping faster. Gripping my hip to control my movements. Bouncing me on his thick cock. "You need it so fucking deep, you can't take any more."

"Yes!" I cry, clutching at his shoulders, holding on for dear life. Every thick drag of his dick inside me is a miracle, the pleasure coiling tightly now, ready to explode.

"But it's not quite enough now, is it?" Saint's voice is thick with lust. "You want a little more . . ."

He bends his head to my breasts again, and sucks one nipple into his mouth. Hard. I yelp, as the pressure only intensifies. *Too much.* "Saint, please—*Oh.*"

He nips the stiff bud sharply as he thrusts up inside, and *fuck*, sensation shatters through me, a heady mix of pleasure edged with a sting of pain.

"You need both," Saint growls, possessive, turning to my other breast. He grazes his teeth over the tender flesh, making me mewl. "We all do, darling. Nothing makes us feel more alive."

He lands a stinging slap on my ass, then smooths over the wet, aching flesh. His fingers stray between my cheeks, caressing the taut flesh as I shudder and sob, lost to it now. Arching against him. Out of my goddamn mind.

"I'll show you what pleasure truly means," he vows. "We haven't even scratched the surface. I'll show you *everything.*"

He rears into me, the head of his cock finding some sweet spot, deep in my inner walls. And then he grinds, relentless, as my body shudders in his lap. Over and over, he rubs me deep, playing my body like an instrument he owns, until there's nothing I can do but let the wave break over me, swift and sweet.

"Saint!" I scream, climaxing with a howl. "Oh God, oh my God!"

The pleasure slams through me, but Saint doesn't stop. He fucks me right through it in a frenzy, using my convulsing body for his pleasure as I come again, and again, screaming his name as I spasm around his cock.

"Tessa!" He sounds my name in a hoarse roar, rearing up one final time to impale himself deep; his body taken over by a shuddering climax as his mouth finds mine in a desperate kiss.

We cling together, wet and breathless, and fuck, I couldn't move to save my own life. I'm liquid, melted into his arms, shaken by the intensity of the moment.

Because now I know that I'm not alone anymore.

We're in this together.

Chapter Twenty-Four
TESSA

I t's all led to this.

Saint agrees to take me to the Blackthorn Society event, to finally find the answers about Wren. As I dress the next evening, it feels like my whole body is tangled up with nerves. But when I check my reflection in the mirror, I can see only determination written on my face. Because the anonymous notes, the secret society clues, everything Wren was able to tell me, it's all led me here, to this moment. Tonight.

I'm finally getting answers.

I hear footsteps, and then Saint is in the doorway. He's dressed up in a tux, looking impossibly dashing as he fumbles with his bowtie.

"How can you not tie one of these by now?" I smile, going to fasten it for him.

He grins. "Maybe I can, and this is just a ruse to have you touching me."

Saint yanks me into his arms, running his hands over the curves of my body beneath my silk dress. "Have I told you yet how much I love this outfit?" he says, stroking over the fabric. "I have *very* fond memories of you in this dress . . ."

I flush. It's the same classic black slip I wore to the Midnights party, the first night I realized there was more to Saint than I'd imagined. I can't believe how much has passed between us since then. That night, he was still a stranger to me, an enticing man who somehow knew my most sinful desires. Now, there's more between us than simply a sexual bond.

As I lean up to press my lips against his in a slow, sweet kiss, I feel a wave of trust and reassurance. "You won't leave my side?" I check, still not sure what to expect. If these people were all at the same party last year, when Wren was taken . . .

Saint nods, looking just as determined as I feel. "I promise. I won't let you out of my sight. The first part of the event is always members only," he adds. "Then, later, security usually gets lax. Everyone's having too much fun to pay attention, so sometimes people sneak in other guests."

"Like an after-party?" I ask, thinking of Max Lancaster. He seems the kind of guy who would want the party to last all night.

He nods. "That's probably how Wren got in. *If* she was there at all," he adds.

"She was," I insist. "I showed you the photo. And the dates match."

"But . . ." He pauses, looking concerned. "What if you don't find anything? You don't know for sure that any of it is connected," he adds gently.

"It is. And we'll find out," I insist. The alternative is unthinkable to me right now, not after all the time I've spent searching, and planning, and burning for revenge. "Whatever happened to Wren, this party is the key to everything."

Saint squeezes my hand. "Then let's go."

* * *

THE BLACKTHORN SOCIETY party is held in a different location each year, and this time, it turns out it's being hosted at Ashford House.

Saint's family home.

"Well, I was curious to see your family's place," I venture, trying to make a joke as we make the drive out to Sussex. "Now I'll get the guided tour!"

We arrive in late afternoon, the sinking sun casting a warm glow over the hills and woodland. Saint gives our details to the security posted at the gates, and then we drive up the long, tree-lined driveway to the main house.

But, of course, "house" doesn't even begin to describe it. The estate is even larger and grander than the Lancaster Manor: a sprawling red-brick Tudor house with so many wings, and turrets, and glittering, iron-paned windows that I'm dizzy just looking up at it.

"*This* is where you grew up?" I ask Saint, wide-eyed. It's like something from a period drama on TV, the kind of estate that even Mr. Darcy would be impressed by.

But Saint doesn't look so thrilled to be back. "It's a nightmare to keep heated," is all he says, as he steers me to the wide, ceremonial front steps, with a line of security in black uniforms keeping watch at every level.

OK then.

"There are a lot of people here . . ." I add, frowning, as I clock the rows of expensive, gleaming vehicles already parked out front.

"Not so many," Saint says, taking my hand. "It's early yet."

I follow him through the lavish main foyer, distracted for a moment by the grand staircase and double-height wood-paneled walls lined with oil portraits and historic suits of armor. The house is incredible, and I hope we have a chance to explore it, but as we emerge out to the back terrace and survey the party gathered there, my heart sinks.

There are *hundreds* of people in attendance.

I take in the scene. People of all ages from nineteen to ninety are dressed up in swanky formal-wear, talking and laughing happily, the crowd spilling over the huge main terrace area and down a wide stone staircase to the rose-lined patio and lush grounds below. There's music, an open bar, even amusements like croquet and badminton on the lawn, which stretches for what must be a full acre, down to the edge of a lake which is glittering in the sinking sun.

It looks like any other fancy reunion party. A stunning and lavish display of wealth and influence, sure. But the place where dark deeds are plotted, and I'll finally discover the truth?

"What?" Saint murmurs, noticing my crestfallen expression.

"I thought . . ." I flush, feeling foolish. "I guess I just thought a secret society gathering would be more . . . *secret*."

"You mean, gathering in a gloomy crypt somewhere to make a sacrificial offering to some demonic power?" Saint asks, looking amused.

My blush deepens. "No," I lie. But as two polished women in their thirties rush past us to hug, loudly shrieking their delight at catching up after all these years, I feel my determination slip. Ever since I found the first whispers about the Blackthorn Society and their vast power and influence, they've loomed large in my imagination—something ominous.

Something deadly.

I thought gaining entrance to their annual gathering would point me to the answers I need.

But these aristocrats gushing over the amazing Botox the other had done?

This wasn't what I was expecting.

I shake my head, trying to think clearly. Just because things look perfectly innocent on the surface, it doesn't mean nothing bad is lurking out of sight. Everyone has secrets, I remind myself, as Saint leads me deeper into the party.

I just have to dig deeper to find them.

* * *

WE CIRCULATE, AND Saint introduces me to a few people, stopping to chat and catch up with old friends. "We haven't seen you in a while," one red-faced man grins, squeezed into a shiny dinner jacket.

"You know me." Saint gives a vague shrug, and the man chortles.

"To tell the truth, I was going to skip this year, too. Formula One in Monaco, half the old gang is out there, but the wife insisted we show. She's all-in on the Ambrose campaign." He nods. "As are we all. Gearing up for the final push."

"Uh-huh. Good seeing you." Saint slaps his back, then moves on, but the man's words stick with me.

"So this event isn't a mandatory thing that all society members have to attend?" I ask, and Saint gives a shrug.

"Technically, yes, but sometimes people have other commitments. You can't miss more than a couple of years though, without getting a stern talking-to. You know, sacred bonds and all."

"Oh."

My hopes sink even further. I'm realizing I didn't think this through at all. It's not some tiny, exclusive group here tonight: People from all generations are gathered, and I have no way of knowing which of them was even around at last year's reunion to meet Wren—or who's missing, who might have met her, who would have any connection to what happened . . .

"How about that tour you wanted?" Saint offers, as my disappointment takes hold.

"Sure." I sigh. "Why not?"

I follow him back inside, relieved to have a break from the crowds. Here, every room is vast, and lavishly furnished in antique pieces, the history clear with every step. "It's like a museum," I comment, wide-eyed, as Saint shows me through a series of grand halls, all displaying glass cases of priceless artifacts and art.

"Yes. My parents don't exactly prioritize comfort in their living environment," Saint remarks dryly. "The cellars have been off-limits for years. Black mold. And we were supposed to keep well clear of all the antiques up here. Although, the polished floors may have seen a few rebellious hockey matches in their time," he adds with a mischievous smirk, that looks awfully familiar . . .

I pause, looking up at a wall of portraits. "That's you!" I exclaim, seeing a picture of a younger Saint, the same smile on his face, posed in stiff, formal clothing next to Robert. There's a third boy in the picture, too. Blond and smiling. Edward.

"The future of the Ashford dynasty," Saint says, his voice twisting on the words. "And just look at us now . . ."

I feel a pang. "So if you weren't allowed down here, where did you do your homework, and watch TV?" I ask, changing the subject for him.

"Ah, that's the part they don't show to the National Trust."

Saint guides me upstairs, to the family apartments, which turn out to be fairly normal. If normal means huge fireplaces and designer furniture, with modern touches. His childhood rooms are buried under the eaves, near a back servant's staircase where I just know he used to sneak out all the time. I could spend hours hearing stories about his childhood here, but I know that I can't be distracted from my task tonight, so I follow him back downstairs to the main historic part of the house, ready to return to the party.

". . . and there are the grand old Dukes of Ashford," he says, nodding to the row leading down the main grand hall. There's an array of older men, in suits, and then further back still, in extravagant period attire: cravats, and robes, and even a suit of armor.

"Is that where your portrait will hang?" I ask, nodding to the end of the line. There's a space beside his father's painting,

"Fate would say yes," Saint replies, and I know he's thinking of his dead brother, the man who was supposed to inherit it all.

I squeeze his hand. "You should mix things up, all these somber oils," I tease, trying to lighten the mood. "How about something more modern, a graffiti artist? A nice Banksy, it'd fit right in."

Saint manages a wry laugh. "Oh, they'd love that one."

He looks around, and then draws me back into the shadows of the velvet drapes, claiming my mouth in a slow, sizzling kiss.

I shiver against him. Despite all the emotions whirling inside me, there's still nothing that transports me like the touch of his lips—and the slow, intoxicating slide of his tongue, delving sensuously into my mouth.

"Fuck, you're delicious . . ." Saint nips my lower lip, his hands already skimming over the silk of my hips. "I've half a mind to yank this dress up and eat your sweet cunt right here. Give those dusty old men on the wall something to watch," he adds, with a playful squeeze of my ass.

My pulse kicks. "Saint," I whisper, a little scandalized. "We can't."

"Why not? Nobody's around," he adds, smirking at me with a dark seduction in his eyes. "No one but the portraits to watch you come undone . . ."

He inches my skirt up my thighs, fingertips creeping higher as I sway closer, ready to surrender—

"Excuse me, this wing is—Anthony?"

An icy voice rings out across the hall, making me freeze. Saint releases my skirt, letting it fall back into place before he turns, sighing.

"Mother."

Oh shit.

I gulp. It's Lillian St. Clair herself, outfitted in pearls and a chilly smile. She moves closer, eyes shooting between Saint and me. It's clear from the purse of her lips that she knows exactly what we were doing just now—before we were interrupted.

And how I would be halfway to mindless pleasure against her son's mouth if she hadn't just walked in.

"Teresa," she says coolly, "I wasn't expecting to see you join us tonight."

"It's Tessa, Mother," Saint corrects her. "And I cleared it with the committee."

"Oh."

I look back and forth between them, confused. "You have a lovely home, Lady St. Clair," I say politely. "Saint was just showing me around."

"Thank you. It's been in the family, safeguarded for almost five hundred years," she replies. "Many outside forces have attempted to wrest it from us, but we stand firm against all invasions. Some more subtle than others," she adds with a glare.

It's clear she sees me as one of those outside invasions.

"Your father is looking for you," she says, turning to Saint.

"He always is," he replies blandly. "Mother."

He yanks me away, back out to the patio, and grabs a drink from the nearest waiter. "And *that* is why I moved out after boarding school, and rarely return," he says, swallowing with a gulp. "Too many fucking ghosts in this house."

Before I can reply, an excited shriek echoes across the terrace. "Tessa!"

I barely have time to react before Annabelle is smothering me in excited air-kisses. "Come on, Max has commandeered the good whiskey, and we're all avoiding all the olds."

She takes my hand and drags me through the crowd, as Saint follows. We find Max and Hugh posted up on the edge of the terrace, sprawled comfortably on the elegant chaises.

"Tessa, darling, what a vision you are!" Max greets me.

"He's already drunk," Annabelle whispers loudly. "Buckthorn gin fizz, gets him every time."

"Au contraire, mesa mi," Max says theatrically. "Merely getting started for the long night ahead. *In vino, veritas*, and all that jazz."

"When he starts quoting Latin, you know he's trouble," Hugh says, with a conspiratorial grin. He greets me warmly and makes room on the chaise beside him. "Although, I might ply you with booze myself tonight, see if I can't talk you into accepting that job at the Foundation. What's the holdup?" he adds, teasing. "Playing hard to get? Saint, I thought you were going to talk her round?"

Saint holds his hands up. "Hey, it's nothing to do with me.

Tessa's got a mind of her own. A stubborn one," he adds with a smirk.

"Is it the package?" Hugh asks me, and Max snorts.

"We have heard complaints about Hugh's package!"

"So mature." Annabelle rolls her eyes.

I smile carefully. "It's a generous offer, and I'm not playing hard to get," I assure him. "I just have a lot going on right now. I'm not sure I can give it the focus it deserves."

After my attack, and warnings from the college about my studies, and everything to do with Wren, that job has been the furthest thing from my mind. No matter how much I enjoyed it, it seems like a different life to me. A life where I'm not set on discovering Wren's attacker as the only priority on my list.

Hugh sighs. "Well, let me know when you make a decision. Or if there's anything I can do to sweeten the deal. Priya is raving about your influencer fundraising proposals," he adds. "And that's not a woman who raves."

I smile, pleased. "I'm glad I could help."

"So what's all this buzz I'm hearing about a big Ashford announcement?" Max changes the subject, giving Saint a sloppy kick. "Do I need to call my stockbroker and get in on the deal?"

Saint gives him a look. "Are you looking for insider trading information?"

"Always," Max says cheerfully, as Annabelle bounces up.

"Bathroom," she trills. "Come on, Tessa. Let's leave these men to their gossip."

"If it's about money, it's not gossip," Max protests. "This is serious business talk here."

"Gossip," Annabelle repeats with a smirk.

She leads me through the crowd, into the house. "Whoops, watch for the blackthorn," she says, steering me around a floral centerpiece with sprigs of white flowers. The same ones that were sent with the note, at the Midnights party, I realize. "I get that there's all sorts of symbolism," Annabelle continues, rolling her eyes. "Poisonous fruit and all that, but honestly, the dresses I've torn on those damn thorns. Not that the guys ever care. It's so nice having another girl as part of the group for these things," she adds, looping her arm through mine.

"What about Imogen?" I ask, realizing I haven't seen her here this evening. "Isn't she a member?"

Annabelle shakes her head. "Her mother is from an excellent family, of course, but Blackthorn is *very* selective. The people at this event represent the upper echelons of British society. The guest list is strictly monitored. Plus-ones are absolutely forbidden," she continues, giving me an assessing look. "Even wives or fiancées have to be granted a special dispensation to come. Saint would have had to be *very* convincing that you two were on the marriage track for the society bigwigs to let you in."

"Marriage?" I repeat. No wonder Lillian was so appalled to see me. "What? I mean, that's crazy, we've barely known each other a month."

"But he brought you here, didn't he? And everyone can see that he adores you," she continues breezily. "Just say the word, I'll refer you to all my wedding people. The florists are just incredible. You know, they're managing to fly in tulips from a special hothouse in Antwerp, just for the big day?"

Annabelle chatters on, but her words linger, whispering in the back of my mind. Not marriage, that part is crazy—that I would be one of those women up in the oil paintings, smiling demurely. Duchess of this estate. It's insane.

But a future with Saint . . .

That part is more tempting. I can't deny the way my body responds to him, and the wild heights of pleasure we share, but there's more than that, too. A bond that's forming, a connection that's been there right from the start.

I'm drawn to him, despite everything. And even with so much in a state of confusion over Wren and the answers I'm searching for, that bond feels stronger than ever. A lifeline, to hold on tight.

A North Star, guiding me to the truth.

But can I trust it?

Chapter Twenty-Five
TESSA

We return to the party. They're all having fun, drinking and catching up with old friends, but as pleasant as the vibe is tonight, my impatience is growing. I keep waiting for some special moment or sign, anything that might be a connection to Wren. I've been thinking her attack was some hazing ritual, or an initiation to the society, but looking around, it doesn't seem like anyone's expecting a big event.

Then, just as I'm about to explode, there's the sound of metal ringing out against glass. The crowd hushes, and everyone turns to the top of the stone stairs, where Cyrus Lancaster moves to address the crowd.

My heart leaps, but Max sighs loudly beside me. "Some stirring words his speechwriter whipped up, no doubt."

Someone hushes him, as Cyrus begins to speak. He's just as imposing as when I met him at the last party, outfitted in an impeccable suit with his steel-gray eyes looking around the audience, like they see everything.

"Welcome, brethren, to our four-hundred-and-fiftieth gathering. Give or take a few."

There are chuckles. I lean closer, anxious to hear what's coming next.

Is this what I've been waiting for?

"Some people might wonder why we keep these rituals and traditions alive," Cyrus says, his voice ringing with importance and authority. "After all, we live in a very different world now than the one seen by our forefathers when they first joined together and swore their oaths. Progress has been made, fortunes built and lost, and then built all over again. Our members don't just span the nations now, but the globe, reaching the highest echelons of power in every corner of industry and politics . . ."

Around me, there are solemn smiles and nods. I just feel a shiver of unease. So much for democracy and equality, when the people on this terrace apparently determine the fate of the free world.

"But I say to you," Cyrus continues, "this ever-changing world requires our loyalty more than ever. Loyalty to one another, to upholding the virtue of those who have come before. Sacrificed their blood and sweat to remake this world for us, the keepers of their legacy. For as we say . . . '*Legatum donum est, et juramentum nostrum!*'"

He chants in Latin, and everyone around me echoes the refrain.

"Legacy is our gift, and our sworn bond," Cyrus repeats, translating. "The past points our way to the future. Enjoy the evening, everyone, in good health."

He raises his glass in a toast, and the whole crowd cheers. "Hear, hear!"

There's applause, and then Cyrus steps back. The party resumes, with drinks brought out, and food circulating. A band takes up position on the patio below and begins to play.

I blink.

"So . . . that's it?" I ask Saint, confused.

He gulps champagne. "I think there might be karaoke later."

I look around at the elite crowd with their drunken revelry and feel a chill settle in my bones. I came to Oxford for answers, and ever since that mysterious note arrived with the secret society motto, I've been imagining some vast conspiracy connected to Wren's attack. Villains plotting dark deeds that would somehow reveal themselves, so I could bring them to justice. But instead . . .

It's just a bunch of rich idiots sipping champagne.

Tears sting in the back of my throat, the bitter taste of humiliation. I'm a fool—and I'm no closer to getting answers for Wren.

With a sob, I turn on my heels and flee, slipping down a side staircase and racing through the gardens, out of sight of the party, to where a small woodland looks over the lake.

"Tessa, wait," Saint calls after me, but I don't stop, not until I'm hidden in the trees, gazing out at the placid water, where I can finally give into my aching sobs and let the tears flow.

What the hell am I even doing here?

Lying to Saint's friends, making a liar out of him, too . . . searching every stranger's face I see for some sign of guilt or evil intentions. I'm acting crazy. Maybe I *am* crazy. All I want is to make sense of Wren's horrors, the nightmare that drove her to her death.

Give her the justice that she never lived to see.

I weep with the grief of it all, and my own futile hopes, until finally, footsteps come through the trees, and Saint finds me by the water's edge.

"Tessa . . ." he says softly, tenderness on his face.

I lift my face from my hands. "I'm an idiot," I sob, still wretched. "What was I thinking, Saint? That these people arranged to hurt my sister, and I could just poke around, asking a few questions, and somehow uncover the truth? I just . . . I thought there was a reason. A reason she's gone. Someone I can blame."

"There is," he says immediately. He wraps his arms around me, holding me close. "Whoever hurt Wren, they're scum. You're right about that. And I wish I could find them, I really do. They deserve justice, for what they did. They deserve hell," he adds grimly as he cups my face in his hands. "But sometimes there is no grand conspiracy." Saint gently wipes my tears away. "Sometimes it's just evil men, acting out their own sick fantasies. Wren's not the only one who's been hurt, who's had to endure that kind of pain.

It happens too often. Without any secret society, or powerful people pulling the strings."

"I know," I sob, feeling like everything is slipping away from me, the rage that's fueled me all this time, burning in my heart, making me keep going in a world without her. "But don't you see? If that's true, if it was just a random attack, then I have no chance of finding them. I'll never be able to make them pay for what they did."

My voice cracks with emotion, and Saint looks down at me with heartbreaking tenderness.

"I know, sweetheart. But maybe . . . maybe somehow, you'll be able to let it go."

A sob breaks free at those words, and I bury my face against his chest and howl, shaken with a fresh wave of grief.

"She wouldn't want you to hurt like this," Saint murmurs. He moves us to the ground, so he's sitting with his back against a tree, cradling me in his arms. "I never knew Wren, but she loved you. She would have wanted you to thrive and be happy, not to spend your life chasing her ghosts. It won't bring her back, baby. I'm sorry. Nothing's going to bring her back."

He's right.

I sob against him, my grief as sharp as a blade in my chest. I know it in my heart that Wren would be the first one telling me to let my anger go and move on. She was always better than me. Kinder, wiser. She wouldn't want me consumed with rage and vengeance, and certainly not on her account. My whole life, she looked out for me, and wanted only the best for me.

And now she's gone forever.

I'm not sure how long I sob in Saint's arms, but finally, my tears ease, and I suck in a ragged breath, exhausted.

"I'm sorry," I mutter, self-conscious as I lift my head. I try to wipe my face, certain I've just smeared mascara all over his very expensive tux. "I must look like a mess."

"You look beautiful." Saint drops a kiss on my forehead, and I manage a hollow laugh.

"Liar."

I take another breath. My head is aching from my crying, but I feel different now. The tight grip of grief in my chest has loosened, and I feel lighter somehow, as if a weight has lifted.

"Thank you," I whisper. "I guess . . . I needed to hear that."

Saint smooths my hair back from my face. "I know what it's like to grieve," he says softly. "And do whatever the hell you can to avoid that grief. After Edward died, it felt overwhelming. Like if I looked at it head-on, or allowed myself to feel the full force of the loss . . . I wouldn't be able to bear it."

"What did you do?" I ask, gazing up at him.

He gives a rueful laugh. "Anything I could to block out the pain. Whiskey. Women. God knows what else. But in the end . . . I knew, I was just punishing myself. And Edward . . . he deserved more than that from me."

I nod slowly. "It just feels wrong, that I'm here to experience all of this, and she's not." I look out across the water, glittering in the sinking sun. It's an unseasonably warm night, with the breeze dancing around us, and the sound of birdsong, and the distant music from the party. Beautiful.

"You can't hide from life," Saint says softly. "Denying yourself the things you want won't bring Wren back."

"I know," I breathe, leaning back in the safe warmth of his embrace. "I just don't know how to do this. To let go of the anger and move on with my life."

"Start small," Saint suggests. "What's the one thing that makes you feel like *you*? The woman you were, before all this happened."

I know he's probably expecting me to say something like "reading my favorite novel" or "eating great pizza," but instead, I twist around so I'm straddling his lap, and kiss him, hard.

"Wait—" Saint draws back, frowning. "Tessa, you've just had an emotional moment—"

"You asked what made me feel like me," I say, gripping his shirt collar. My emotions are whirling inside me, and everything feels like it's shifting beneath me. I need him. I need the release only he can provide. "You do, Saint." I look at him, run my fingers over his cheeks, and feel the contours of his face. "When you're touching me . . . when we're together . . . that's when I feel most like myself. Like nothing else exists in the world, just you, and me, and *this* . . ."

I kiss him again, deeper this time. Saint sounds a low groan against my mouth, and then he's kissing me back, slow and sweet, taking his time. Heat burns, rising through me as his hands slide over my body, and his tongue delves, deep between my lips to tangle with mine in a sensual dance.

I hum with satisfaction, already sinking into the glittering rush. He shifts me in his lap, and I feel his cock, hard against me. Anticipation flares.

I rock back on my heels. "I want you . . ." I whisper softly, nuzzling at his neck. Breathing in the scent of him. "I want to *taste* you . . ."

Saint curses under his breath. "Tessa . . ."

I push him gently back, moving down his body to undo his belt, and peel away his pants. His body responds as I tug down his zipper, and I feel a sharp thrill of anticipation. His cock is straining against his briefs, and I tease him through the fabric, closing my hand around the hard length of him and pumping slowly.

Saint groans. "Fuck . . ." He's sprawled back now, eyes hooded with pleasure as I run my fingertips over the bulge. I meet his gaze and give a flirty smile.

"Now you're the one who needs to keep quiet," I murmur, as power begins to buzz in my veins. This is what I need, to lose myself in the rush of pleasure. To forget that the real world exists. "You don't want anyone to hear . . ."

Saint inhales a ragged breath as I slip my hand beneath his briefs and close my fingers around his cock, skin on skin. "Now, don't tease, baby," he says in a low growl, eyes dark with lust.

But I'm enjoying it too much to stop. "You know, I think it's time for *you* to strip," I coo, running my gaze over him appreciatively. For the first time, we're not in the dark shadows of a club or covered in bubble-bath. "I want to see it all. Come on. Off."

Saint chuckles, and obligingly strips off his jacket and shirt, as I make short work of his pants, pulling them all the way off. "Satisfied?" he asks, when he's almost naked.

"Very." I smirk, caressing his bare stomach, admiring the ridge of his abs and the trail of dark hair, leading down to his briefs. I snap the waistband, and he chuckles.

"Go ahead, baby. Be a good girl and let me feel that wet mouth. Suck it, nice and deep."

I bite back a moan, finally peeling his briefs off, too. Saint lifts his hips, letting me pull them away to reveal his cock: standing tall and thick, straining for my touch as his thighs tense, and—

I stop.

The heat in my bloodstream turns to ice. My heartbeat pounds in my ears, louder than thunder as I see it for the first time.

The small tattoo on his inner thigh. A crown, encircled by a serpent.

The one thing Wren remembered from her attacker.

It's him.

Acknowledgments

A huge thanks to Alessandra Roche and May Chen, and everyone at Avon. To my team standing on business: Gary Ungar, Tanya Mallean, Anthony Colletti, and Sue Carls and the team at CAA.

To my cheerleaders and confidantes, Elizabeth L, Ava H, Ally C, Elisabeth D, Riann S, Ann M, Zach A.

And finally a huge, heartfelt thanks to all the spicy romance lovers and #BookTok creators who have championed this trilogy, to Bria (@readingoveradulting), Laura (@elitereading), Kylie (@buriedwithinpages), Anna (@thatblondebookworm), Marissa (@thatssodavis), Chelsey (@chelseyjreads) and so many more!

TO BE CONTINUED . . .

What happens next? Tessa and Saint's

explosive love story continues in

Break My Rules,

the next book in the Oxford Legacy trilogy.

Coming in December 2024!

About the Author

ROXY SLOANE was born and raised in England, and got her bachelors degree at the University of Oxford, where she absolutely did not attend any scandalous parties or secret society events. Not at all. She currently lives in Los Angeles, where she enjoys recklessly writing spicy scenes in public places.